THE FINAL
REALITY

AN ALEX PELLA NOVEL
STEPHEN MARTINO

Light Messages

Durham, NC

Published 2017, by Light Messages
www.lightmessages.com
Durham, NC 27713
Printed in the United States of America
Paperback ISBN: 978-1-61153-165-7
Ebook ISBN: 978-1-61153-164-0
Library of Congress Control Number: 2016956068

This is a work of fiction. All characters and events appearing in this work are fictitious.

"My reading of history convinces me that most bad government results from too much government"
–Thomas Jefferson

PROLOGUE

October 4, 1944
Somewhere in the Tsang Po River Valley Southwest of the
Tibetan Capital, Lhasa

THOUGH ACCOMPANIED BY FOUR other companions,
Ernst Schäfer felt alone on the barren, salt-crusted sands of
the Tibetan desert. Even now as he entered the drab brown
mountain valleys once forged by a long-forgotten river, the
change in scenery only proved to heighten his feeling of
complete isolation from both humanity and his own self.

The pain of each footfall ignited his soles and exploded in
his legs. Walking over thirty miles a day for the last month had
certainly taken its toll on his body. Though almost paralyzed
at times by the pain, he knew that the success of this mission
made his personal suffering inconsequential.

"We must be getting close," Ernst's guide noted, pointing
towards a few boulders on the ground, each with the word *Tsan*
etched on them.

Ernst nodded in acknowledgement. Though limited in his
Tibetan vernacular, he knew the word meant *border*. Serving as

a warning as opposed to a designation of property lines, it was meant to frighten off any unwanted trespassers. Because most Tibetans were afraid of ghosts, spirits, or other supernatural beings, such a warning would scare even the most curious travelers who unknowingly stepped foot in this part of the valley.

"Thank you, Illion," Ernst said.

"The City of the Initiates must be ahead," Illion responded matter-of-factly. Dressed in a long sleeve wool gown known colloquially as a chu-pa with thick leather boots that fit snuggly up to the knees, their guide donned both himself and the rest of the expedition in the native garb of a Tibetan nomad.

Because of the war and the distrust towards Westerners, Ernst's expedition was forced to travel undercover so as not to rouse local suspicion. They even had to lather their faces with a tincture of iodine and oil to disguise their fair skin.

"We must be entering The Valley of Mystery," Illion added.

Well acquainted with Tibet, Illion had traversed the land alone and by foot about ten years prior to this expedition. In fact, he enjoyed such international popularity from his excursion that Ernst Schäfer sought him out one year earlier specifically for this mission. Though distrusting anyone who bore the SS skull and crossbones insignia on their uniform, Illion respected Schäfer for his groundbreaking botanical and zoological discoveries he had previously made in Tibet and agreed to be their guide.

Unlike the fifty-mule caravan, interpreters and porters who accompanied Ernst on his previous Tibetan expedition, this time, he brought a mere pittance of supplies in comparison. In fact, Illion needed to train both Ernst and the rest of the team to carry everything they needed, including food, personal needs, a tent, and some water underneath their chu-pas. It took nine months of grueling preparation in the lower-oxygen

Scandinavian mountains, eating raw meat and drinking murky water disinfected with a hint of radioactive earth before Illion felt comfortable escorting the team into Tibet.

After all the training, there was still a significant risk of being captured while in British-controlled India, especially during the height of the war. With fake passports disguising their German origin, they were able to travel undetected even in the most well patrolled northeastern Indian region known as Sikkim. Once entering Tibet, they needed to hike by foot like desert nomads, without any beast of burden so that they would not draw the attention of the local authorities.

Ernst continued to walk next to Illion without saying another word while their four other undercover SS companions followed silently behind them. Selected from the purist of Aryan stock, Heimlich Himmler had personally recommended them for the mission.

Though no one in the expedition believed, like the Tibetans, in evil spirits, they each felt spooked by the eerie valley. As they entered, a thin white mist seemed to ooze up from the white sand and muffle all sound around them. Even their footsteps and the bustle of their chu-pas became more distant the further they walked. Though the sky was clear, the sun seemed to dim and the air chill.

Despite their harsh training, each member of the expedition could not help but give some credence to the local Tibetan myths and warnings about this valley.

What if evil spirits really did preside in the area? Could this place be cursed?

Though no one spoke it aloud, a chill ran through them. It was as if this whole area exuded some form of strange energy.

The valley widened in front of them, revealing a brown, circular stone wall about four feet high. As the group cautiously approached, they were able to understand its diameter to be about twenty-two feet; its stone slabs were most probably quarried from the local mountainside.

"Slowly," Illion whispered. "You must show utmost respect upon entering this holy City of the Initiates."

"Remember our objective," Schäfer reminded the other four members of the group. Behind Illion's back, Schäfer then nodded specifically to each of them, as if giving a signal.

The ground gently sloped downward from the centrally located wall. About 200 feet from the wall and spaced equidistant from one another were seven massive slabs of glass positioned around its perimeter. The sun glistened off their surface as if amplifying the dull light penetrating into the dried-up river valley.

"Not the city I expected," Ernst mouthed to Illion. "Where are the houses? Where are the people?"

"There is much we don't know about this place," Illion responded. "Tibet still remains shrouded in mystery."

Ernst and Illion walked over to one of the glass slabs. Upon their approach, the men noticed a long staircase descending into the Earth just in front of the slab. After closer inspection, it appeared that each of the other six slabs also had an adjoining staircase.

"The city must be underground," Illion surmised.

Ernst gestured to the group to follow him as he walked over to the stone wall. The closer he approached, the more nauseated and lightheaded he became. Though his body willed him to stop, his mind pushed forward. The others joined him around the wall's circular perimeter. They had trained too hard and endured too much already to be intimidated by the mounting queasiness.

Ernst looked over the wall. His face was met by a surprisingly cool breeze, which at first left him breathless and made his eyes water. After blinking a few times, he noticed the wall surrounded what appeared to be a deep pit.

Maybe a well?

Ernst took a loose stone from the wall and dropped it into the pit. Counting on his fingers, he attempted to estimate its depth by listening to when the stone struck bottom.

Ten seconds.

Making a fist with both hands, Ernst then started to count *eleven* as he raised his pointer finger.

Twenty seconds.

Ernst looked mesmerized at his companions as he then uttered, *"Sixty,"* a little louder and more robust than the other numbers.

"Chi la iru dung?" a voiced echoed from behind them, startling the entire group.

A distinguished man with a long, wrinkled face, large eyes and beaded white hair emerged from one of the staircases. Wearing a pure silk chu-pa embroidered with decorative, red designs, he sounded as if he were chastising a group of wayward children.

Illion walked over to the man and bowed for his forgiveness. As he was the only member of the team fluent in the native Tibetan tongue, Illion explained why he and his companions had entered the sacred city.

After a curt discussion, the man in the silken chu-pa abruptly turned and descended the staircase.

Before Ernst could ask Illion any questions, one-by-one men, women, and children began exiting different staircases around the courtyard. Unlike the first man, these inhabitants wore drab, cotton chu-pas and walked almost mechanically along the desert sand. Their faces were devoid of expression and appeared at times grotesque in nature. Even the children seemed to be lacking a soul, conducting their chores as if programmed by some omnipotent being that resided in the city. None noticed the visitors amongst their midst.

Illion could not help but draw a comparison between these lifeless human robots and the four soulless SS killing machines who accompanied him on this mission. *Was there any difference?*

An occasional handsome man or woman would exit one of the staircases. Unlike their other counterparts, they wore an ornate silken chu-pa and seemed to control the drably dressed inhabitants with a simple nod of the head or glance in a particular direction. All remained silent.

The scene reminded Ernst of a colony of ants.

Illion slowly walked over to Ernst, avoiding eye contact with the other city inhabitants. Leaning over ever so slightly, he then whispered, "The man said he had received no word that any visitors were expected."

Ernst gulped deeply, gravely concerned now about the success of their mission. The news set his heart racing.

Had they not received the shipment? Was he duped?

Ernst could not but help replay in his mind everything that had transpired since he last visited Tibet in 1938, just prior to the breakout of the war. While in the capital city of Lhasa, he had met with a top-ranking governmental official by the name of Reting Rinpoche. Concerned about Russian oppression of the Buddhist religion and possibly even military aggression by the communist nation, Rinpoche had urgently requested an arms deal with the Nazi regime.

For an exchange of weapons, Rinpoche promised Ernst proof of an ancient Aryan culture and access to some of their most sacred texts containing powerful knowledge long forgotten by humanity. It was at that time that Rinpoche informed Ernst about the City of the Initiates and the secrets it possessed. As a high-ranking member of the fraternity known as The Holy Brotherhood who supposedly controlled the City of the Initiates, Rinpoche personally assured that he could grant access to the knowledge about an ancient Aryan race.

Without authority to broker a deal himself, Ernst politely informed Rinpoche that this proposal would be sent to the himself.

As the war progressed, Ernst assumed that the message had been lost in a bureaucratic mess, forgotten by both the SS and the Nazi Ancestral Heritage Foundation, known as the Ahnenerbe. However, as the German war machine ground to a halt on both fronts, Hitler himself commissioned Ernst's Tibetan expedition in the hopes that some lost Aryan technology or scientific information could be uncovered in Tibet and win him the war.

After a brief moment, Illion then added, "He went to discuss our presence with Lha-mo-chun."

"Who?" Ernst whispered.

"The little goddess," Illion answered. "She is the caretaker of these grounds."

The pair waited patiently while the four SS soldiers surrounded their position as if expecting an ambush.

"Must we keep with formalities?" Illion asked.

Ernst ignored the question, indignant to the man's ignorance and his lack of urgency. Despite the propaganda, the war was proceeding very poorly for Germany on both its Eastern and Western fronts. With the Allied forces overtaking the Siegfried Line and advancing eastward by the day and the Russians closing in on them with their westward assault, Germany was on the brink of a catastrophic defeat. Not only would his country be left a desolate wasteland, but after selling his soul to Himmler and the SS, Ernst knew his career would fair no better after the war.

After about a half hour of waiting, a beautiful young woman with long dark hair braided into a single strand behind her head, high cheekbones, large brown eyes, and a radiant olive-hued complexion ascended one of the staircases. Wearing a pure white chu-pa, she made a breathtaking appearance.

"Welcome to our city," she surprisingly greeted in Ernst's native tongue. "Reting Rinpoche notified us that we should be expecting you."

Success! Ernst let out a large sigh of relief. *Rinpoche must have received the weapons.*

"Then I assume you understand the nature of our arrival," Illion responded as he bowed in respect to their new host.

With a smile that proved only to accentuate her beauty, she replied, "Let me assure you that we entombed the body of your fallen compatriot with the utmost respect." Like a feather she raised her flowing arm and pointed to an adjacent staircase next to where they were standing. "Please let me escort you over to the Lha-Khang complex."

Lha-mo-chun walked away as if gliding on the sand. Side by side with Illion, she led them to the staircase.

Again, Ernst nodded to his companions. Upon his signal, they began to adjust what they had hidden underneath the long sleeves of their chu-pas.

Lha-mo-chun turned back to the rest of the group. "Your friend is buried on the second level of our temple complex."

"What is on the other levels?" Ernst asked, hoping to find the answer that Reting Rinpoche had promised.

While descending the stairs, the little goddess responded while looking directly ahead at the arched door. "The first level is where our monks prepare the recently deceased bodies for burial, and the third is our most sacred temple, the Lha-Khang." She bowed when speaking of the temple.

Lha-mo-chun pulled out a set of golden keys from underneath her white chu-pa. Before she could open the door, Ernst asked, "Have you ever been in the temple?"

She turned and with a smile said, "Only high-ranking members of the fraternity, the prince of the city, and I are allowed to enter the temple."

Without further explanation, she unlocked the large door and opened it with little effort.

As the group entered, the intense glare of the light glistening through the glass ceiling initially blinded them. Once their vision came back into focus, they noticed another door at the end of a hallway along with other long corridors exiting all along the path.

I bet this whole complex is connected underground, Ernst deduced after viewing the layout.

"Please follow me," Lha-mo-chun said as she escorted them down another staircase to a large arched doorway at the end of the hall. The glass ceiling above illuminated the area. Although not as bright as the first level, it provided ample visibility. "Your friend's earthly body is behind here."

"Thank you," Illion responded. "If we may pay our last respects and collect his belongings, we will be on our way."

Lha-mo-chun grabbed the keys once again from underneath her chu-pa. Before she could open the door, one of the SS soldiers clutched her hand while a second placed a knife to her throat.

Just as she was about to scream, the SS soldier with the knife placed his hand over her mouth and squeezed down on her face.

'What are you doing?" Illion turned to ask Ernst, flabbergasted by what was transpiring. "What about the mission?"

"So naïve," Ernst responded with a sadistic smile. "This is the mission."

"But—" Illion started then stopped, realizing that he had been duped.

"The body behind this door was a plant," Ernst continued. "A ruse to allow us access to the temple complex."

One of the SS soldiers then took out a Lugar pistol from underneath his chu-pa and pointed it at Illion while another grabbed the keys from Lha-mo-chun.

Illion remained silent, still in shock. Not sure whether to be angrier with Ernst and the other SS soldiers or with himself for being deceived, he kept further comments to himself.

Pointing to a staircase located in an adjacent corridor, Ernst signaled the two unoccupied soldiers to lead the way. Now with their two hostages, they all descended the steps, heading down to the third and most sacred level. Evenly spaced along the wall, golden torches burning smokeless flames lit the way.

Upon exiting the staircase, they were met by three men donning elegant silken red chu-pas standing motionless in front of a magnificent golden door. It was almost as if the men were in a trance as they made no indication of noticing the group's arrival. Etched in white upon the door and also sewn into these men's gowns were elaborate depictions of bulls along with what appeared to be magical symbols.

More torches with smokeless flames adorned the walls of this narrow hallway. Unlike the two levels above them, this level possessed no glass ceiling.

The group slowly approached as the three men ahead of them remained stationary, as if carved from stone.

Ernst cautiously pointed to the door.

Without hesitation, one of the SS soldiers slowly moved forward in a crouched position. With a knife in his hand, he gradually approached the men. Unsure if they were actually alive, he wanted to be as careful as possible. Steadily he reached out his left hand, ever so slightly, moving it towards one of the men's face.

Just as he was about to touch him, one of the other guards sprang to life. Swinging a sword he had hidden behind his back, he swiftly chopped off the SS soldier's arm at the elbow with one clear swipe. Blood began to squirt from the stump, spraying on the floor and staining one of the men's red chu-pas.

Ernst and the remaining soldiers immediately pulled out their concealed Luger pistols and opened fire, emptying all eight rounds in their magazines. The shots reverberated in the small confines of the hallway and continued to echo in their ears even after the last bullet had been fired. The guards were quickly killed—even their fellow SS soldier lay motionless on the floor, riddled with bullet holes.

Lha-mo-chun ran over to the fallen bodies and knelt down, staining her chu-pa in the growing pool of blood. The little goddess placed her hands together and bowed forward, whispering a prayer as she gently rocked back and forth.

Illion walked by her side and placed his hand on her shoulder. Stunned by what had just transpired, he had trouble uttering a sound. After a brief moment to compose himself, he whispered, "I am so sorry. I did not know." Illion's lowered lip quivered. "You must forgive me."

Ernst marched over the fallen bodies. With a freshly loaded Lugar in one hand and the golden keys in the other, he turned to Illion. "Don't forget the motherland Illion. You know as well as I that the war is all but lost." Pointing at the golden door, he added, "Unless what we find behind here is a miracle, Germany as we know it will cease to exist."

"If men like you represent the Germany of today, sir," Illion replied, "I certainly look forward to the Germany of tomorrow."

"Then you are nothing but a fool." Ernst fumbled with the keys in the lock until he found one that fit. With a loud click, the door split vertically down its center and opened automatically away from him. The light from the adjacent room poured out like a tsunami and flooded the hallway. Ernst shuddered as the light's cool presence chilled him to the core, as if it were attempting to reach deep inside him.

"Please," Lha-mo-chun pleaded, still on her knees and wringing her hands. "You must not enter. You know not what you are about to do."

Illion placed a soothing hand on her shoulder, realizing her pleas fell on deaf ears.

Ernst and the three remaining SS soldiers slowly entered the room. As if a veil had lifted from the intense light, the glory of this inner sanctum clicked into focus. The room radiated light without any visible physical source. Golden cases filled with scrolls were perfectly aligned around the room's circular perimeter. On its walls were long, beautiful tapestries and rugs decorated with geometric designs, depictions of bulls, and what appeared to be the same magical symbols seen on the chu-pas of the temple guards. Vases with similar portrayals stood on marble pedestals next to most of the shelves.

What is this place? Looking at all the scrolls, Ernst could only assume that this room represented some sort of ancient library or possibly even a long-forgotten repository of knowledge.

Ernst was momentarily taken aback by the presence of a football-sized, perfectly clear crystal levitating in the center of the room. Its presence captivated his attention. As he watched it rotate methodically, he felt at ease, as if his whole body were at peace with both itself and nature.

Approaching the crystal, Ernst noted that directly underneath it, inlaid in the floor, was what appeared to be a ten-foot circular representation of the Earth. While the undulating gold most likely symbolized the world's continents and their actual topographic landscape, a naturally flowing sea of silver appeared to represent the planet's oceans, rivers, and lakes.

However, the world on the floor looked much different than the planet Ernst was familiar with. *Is this the Earth?* Ernst asked himself, vaguely recognizing a few familiar continents.

"Should we take some of these scrolls?" asked one of the SS guards.

Ernst ignored the man, knowing the real prize levitated just beyond arm's length. He then slowly stepped onto one of the golden continents. As he entered the inner sanctum of the circle, he felt the same strange sensation he experienced after first stepping foot into the Valley of Mystery. Ernst's hair began to stand on end, and his body felt as if electricity coursed throughout it.

Now edging himself closer to the crystal, Ernst slowly reached for the prize as if he were Eve plucking the forbidden fruit from the Garden of Eden. Inside, Ernst knew that what he was about to do was wrong. He also knew that for the sake of his homeland, family, and career, he must proceed.

"Stop!" Illion screamed from the room's doorway.

With blood covering her chu-pa, Lha-mo-chun stood next to his side. Tears still in her eyes, she pleaded, "The crystal must not be touched. For the sake of the entire planet, please leave this place."

One of the SS soldiers pulled a knife on the two, impeding any further entrance into the room.

With both hands, Ernst grabbed the crystal. For a brief second, his mind transcended this mortal plane and entered a different state of existence where time ceased to exist—a place whereby all that ever occurred in the universe's past and future was commencing in that exact moment. The entirety of the war flashed before his eyes.

"What have I done?" Ernst lamented, finally coming to his senses.

The silver seas around the continents on the floor stopped flowing and grew eerily calm. Dropping into his hands, the crystal collapsed into Ernst's grasp, losing its ability to levitate. The chills and sense of electricity that once ran down his spine had left.

Slowly, the ambient light emanating from the room began to dim.

A rumble from the earth underneath their feet made all in the room stumble slightly to their side.

"We must leave this place," Lha-mo-chun insisted, "before it is too late."

With the crystal in hand, Ernst ran out of the room just as it went completely dark. After grabbing a few of the scrolls, the SS soldiers followed him along with Illion and Lha-mo-chun up the flights of stairs and above ground. The underground city complex shook as it crumbled.

As they reached the surface, Ernst saw the glass plates circling the stone wall in the center of the valley shatter into countless pieces. One by one they fell into the earth as if engulfed by a sinkhole. Only about 100 of the city's inhabitants were able to make it above ground before all of the staircases also collapsed into the earth.

The mountain valley around them began to shake as boulders came tumbling down from the earthen embankments around the city. While the robotic men, women, and children walked methodically away from the danger, those donning the silken gowns ran frantically.

Ernst instinctively followed the silken-gowned inhabitants, presuming that they most likely knew the safest route out of this crumbling mountain valley. Boulders crashed into the city, killing or maiming many in their paths of destruction. One of the SS soldiers behind him took the full brunt of one boulder and was crushed to death by its massive weight.

The two other SS soldiers were lost in the commotion, running haphazardly among the city's inhabitants and falling debris.

As Ernst exited the valley, the land behind him crumbled to the ground, most likely killing everyone who had been left behind. Smoke and dust swirled in the air, dimming the sun and bringing darkness over the land.

What have I done? Ernst lamented.

As he entered further into the desert, the earth continued to shake around him. Keeping a foothold grew increasingly difficult as the ground seemed to escalate in volatility.

Seven, eight, or even nine? Ernst contemplated, attempting to gauge the size of the earthquake. Now alone in his journey, he then set out cautiously in a southern direction, hoping to find India.

Two figures caught Ernst's attention from the corner of his eye. Surprised by the sight, he noted Illion carrying Lha-mo-chun in his arms.

No matter, Ernst thought. *The war is lost.* As he continued to run, a brief and vague vision entered his mind. He recalled seeing it when initially touching the crystal. Most of what he had glimpsed now seemed a blur, but this one image continued to grow in clarity.

Ernst stopped running and stood still, shuddering as the image came into focus. Looking at the crystal in his hands, Ernst could not help but focus on one thought: *Humanity is doomed.*

CHAPTER 1

May 2, 2086
Philadelphia Art Museum

CHILLS RAN DOWN Benjamin's spine, making him shudder as the tingling progressed, unadulterated, throughout his body. Though there was a crisp chill to the air, the unusually cold spring morning did little to generate such a response. Instead, the putrid smell of sickness and disease inundated his senses. The horrid odors seemed to cling to every part of him; he could almost taste the air.

Benjamin ran his fingers through his dark brown hair, attempting to get a few strands out of his eyes. Used to a buzz cut all of his life, he felt as if he needed to constantly scratch his thick hair, which was in desperate need of a cut and wash.

Looking around the room, Benjamin attempted to imagine how this brilliant museum once appeared. He recalled how as a child he had once visited this place during a seventh grade school trip. That was ten years ago; he could hardly fathom now how much excitement and joy he had felt running into this particular room, looking at all the armor and swords with such amazement.

Ben, walk don't run, he recalled one of his teachers cautioning as he sprinted from exhibit to exhibit. *Don't touch that*, another scolded as he ran his hand along the metal armor of a fully suited medieval knight sitting on an equally fortified black replica of a horse.

As he looked at the floor, Ben saw what was left of this once mesmerizing exhibit. A few stray metal plates and shattered pieces of the horse lay strewn across the white, porcelain tiles, already cluttered by broken glass debris from all the shattered windows. Though saddened about its destruction, he felt overwhelmed by the memory of how excited he was to tell his mother and father about what he saw during his museum tour. When he arrived home later that day, he could hardly catch his breath.

The swords, the suit of arms, the guns, he sputtered to them over a home-cooked dinner. He could barely eat as he went on and on that night regaling them with the details of what he had spotted during the day.

Innocence lost, Benjamin lamented.

Benjamin took a deep breath, momentarily forgetting he was in the present and not the past. His lungs were overwhelmed by the unfettered smell of urine and stool. Attempting not to gasp, he almost vomited.

He zipped up his jacket, struggling to stay focused, but the memories persisted in his mind's eye. He remembered how vibrant both his mother and father looked at the time. Always impeccably dressed, his mother wore a beautiful floral dress and had her blond hair tied into a bun. In addition, he could recollect how intently his father listened to his stories that evening. A hulking man dressed in a gray jumpsuit with *Armor Assembly* written on the sleeve, Benjamin's father was jolly despite having just finished back-to-back grueling shifts at work.

The Disease it was simply called. Benjamin shook his head in disgust. His mother was the first in his family to be claimed by the plague that had engulfed the planet just four years earlier. Before claiming the lives of its victims, *The Disease* first took their dignity and sanity. Benjamin recalled how his beloved mother had withered away helplessly in their home. With no cure at the time and the hospitals overwhelmed by infection, most people were left to die in pain without any medical assistance. Two of Benjamin's grandparents and one uncle soon followed his mother.

The sick and wounded lying around Benjamin on the floor, huddled under blankets, had triggered the memory. Having been barricaded in this room for almost four days with little food and water and no medical supplies, they were trapped. Two had already died while a few others were soon to follow. Without access to any form of sanitary facilities, the sick were forced to wallow in their own excrement.

The Disease, Benjamin sighed. He had naively believed that its cure would be the end of the suffering. Instead, it had proved to be just the beginning—for not only him but also the entire planet. What most angered him was that *The Disease* was manmade and supposedly released inadvertently. *The New Reality*, Benjamin cursed, knowing they must have been behind it.

Benjamin stood up and stretched his back and legs. Though he had been a Boy Scout in his younger years, he certainly was no longer prepared to sleep three nights on a cold, hard floor. He felt stiffer than the pieces of armor that used to adorn this very room. Looking down, he grabbed a Spanish era sword that was lying next to him.

Just in case.

"Ben, I made some coffee and picked up a dozen donuts," Christine jested as she sat against an empty glass case. Taking a bite from a ration bar wrapped in foil, she reached out and offered, "You want some?"

"Is that jelly filled?" Ben responded, with a slight smirk. "You know I would prefer the Boston Cream."

Christine smiled. Her big blue eyes and vibrant red hair seemed to illuminate the room. Though she had only known Ben for a few months, she felt very comfortable with him. She knew that as the de facto leader of this rag tag bunch he had done everything he could to keep them alive. Now outcasts in their own home city, they, along with many others just like them, fought for their own survival. With the Art Museum now surrounded, she knew it was just a matter of time before they all met their creator.

"You have to eat something," Christine insisted. "What if the Lopers break through before help arrives? You need to stay strong."

"How much food do we have left?"

"If we're lucky, maybe another day."

"Is that it?" Ben asked. "What if we reduced rations by half to stretch things out a little longer?"

Christine's eyes said it all. With a tilt of her head and one-raised eyebrow, Benjamin knew what she meant. The rations were almost completely gone. They could be stretched no further. With the cold weather, starvation would set in sooner rather than later. Thankfully, a sole water fountain provided them with all the liquid they needed. Though the water was tinted brown and emitted an unusual smell, it served its purpose.

Christine took one final bite of her ration and threw the wrapper on the ground. Wearing a ragged and torn blue coat and equally tattered pants, she stood up and gave Benjamin a hug. Looking up, she asked, "Any word on help?"

Benjamin smiled. "Maybe today," he said, attempting to respond optimistically. But he knew the truth. The chance that they were to receive any form of help, especially within the next day or two, was slim to none. Most groups like his were also in hiding, scared to show their faces.

Looking past Benjamin's smudged glasses and into his hazel eyes, Christine wished she could believe him. Deep down, she knew he was attempting to be optimistic and provide her and the rest of them with a tiny hope. Despite the lack of substance to his words, his optimism did bring her some solace.

Christine took her right hand and lightly caressed Benjamin's stubbled face. Right now he and the rest of the group here were all she had left. She especially appreciated Benjamin who had taken her in after her entire family had been murdered. Traumatized and nearly suicidal, she felt grateful how he had personally nursed her back to both physical and mental health.

"Thank you," Benjamin responded, enjoying the momentary tranquility.

Benjamin then looked around the room at people huddled amongst the broken glass display cases and the bits and pieces of history cluttering the floor. Many were bunched together under blankets or simply leaning against a wall as they awakened to another cold morning.

"How's Bruce?" Benjamin asked. "I don't see him."

Christine grabbed him by both arms. "He passed last night." She let the news sink in before continuing. "Sepsis got the best of him"

She then pointed to the corner of the room where a few large quilted blankets covered the silhouettes of three bodies underneath.

Shocked, Benjamin was left speechless. Bruce's death had been so quick. It was just yesterday that he accidentally cut himself on a jagged piece of armor on the floor. Now, not even twenty-four hours later, sepsis had taken his life. It seemed so appalling and senseless—especially now in 2086 with modern science. A simple antibiotic could have easily saved him.

Benjamin shook his head. *What type of leader am I?* he lamented. *People die under my watch, and I don't even know it happened.*

"Ben, it's not like you could have done anything," Christine responded, lifting up his head. "I thought it best that you slept. We need you at your finest."

Benjamin knew Christine was rationally correct. However, the shallow feeling that dug through him did not abate with her words. The rapidity of Bruce's death reminded him of the passing of his own father; the agony of that event resurfaced involuntarily.

Bruce had reminded Benjamin so much of his father. Not only did they share the same name, but also physically they were both large, strong men with the kindest hearts and a great sense of humor. Even in death they were alike: Bruce and Benjamin's father had both died within twenty-four hours of falling ill.

"Stay focused," Christine implored, recognizing Benjamin's blank stare. She gently squeezed his chin. "I know he reminded you of your father."

She stopped talking, suddenly realizing that she had said the wrong thing. "I'm sorry," she quickly responded. "It's not what I meant."

"Don't worry about it," he said, attempting a smile. "It's what you were thinking." He paused a moment. "It's what I was thinking."

"The nanosplicers took so much from us all," Christine commented. "We all had to bury at least one person dear to us."

Even the word *nanosplicer* sent chills down Benjamin's spine. Released onto the entire planet, these self-replicating microscopic, half biologic, half robotic devils tore up the DNA of over a billion people and sent them prematurely to their graves.

"Myra Keres," Benjamin said with revulsion. How he wished that he could have personally killed her and watch her whither away just like his father. Her instant and painless death by poison was far too easy for such a callous monster. Her thirst for power and control had left over a billion dead in her wake.

"She's gone now," Christine said.

Benjamin pointed to a poster hanging on the wall. Still in reasonable shape, it covered an unfaded rectangular area that might once have boasted a painting or other piece of art.

"By coming together and accepting each other's beliefs, we can come to ultimate truth," he read.

Christine looked over at the poster. Until now she had not noticed it clinging to the wall. The slogan was set in front of The New Reality insignia, a diamond with a gold circle in its center. The ignominious symbol had replaced the country's national flag and all the flags of the sovereign nations around the world.

Though she despised the company, Christine knew that they, the people, were to blame for its rise to power. When the countries around the world had reached an unfathomable deficit spending and accumulated insurmountable debt to The New Reality, the company called in their loans, taking advantage of havoc wreaked by *The Disease*. When the countries were unable to repay even a pittance of their debt, The New Reality usurped their sovereignty, creating a New World Order that fundamentally changed the planet.

Personal freedoms and individual thought had become a relic of the past. Central planning, massive regulations, and insurmountable taxation had made the accumulation of personal wealth almost impossible. The bankers and businessmen who ran The New Reality became richer by the day while the rest of the planet's population wallowed in servitude and fought for the economic scraps left behind.

The middle class had been eradicated and an "even playing field" had been created for everyone except the extremely rich bankers and businessmen who essentially controlled everything. Well over 99% of the world's population lived in the same economic misery.

"Everything was supposed to change after Myra Keres' death when The New Reality instituted their Open Society Initiative," Benjamin commented. "Instead, it became worse. We turned on ourselves, devouring one another for the scraps left behind by the elite."

Christine agreed. Once Jules Windsor grabbed power from Myra Keres and gained control of The New Reality, things were supposed to be better. The world he promised to all based upon the philosophies of his hero Karl Popper, was supposed to create a veritable utopia on Earth. The thought that a new, greater society would emerge out of the collective, shared values of the many proved to be a farce. Instead of keeping the morals and values that held civilization together for hundreds of years, a new morality and value system was created, one based upon the masses.

It was a system where borders, religion, and traditional values were eradicated and a new moral construct arose. In but a year, civilization completely changed. Absolute value was based upon mass belief. What is right or wrong could change on a whim.

Plus, everyone had equal say in this newly-created society. All the criminals, deviants, anarchists, racists, militants, and radicals now had an equal seating at the worldwide table. Without a true moral compass to guide this new Open Society, people self-segregated themselves into individual groups, fighting amongst each other for their voices to be heard. Instead of lobbying The New Reality for change or holding them accountable for their actions, the people turned on one another and fought amongst themselves, each faction hoping their will and beliefs would win.

Most never understood what was happening to them and their previously sovereign countries—they blindly supported Jules Windsor without hesitation.

"It led to this," Benjamin grieved.

Ever since *The Disease* had taken his mother, he never trusted The New Reality again. Left to fend for himself, and homeless after the death of his father, Benjamin quickly learned how things worked on the streets. He soon realized how this Open Society was merely a ploy—a means for The New Reality to keep control of its citizens without the mass surveillance and global military force it once needed to stay in power.

As humanity's usefulness was becoming more obsolete by the day with the rise of automatization, a massive population reduction was not frowned upon by the global elite. In fact, with less of a working population and more robots doing the labor, they could wield a much stronger stranglehold over the planet than ever before—just like their Illuminati guidelines mandated.

A rumble shook the Art Museum, sending a few loose shards of glass precariously hanging from the windows on the ceiling crashing down to the floor.

Christine jumped back, startled.

Benjamin quickly reconnoitered the entire area, looking for any signs that they were somehow under attack. The doors were still boarded shut, and all the armor and tables behind them continued to bolster their defenses.

The people in the room snapped to attention. The worn and tired looks on their faces quickly subsided with the thought of a possible battle at hand. Many instinctively grabbed a vintage medieval sword lying next to them or a piece of metal pipe to defend themselves.

"Calm down," Benjamin assured. "I think it was just an earthquake."

"Like that's any relief," grumbled a man in the far corner of the room. With one arm in a makeshift sling and a poorly healing scar on the side of his face, he continued to heckle, "It's not like dying from this building crumbling down upon us all from an earthquake would be any worse of a fate than we all face right now."

"Jeremy," Benjamin pleaded, "now is not the time."

"Listen, Ben," he continued, "now *is* the time. "If those bastards outside don't come in here soon and kill us all, starvation will do it for them."

Benjamin could see a few heads nodding in agreement.

"You got that right," agreed a middle-aged emaciated woman.

"Lord God, take us all now," Jeremy pleaded, looking up at the ceiling. "Send down the fire and brimstone and take us all out of our misery."

Benjamin did not know if this outburst were out of pure frustration, post-traumatic stress, starvation, or a combination of all three. However, he did realize one thing: He needed to take control. If they were to survive, they must remain cohesive.

Utilizing a technique that he learned on the streets, Benjamin raised his voice and tenor to meet the anger projected by Jeremy. "Do you want the Lopers to win?"

Benjamin looked around the room, meeting the gaze of each and every man and woman before continuing. "When *The Disease* struck, who did we rely on to get through it?"

Silence echoed throughout the room.

"We here in Philadelphia stuck together. We took care of one another and made sure our neighbor's best interest was that of our own." He stopped a second. "What happened when the nanosplicers decimated our population? Did we sit and cry? What did we do?"

"Stuck together!" Christine added with a little enthusiasm. A few others joined in, echoing her words in agreement.

"That's right. We stuck together," Benjamin added.

A few of the people in the room held up their swords.

"You all here are my family." He looked around the room again. "This is our family. We have—" he attempted to continue.

The entire building began to shake. This time the tremors proved much more violent. What was once a simple rumble turned into a roller coaster ride. Parts of the ceiling began to crash down upon them as the wall Jeremy had been standing next to crumbled down on him, crushing the man.

"Jeremy," Benjamin pleaded as he touched a two by two mm auricular chip implanted in his outer left ear canal, "are you alright?"

He repeated the request twice but received no response. The crackles emitting from the chip gave him the only answer he needed: Another friend had been lost.

Over the rubble from the collapsed wall, Benjamin saw the glint of the sun flicker off what appeared to be a shiny metal object. A few more reflections of sunlight again glimmered in the distance.

Recognizing the danger, Benjamin yelled, "Prepare your weapons!"

CHAPTER 2

A STRING QUARTET consisting of two violinists, one viola player, and a cellist, all dressed in Renaissance-era tuxedos, played a tune from one of Jules Windsor's favorite composers, Cesar Frank. The song, "Panis Angelicus," soothed his mind, and never an event went by without its performance.

Aboard his massively large and equally expensive yacht, fittingly named *The Caligula*, Jules enjoyed the music and soaked in each harmonious note. He drew great inspiration from the song and breathed in deeply so that he could not only hear but also feel the notes.

"Jules," interjected an older woman donning a luxurious, tight-fitting hazel dress that flowed out as it grazed along the floor. "My, you did not disappoint tonight."

Though in her late sixties, she could easily be mistaken for someone half her age. With a combination of plastic surgery and selected genetic manipulation, the woman's appearance certainly did not mirror her chronological clock. Only a few wrinkles on her eyelids and elbows allowed Jules to astutely guess her age. As one of his more robust financial partners over the years, Elizabeth proved not only beautiful but also cunning in the cutthroat business world.

"Enjoy," Jules responded with a sophisticated English accent. "My dear, this little get together is for you all in thanks for what we have accomplished since I took control of The New Reality."

Elizabeth grabbed Jules by the lapel on his black pinstripe double-breasted suit. She found his power and intellectual prowess intensely attractive. Just above six feet tall with wavy blond hair and an athletic physique, Jules' aesthetic quality was also not lost on her. Though he was almost twenty-five years her younger, Elizabeth did not find the age disparity at all daunting—after all, she had experience on her side.

A waiter with glasses of champagne approached the two of them.

"May I?" Jules said as he took two glasses, handing one to Elizabeth.

Though he dearly enjoyed Elizabeth's company and her business acumen, he definitely had no interest in escalating their relationship. He had a firm belief that business partners and bed partners should be completely separate. Plus, with a veritable harem of woman at his disposal, there seemed no need to take on the complications that would inevitably follow any real romantic relationship.

Jules looked out the port window onto a sister yacht known as *The Billion*, owned by the former French financial minister. Because of *The Caligula's* magnetic stabilizers, it felt as if they were gliding on ice, despite the slightly choppy Atlantic waters below them. Looking at the reflections in the glass, he took note of everyone in the room, not forgetting faces nor to whom they were speaking. He momentarily watched as they enjoyed the generous supply of alcohol pouring out from the four well-stocked bars around the room and partook in the seemingly endless amounts of food.

He watched in the reflection as the former Chancellor of Germany approached him from behind. Though nearly equal to Jules in height, the man appeared to be as wide as he was tall.

"Your uncle would be proud," Helmut sputtered in a jovial, deep voice. With crumbs of food in his grey beard and a jolly tenor to his voice, he continued with only the slightest of German accents, "The New Reality has far surpassed anything Albert Rosenberg would have ever imagined."

Helmut held up his glass of champagne. "Here's to you and the further success of The New Reality!"

They clinked their long fluted glasses and savored the drink. "Well done," Helmut reiterated after finishing the entire glass of champagne. "Well done. You are one hell of a businessman!" With a mighty laugh, he grabbed another glass of champagne from a passing waitress and began drinking immediately.

Jules cringed at the compliment. Though in agreement about the success of The New Reality, he would much rather be thought of as a philosopher or even a philanthropist. He had studied the great works of Plato and Aristotle along with countless other classical thinkers. He also poured over the writings of Marx, Buddha, and even Pope John Paul II.

However, Jules' greatest influence was from Karl Popper. Through Popper's works such as *The Open Society and its Enemies*, Jules created the modern-day version of the man's nineteenth century vision. Unlike the former leader of The New Reality, Myra Keres, who ruled the world with an iron fist, Jules was able to accomplish the same results with a fraction of the cost and manpower. Instead of the company having to constantly patrol the masses, the masses now patrolled themselves.

As people self-segregated into smaller and more militant groups in order to have their own beliefs and ideas be heard, they fought vehemently amongst themselves to improve their financial, social, and political positions. Instead of making any real change in the system that ruled over them, they bickered for the mere crumbs left to them.

"On that note," Helmut went on to say with a slightly more boisterous tone, "I think I see a few more chafing dishes calling my name." He patted Jules on the back before departing.

Elizabeth looked over at him as they both sipped from their glasses.

"You don't like him, do you?" she questioned.

"My dear," Jules responded matter-of-factly, "whether I like or dislike him is rather irrelevant. It would be juvenile of me to conduct my daily business based upon the whim of my emotions. Helmut is a financial business asset whose worth to The New Reality is far more than most aboard this ship."

Raising a quizzical eyebrow, Elizabeth asked, "But do you respect him?"

"As a business man, yes. However, one must never forget how he sold out his country in order to bring them under the governance of The New Reality. If you recall, he willingly bankrupted Germany so that my dear old uncle Albert Rosenberg could usurp their sovereignty through a mere financial loophole."

Jules smiled, thinking of the utter brilliance of his uncle to not only finally take control of The New Reality but also to conquer the entire planet, without a single shot ever being fired.

"Your uncle was a remarkable man," Elizabeth added, knowing what was running through Jules' mind.

Jules turned to Elizabeth. "He certainly was. In a way, he was like a father to me. Though far from a loving or nurturing man, he provided me with more than a mere hug or a simple pat on the head. What he taught me, dear Elizabeth, was how to think."

The boat suddenly tilted, sending a few people and chafing dishes to the floor. Elizabeth accidentally fell into Jules' arms.

"Why Jules," she hinted, "I thought you would never ask."

Jules' company laughed at the incident as if they were on some amusement ride. With so much liquor and food in them, Jules realized that even if the boat sunk, they would still be amused.

"Tried to save some money on cheap stabilizers, Jules?" jested one of the guests, wiping some food off his lapel.

The poke provided all with a mighty laugh.

Despite their enjoyment, Jules knew such a sudden movement of *The Caligula* was more than a whimsical mechanical failure. With redundant stabilizing systems including two magnetic dipole oscillators, such an event should not have occurred.

After a brief interlude, the string quartet began to play as if nothing had transpired.

Still holding Elizabeth, Jules noticed the approach of one of the ship's crewmen wearing a white tuxedo with a black hat bearing The New Reality emblem.

"Sir," the man politely said, tipping his hat in the process. "Your presence is requested below deck."

"My dear," Jules said, looking at Elizabeth, "we shall continue this lovely conversation at a more auspicious time. As always, business before pleasure."

"Promise?" Elizabeth smirked.

Following the crewman below deck, Jules was lead into a circular room with a blackened ceiling. A New Reality emblem was etched into the center of the marble floor, and a golden three-foot pedestal emerged from it.

"If you need anything, sir…" the crewman said, leaving the room. The door behind him materialized into dark mahogany paneling that matched the rest of the wall circling the room.

Jules walked up to the pillar and placed his hand solidly atop it. Upon his touch, the stark interior of the room transformed holographically into an entire scientific laboratory. Shelves piled with different mechanical devices, wires, computer chips, and electrical coils filled the area.

"Mr. Windsor," blurted a middle aged, thin man with thick black curly hair down to his neck and a neatly trimmed dark beard. "There is a problem. The shield. The magnetic dipoles. The grid."

"Drew," Jules said in his most calm voice, "take your hands out of your lab coat and breath in deeply and slowly. I can only assume this is not a social call and may have something to do with what I just experienced here out at sea."

Surprised that it was not the captain of the ship or the Atlantic Nautical Advisor beckoning his presence, he let the man speak. Before doing so, Jules took a few steps backwards as Drew's holograph was uncomfortably close to where he was standing.

"We are disrupting the entire world grid," Drew slowly responded after recouping his thoughts. "This experiment is having unintended consequences."

"Slow down, my boy," Jules insisted. "You must explain yourself better than that."

Trying to speak with one thought in mind, Drew gestured to a holographic globe that appeared next to him. Above the planet ran flowing silver lines much like those of a longitudinal and latitudinal grid. However, these lines intersected in such a way that it created a grid composed of triangles encircling the Earth.

"The world grid," Drew explained with a little more confidence, "is composed of these lines of electromagnetic energy that flow around the entire planet and are generated by the Earth itself." He continued emphatically, "Remember, the Earth was created by gravity, energy, and magnetism. When the quadrillion particles of microscopic vibrating dust and gas coalesced and packed to form the planet, the inherent energy in them was never lost but instead transformed into mechanical, electric, nuclear, magnetic and chemical equivalents. Our planet is a living entity, exuding energy from the very first day it was created."

Jules was quick to understand the implication. "So as chaos theory postulates, out of this complex energetic system, a natural order will evolve. And what I see presented before me is that end result."

"Exactly," Drew responded, not surprised by how quickly Jules understood the topic.

Gesturing to his left, Drew pointed to a clear rectangular case surrounding a shield levitating in the air.

Jules had no doubt the shield was exactly where the conversation headed. As part of his late uncle's prized ancient Greek military collection, the shield once stood as the centerpiece amongst a litany of priceless artifacts. However, Jules knew this famed historical vestige, known as Achilles Shield, was not an ordinary relic. Its historical and scientific significance went far beyond what was once believed. And once he came into possession of it, Jules was determined to unlock its ancient secrets. He feared that if he did not do so, another contender for his rightful place at the helm of The New Reality would.

Plus, if there were other artifacts harboring such unknown scientific potential, what would a possible threat to The New Reality do with such power? Such a thought was completely unacceptable to him. After almost a year of his scientific team diligently working on an answer, he was getting frustrated with the lack of results.

The aesthetic beauty of this artifact was not lost on Jules. The sun surrounded by the Earth, moon, and a few constellations were engraved in the center of the silver-plated shield. Then, like layers of an onion, different gloriously-sculpted scenes encircled this central point. A city at peace lay above the sun and constellations, while a city at war was depicted below it. Surrounding these scenes were three separate engravings of men reaping bushels of corn from a king's estate, workers plowing a field, and young girls picking grapes along a bountiful vineyard. In the following layer, a bull being ripped apart by two lions was engraved prominently at the top while two more pleasant engravings of sheep grazing and young men and women dancing framed each of its lower sides. At its outmost edge, a flowing ocean encircled the inner scenes. A rusted strip of metal wrapped tightly around the edge secured its perimeter.

"As we continue to fluctuate and intensify different electromagnetic fields around the shield," Drew continued to explain, "it is directly affecting the grid." He looked at Jules. "Plus, it's affecting it in a most unpredictable and, may I say, chaotic way. This is why there has been increased seismic activity all around the globe. This is why your ship momentarily lost stability. I saw the grid shift above you and at another hundred spots all along the globe."

Undeterred by the setback Jules asked, "So what have we learned from this little experiment? I'm not financing you and your team to give me a scientific lecture. My boy, I need results."

Exasperated, Drew responded, "I learned that you were still alive. When I discovered the location of your yacht, I called her captain immediately to see if it had capsized. I also learned that we must stop this experiment until I obtain a better understanding of the shield."

Jules was unamused and became more impatient. "There is obviously an awesome power connected to this artifact that we have yet to understand. If you can alter the nature of the Earth's grid by simply tampering with its electromagnetic field, imagine what someone not inclined to embrace the Open Society would do with such power. What if there are other relics out there at this moment that can do the exact same thing or maybe even worse?"

Jules held up his finger. "No. No. Discontinuing this project is certainly not acceptable and will not be tolerated. If you are not up to the challenge, I will accept your resignation immediately."

"Mr. Windsor," Drew gulped, "that is not what I was implying. We just need to do more research."

"Well, then," Jules smiled, "we are in total agreement. If that means fluctuating or increasing the electromagnetic field around the shield, do so. Find out how it works and how to control it."

Content with his orders, Jules stood proudly, undaunted by its potential implications. As a proponent of the Illuminati and New World Order theory, he understood the planet to be far too overpopulated; humanity was by no means living in harmony with the Earth. With billions of people assaulting her surface, thinning the herd was the only solution.

"But you are exactly where one of the last disturbances hit," Drew said sheepishly. "Shall I wait until you are in a safer place before I continue?"

"Chaos gives us no safe place," Jules said brashly. "My reputed safe place may be the most unsafe place of them all. I'll take my chances."

"Yes, sir," Drew capitulated.

Jules ended the transmission as the room returned to its natural décor. After straightening out his jacket, he walked out of the room with the door dematerializing in front of him. To his delight, the party on the entertainment deck had only grown more rowdy.

"One scotch," Jules said, pulling up a seat on one of the deck's many bars.

"Make that a double for him," cajoled the man sitting next to him.

Obviously intoxicated from one too many drinks already, the man downed a huge shot of whisky as if he were in a fraternity drinking contest. Jules recognized him as one of the founding partners of the European National Bank. He also recalled how wealthy he and his bank became with the financial collapse of the world's governments. Overnight they earned the equivalent of more than twenty trillion American dollars.

Not one to miss out on some levity, Jules said, "And divvy up my friend here another shot of whisky. He's seems a little too shy to ask for it himself."

Before either of them had a chance to enjoy their drink, the boat jerked wildly to the left as a massive wave hit the starboard side, obscuring the view out the window. Jules fell to the floor, rolling defensively so as to not be injured. Fortunately, his years of MMA training and constant exercising had kept him limber.

Most of the passengers on the deck did not have the same coordination. Already stuffed to the point of popping or too drunk to walk a straight line on stable ground, they tumbled like dominoes, knocking down everything in their path.

Moans replaced the laughter. Cries for help instead of music harmonized throughout the room.

Jules felt no pity for any of them. *Bloated blokes*, he thought. *Too fat on self-indulgence to keep a clear mind and body.* Plus, in truth, he didn't actually need any of them. Though their business collaborations had been fruitful, another one of their associates would eventually take their place, and it would be business as usual.

Another wave pummeled the port side of the yacht, throwing them all to the other side of the deck. Jules rolled and slid on his feet to stabilize himself. Dodging a few passengers and tables in the process, he managed to position himself in a neutral crouched stance.

I hope Drew is discerning some valuable information, Jules thought. *If he's putting me through this bedlam, I indeed expect some answers.*

As Jules looked up to assess the damage, he thought another wave was about to hit the ship along her bow. However, it was moving too slowly and the closer it came, the more vivid it appeared. Just as it was about to strike, Jules was able to discern two large words written along its side: *The Billion.*

The two yachts collided with a tremendous bang. Glass spewed along the entertainment deck causing water and wind to pelt the passengers through open windows. The cries of agony intensified after the impact.

The Caligula began to lean to its port side and slowly sink into the water. Red lights and sirens blared.

"Abandon ship," the captain announced. "Abandon ship. Head to the nearest safety pod."

The instructions replayed on a recorded loop.

"Grab the crew," Jules said softly to the captain as he touched the auricular chip in his left ear, "and bring them to the stratoskimmer above deck."

"I must insist that you get to the nearest safety pod," responded the captain as his voiced echoed in Jules' ear.

"Do as I say," Jules commanded.

He knew the safety pods would be useless in such a crisis; if he dared enter one of them, it would prove to be his coffin.

Jules got to his feet and began running to the front of the ship as the fellow passengers who were able to still walk headed for the stairs in the opposite direction. Along the way, he saw one of his crewmen stuck under a monstrous wooden table. Wind and rain pelted him in the face. Unable to open his eyes, he flailed helplessly to free himself.

The ship creaked as *The Billion* wedged itself further into his yacht.

Grabbing the table, Jules agonizingly slid the behemoth furniture by himself off the yacht's first mate and grabbed him by the hand. The crewman staggered to his feet with Jules' assistance. Though his right leg appeared either broken or dislocated at the hip, the sailor managed to remain standing.

Jules turned his head as salt water sprayed into his face, feeling as if a thousand pins were simultaneously stuck into his eyes. The sensation was crippling and almost brought him to his knees. Realizing he couldn't stay blind to the chaos around him, Jules forced his eyes open, regaining his vision. Everything was initially red and blurred. As things came into focus he noted Elizabeth lying next to him on the ground. Blood oozed from her mouth as a large shard of glass protruded from her back. Her once elegant dress was now blood soaked, wet, and tattered.

Good by old friend, Jules thought without remorse.

"Let's go," he then insisted to the first mate as he guided him forward to the steps.

"I can't see!" the man hollered as water pelted his eyes.

"Big steps. Move forward," Jules instructed while attempting to deflect with his arm some of the salty water away from his eyes.

The ship began to tip further as the two finally made their way to the stairs. It was a welcome feeling to be in an enclosure, momentarily away from the relentless elements.

"Up the stairs," Jules asserted. "No time to dilly dally!"

The two maneuvered up the tilted steps, slowly making it above deck where they were greeted in full force by the elements. It felt as if they were stuck in a hurricane. The wind and rain instantly knocked over the first mate who collapsed on his injured leg. Jules put his arm under him and pulled him back to his feet.

As the two staggered along the increasingly-tilted deck, the outline of his prized stratoskimmer came clearly into view. It was a long, oval-shaped ship with two large cylindrical engines in the rear and a curved tail fin running the length of the vehicle. The New Reality insignia emblazoned along its length completed the look.

The captain of the yacht stood at the bottom of its stairs waving them over to him. "Mr. Windsor, we're waiting for you to depart."

A few crewmen staggered up the steps and into the stratoskimmer, pulling themselves up on the railing.

"How many crewmen are left on the ship?" Jules shouted through the howling winds.

"We've got about fourteen on board the stratoskimmer already," shouted the captain, "and another twenty opted for safety pods."

Imbeciles, Jules lamented.

"That leaves fifteen still unaccounted for," continued the captain as he held onto the steps while looking at a blurry holographic image of the ship displayed before him.

Reaching the stratoskimmer, Jules asked, "Where are they?"

"It looks like eight are heading up here right now, another two are working their way to the safety pods, while the last five are not moving anywhere." He looked over to Jules. "Presumed dead or injured."

Grabbing the captain by the arm, Jules pushed him and the first mate up the stairs. "But I insist!" yelled the captain. "I must be the last one to leave."

"This is my ship, and you are my crew," Jules commanded, pointing to the stairs.

The captain capitulated, helping his injured first mate into the cabin.

"Wait!" cried two crewmen from behind Jules. Though he could barely discern their voices, he could almost feel the terror in their cries.

Jules yelled up to the captain who was standing at the stratoskimmer's entrance, "Tell the pilot not to leave until I say so!" He looked over to his crewmen fighting the elements to reach the stratoskimmer and spurred them on. "Faster! We need everyone aboard."

A loud creek began to drown out the roar of Mother Nature. In response, the ship began to tilt at an even more precarious angle until standing became problematic. Jules held on to the stratoskimmer's railing as the vehicle began to slide down the deck.

The more quickly it slid, the more precarious Jules' grip on the railing became.

The captain flew over Jules' head, crashing down into the water. His screams were drowned out by the waves pummeling the ship's deck. Jules knew that without a life preserver, he would last less than a minute in such violent waters.

A few other crewmembers scrambling to get to the stratoskimmer followed overboard as they, too, crashed helplessly into the water.

"Throw them a life vest," Jules attempted to say as a wave pummeled his body. It was as if someone dropped a ton of bricks straight onto his chest, knocking the wind out of him in the process.

Jules tried to regain his bearing as his tenuous grip on the railing started to fail. He coughed up water, trying to take a breath of air without choking. His eyes burned from the salty water; with the loud commotion surrounding him from every direction, he felt lost and confused.

As Jules attempted to pull himself up on the railing, he lost his grip and plunged into the cold ocean. Beaten by a tremendous gush of wind, he was now at Mother Nature's mercy. The stratoskimmer followed suit, sliding off the deck as *The Caligula* continue to sink.

The sea roared and rose up in great fury.

Struggling to surface, Jules' endeavors were met by the crashing of his prized stratoskimmer into the water above him. Trapped, and without means to escape, the unrelenting sensation of drowning began to overtake him.

CHAPTER 3

BENJAMIN GRIPPED THE SWORD in his hand a little tighter. The weapon's historical relevance meant nothing to him at the moment; his only thought was that of survival. Never having wielded such a weapon, he hoped mere determination and anger would propel him to victory.

Benjamin swiftly assessed the unfolding situation, considering all possibilities. He measured who among them was still viable to fight and where they may be best utilized. He also assessed that a previously barricaded door on the north end of the room had crumbled in the earthquake, leaving another opening for possible entry into this part of the museum.

"The Lopers are here!" alerted an older gentleman in the room, brandishing a metal pipe.

Benjamin wielded almost as much disgust for the Lopers as he harbored for The New Reality. Short for the word *interlopers*, the abridged version had their given name.

This had been the city of brotherly love until *they* arrived. The citizens of Philadelphia helped each other through the worst times in recent history, and there was a true camaraderie amongst the residents.

Benjamin looked on with repugnance as the first ones stumbled upon the rubble that had been the wall. Originally received into the city with open arms after the nanosplicers decimated the world's population, the Lopers quickly wore out their welcome. Failing to integrate and attempting to force their will on the same people who so graciously allowed them into the city, the Lopers attempted to make the city theirs.

After Philadelphia had lost nearly thirty percent of her inhabitants to *The Disease* and nanosplicers, the Lopers quickly repopulated the numerical losses. Unlike those who were native to Philadelphia, they did not possess the same work ethics and values. Theirs was one of subservience and dependence on The New Reality; they were bureaucrats working for the new state, content with the status quo and government dole.

Producing little and working even less, the Lopers' main concern was for themselves. The idea of brotherly love was a concept they chose to ignore.

As The New Reality rolled out the Open Society initiative, government jobs declined and the Lopers' source of income was lost. Instead of creating businesses or taking on private sector jobs, they blamed those who already lived in the city for their new lot in life. Tensions rapidly escalated the faster their jobs disappeared until violence broke out as they sought to take over the city for themselves.

Benjamin lamented all that had brought them to this point. The New Reality and Open Society had failed her people, and now all of them were left to suffer. Few understood what The New Reality had perpetrated as most lived their lives blindly, lead like sheep by this world-wide behemoth.

"Ken, Sue, Darrel, Jake" Benjamin commanded, placing a pinky on his auricular chip, "get to either side of the hole in the wall; hit them as they attempt to climb the rubble."

He knew these were the most limber and quickest of the bunch. Unless a mass onslaught awaited them, they would definitely prove to be a valuable deterrent.

"Christine," Benjamin pointed with his sword, "take Murph and Glenn over to that open doorway. Make sure no one is on the other side."

"And if there is?" Christine asked.

"Stay alive," Benjamin said.

Ben knew he had no other options. He hoped that Christine's agility from dance and gymnastics would prove advantageous. Plus, her speed would complement the brute strength of both Glenn and Murph.

"Get the Natives," yelled the first Loper as he stumbled over the rubble, pointing into the room.

Benjamin cringed at the term. Used by the Lopers to identify anyone who lived in the city during *The Disease* or nanosplicers infestation, the name was hurled upon them with disdain. He loved this city, what it stood for, and the people in it. And he was ready to fight to the end to defend it.

Before the first Loper could gain a footing, Sue dexterously impaled his throat with her sword. Now choking on his own blood, the man fell to his hands and knees gasping for air. Another Loper attempting to enter behind him stumbled over the man. Taking a baseball swing with a metal pipe, Jacob bashed in the man's skull as he attempted to grab the wall for support. The Loper fell backwards and onto a husky woman also making an effort to enter.

Since all weapons had been confiscated by The New Reality, people were left to fight with whatever they could find. If they didn't have a sword, stick, or pipe, they were prepared to rip each other apart with their bare hands if necessary.

"Don't let them enter the room!" yelled Benjamin. He knew the bottleneck in the wall was his only advantage. Allowing only a certain number of people through at a time, it would give him and his people a fighting chance. But if enough Lopers were able to gain entrance, their superior numbers would prove unbeatable.

A few more Lopers were bludgeoned or impaled as they attempted to enter. Benjamin knew that if they continued this haphazard assault, the only thing that could impair him and his friends from defending their position would be pure exhaustion.

Maybe we should take shifts, Benjamin momentarily contemplated, *to make sure we don't fatigue ourselves.* As another Loper lurched over the rubble, Ben personally struck the man on the neck with his sword. Due to the artifact's age, the blade broke near its hilt, leaving him with what appeared now to be a dagger.

The man was then kicked and beaten by those surrounding Benjamin until he was no longer moving. All able-bodied people still in the room stood guard in a semicircular position around the breach in the wall. In certain places, they were two to three deep, each prepared to defend their stronghold.

Benjamin looked over to the open door and saw Christine with her two companions clamor through the rubble into the adjacent room. *God help her,* he thought, hoping it would be empty.

After another few Lopers met their quick demise after attempting to enter the room, all momentarily went quiet. The attack had suddenly ceased.

Have the Lopers left? Benjamin wondered. *Were they deterred by the early losses? Did they simply move on overnight?*

Benjamin held out his arms. "Stay back," he said while slowly walking on the rubble to obtain a better view of the outside. Because the Art Museum stood on a hill, he could not ascertain how many people were outside the building. With only a view of the sky, he needed to be standing on top of the rubble to obtain a better view.

His friends in the room cheered at their initial victory. "Give 'em hell!" yelled one. Benjamin's enthusiasm certainly did not match theirs. Forced to barricade themselves in the museum just a few days ago, he recalled how over 100 Lopers had forced them into confinement, hiding for their lives.

The chirps of a morning bird and the crisp smell of a new spring day greeted him as he stood on top of the rubble looking down towards the Susquehanna River. For a brief second he remembered rowing along the water with his friends, enjoying a beer or two they smuggled on board.

The harshness of the reality now afoot crushed any fond memories. The Lopers' numbers had drastically risen. What was once 100 now seemed like thousands. Benjamin quickly realized why any reinforcements for his group had not come. If they had, they would have all met an unceremonious death or fled before daring to proceed any further.

Usually the optimist, Benjamin realized there was no hope. As he watched what looked like an endless sea of Lopers ascend the hill, he knew all was lost. The brief hope that the bulk of the Lopers had left the premises was crushed. Instead, he saw they were simply regrouping for their true assault.

✶✶✶

The dim light twinkling in through a dirty window on the ceiling provided little illumination for Christine to see. Between the dust and darkness, any number of people could be hiding in it, and she would not know.

Murph shined a flashlight over her shoulder, brightening up the room. To her delight, they were the only ones in it.

"Glenn," Christine said, "watch our backs."

"Sure," the former machinist responded, clenching a piece of wood with a dirty nail hanging out of it. More than eager to use this weapon against one of the Lopers, he was looking for a brawl. These invaders had taken his house, his belongings, and everything he owned but his dignity. He was ready for payback.

A slight rumble again shook the museum; the aftershock only proved to heighten Christine's alertness. Murph's flashlight jiggled in the process, making the movement a slightly nauseating experience.

"This must be some sort of storage closet," Christine surmised, looking at all the shelves and massive filing cabinets. Some of the drawers were missing or half open. Trash littered the floor, and only a few parts of medieval relics remained.

"You see anything in there?" Glenn asked. His voice echoed from the other end of the room.

"Nothing useful," she admitted.

Though narrow, the storage area was long and wound around the back of the building.

Turning to face Glenn, Christine hollered from the distance, "How's Benjamin?"

"All's quiet now," he said enthusiastically. "I think we scared them off."

Christine breathed a sigh of relief. She hoped that the rest of the Lopers had left long before the wall fell.

While she looked further into the room, she pondered the inevitable: leaving her beloved city. Even if they managed to escape, Christine knew it was time to flee the city. Philadelphia was long lost. Most of the original inhabitants had already bolted once the Lopers grew violent.

She knew it was time to begin a new life in a new place. She just hoped there was somewhere she could find, maybe even with Ben, that the Open Society had not infected, and where she could finally live a normal life once again.

An aftershock threw Christine and Murph to the floor. In the distance, she could see the roof and opposite end of the room collapse. Wood and stone then began to fall around her like an avalanche. Everything went dim after she was struck by falling debris; she could hear Murph's voice implore her to get under the desk before all went dark.

CHAPTER 4

THE LACK OF OXYGEN burned Jules' chest. Submerged under water, he fought off every bodily instinct to open up his mouth and breathe.

Must get out from under the stratoskimmer.

Clawing his way underneath it, Jules desperately needed air. His focus blurred by the second while consciousness slowly slipped away. As the world began to blacken around him, his hand thrust out of the water.

With his last effort, Jules propelled himself to the surface and gagged up a staggering amount of water before taking in a deep breath. His vision began to clear, but a pounding headache took its place.

"Mr. Windsor!" yelled the captain.

To his surprise, the captain of *The Caligula* was standing in the stratoskimmer's entrance beckoning him to come aboard.

Good show! Jules applauded at both his captain's survival skills and pilot's ability to stay afloat as the ship plunged into the waters.

"Mr. Windsor," he again pleaded. "Take hold of the leverage raft."

Realizing that Jules would never be able to board the stratoskimmer in such choppy waters, the captain threw down what appeared to be an orange log. Jules had stocked hundreds of these modern flotation devices on all his boats and aircrafts. Utilizing both its buoyancy and electromagnetic hydrophobic properties, the device not only floated but could also levitate on the water if activated.

The leverage raft struck the water as if it were a log. He had hoped the captain activated its hydrophobic charge, but to Jules' dismay it appeared as if he had forgotten. Grabbing it, Jules looked around for any other crewmembers adrift in the waters.

"Throw them a raft," Jules yelled as the waves battered him.

He could see a few crewmembers treading water. The waves must have pushed them further out to sea as they were at least fifty yards now from the stratoskimmer. Each looked like they would not make it much longer without help. Pummeled by the water, they were desperately clinging to life.

Bright yellow circular boats surrounded both him and the ship at a distance. These safety pods bobbed up and down in the water with their passengers harnessed securely inside of each of them.

The ocean began to grow eerily calm, almost as if someone turned off a switch, and the waves and rain quickly subsided. Jules tapped the auricular chip in his ear, hoping to order Drew to cease further experimentation on the shield until he had reached safety. However, there was no response.

Where are the lights on the pods? Jules thought, looking closer at the small boats. *And why were they bobbing so erratically? Weren't their stabilizers working?*

After repeatedly attempting to activate the raft in his hand, Jules noted that it also was not working. Looking around, he realized that nothing was working.

Jules swam over to two crewmen closest to the stratoskimmer and pulled them towards the steps leading up to the ship. With the sea momentarily calm, he knew it may be his only opportunity to save them.

"Thank you, Mr. Windsor," gasped the first man, grabbing hold of the stratoskimmer's railing.

"There are two more crewmen out there," Jules shouted while the captain and a few other crewmembers aboard the ship helped all three of them up the stairs. "Grab me the rope in the supply chest under the conference table."

A crewman waiting at the entrance of the ship attempted to place a towel around Jules. He shunned the gesture and slipped the straps of two leverage rafts over his right shoulder. Looking towards the cockpit, he noted the entire elegantly-designed hull filled with crewmembers. Some were lying on the floor while others leaned on the walls or had collapsed on one of the white leather chairs.

Jules placed his hand on the wall to activate the telecommunicator. "George, what's the status of the stratoskimmer?"

"Sir," a crewmember interrupted, "the rope you requested."

"George," he then bellowed through the ship's hull, realizing the error in his action, "status please!" Grabbing the rope, he peered over the black, oval conference table in the center of the room, awaiting an answer.

The pilot wearing a blue jumpsuit and cap gazed through the open cockpit door and succinctly responded, "Dead in the water."

Before the pilot could continue, Jules reached out of the stratoskimmer and grabbed the tailfin above the door. Though slick, he took his other hand and pulled himself up and onto it before climbing to the top of the ship. In the distance, he could see *The Caligula* and *The Billion* slowly sinking. They both creaked as the sea pulled them to their deaths.

The two crewmembers he had spotted earlier were still alive. Both pleaded for help and waved their hands, hoping to bring attention to themselves.

"Grab these!" Jules yelled. After tying the straps of both rafts about five feet from one another at the end of the rope, he spun them around his head and threw the line into the water. The rope unwound until the rafts hit the water. Taking the loose end, he wrapped it a few times around his waist.

"Take hold," Jules said.

A safety pod bobbed closer to the stratoskimmer. As it drew near, Jules could see the scared look on the four occupants' faces. Strapped into their seats, these European bankers were used to being in control. Now adrift at sea, they were as helpless as a baby without a mother.

As both crewmembers lurched onto the rafts, the ocean began to swirl around a central point a few miles from their current location, dragging the stratoskimmer in its wake. Jules ran down to the nose of the ship and pulled in the slack on the rope, dragging the sailors closer to the stairs.

The captain and the first mate reached out and grabbed hold of the two crewmembers before they floated by the ship. As Jules leaned back on the rope, the captain and first mate, despite the injured leg, yanked the two out of the water. Assisted by a few others who joined to help, the waterlogged crewmembers were carried up the stairs and into the ship.

Untying the rope from his waist, Jules watched as the waters began to churn more violently around this central point in the ocean. The larger the waves became, the quicker the stratoskimmer, the escape pods, and the sinking boats moved in the water.

Jules sidestepped down the length of the ship until he reached the door. His eyes were on the ocean the entire time, considering what options he had available for escape.

"Bloody hell," Jules commented, amazed at the raw beauty of Mother Nature.

The ocean at the focal point around which the water swirled began to rise up out of the water and spin as if it were a tornado. Instead of descending from above, this natural terror reached for the heavens in its devastating display of might.

Jules jumped onto the tailfin and swung himself into the ship.

"We're going to have to close this door manually," Jules said, sliding open a panel on the wall. A two-foot padded, cylindrical handle was located behind it. Grabbing it with both hands, he thrust it to the left until he heard a clink. Then, arching his back, he pulled on the handle and yanked it back towards him.

A cylindrical portion of the wall attached to the handle opened downward until another loud thump that echoed through the ship's hull indicated it was in position. Jules then began to crank the handle in a clockwise rotation. Because of the mechanism's counter-weighted system, Jules was quickly able to make the stairs ascend back up to the ship and seal the doorway in the stratoskimmer's hull without much effort.

Jules then pushed back the crank mechanism into the wall and closed the panel behind it. As he turned, the boat began to rock.

"The ship's still dead," commented the captain.

In the commotion, Jules had not noticed how dim the ship's hull looked. With little light filling its interior through the side windows, the area took on a bleak gray color. The dreary pallor of his crew's faces only added to the overall dark ambiance.

The ship then lurched forward again as it rode what seemed to be a bigger wave. Everyone in the stratoskimmer's hull hung on to anything secured to the floor, attempting not to fall.

"What is that?" shouted the ship's first mate. Pointing outside the port window, he noted the large water funnel rising from the ocean as if conjured up by the mythical Poseidon himself. Other crewmembers lurched over to peer out the window. Careful to keep a grasp on anything to stabilize themselves, they gasped in horror at the site.

Jules took off his jacket and carefully folded it over the bar next to him as if he had nonchalantly returned home from an uneventful day's work. Without any apparent urgency, he then paced over to the cockpit while contemplating potential options.

This trait to remain calm even under the most inauspicious circumstances was Jules' trademark and had brought him great notoriety within the company.

Jules entered the cockpit and strapped himself into the copilot's chair.

"Admirable what you did out there," the pilot applauded.

"Any other action," Jules rebutted, "would not have been honorable."

He then peered forward through the windshield and noted that the massive rotating water funnel had now reached all the way up to the clouds and caused them to also spiral in unison. He also perceived how a few safety pods caught up in this mighty water vortex would spin around the funnel until they almost reached the top before being jettisoned violently back towards the sea. As they neared the clouds, their red beacon lights would flicker on for a few seconds before their inevitable deadly drop into the ocean. As they smashed down upon the roaring water, the pods would crumble much like a plastic cup under a hand.

"I was able to utilize the natural polarity of the ship's engine," the pilot went on to explain, "to create a manual technique to at least steer the ship away from that massive funnel." He shook his head. "I don't know how much longer I can do it though. As that monstrosity gets bigger, so do these waves. Let's just hopes that whatever's going on stops before it's too late."

"You say you can manually maneuver this stratoskimmer of ours?" Jules asked.

"Yes, sir!" the pilot answered proudly.

"Then I want you to steer the ship right into the heart of the beast," Jules said with a sadistic smile on his face, as if he were looking forward to what was in store for them.

"But that would be suicide!" the pilot exclaimed. "Just look at what it's doing to the safety pods."

"I am looking," Jules answered without much sympathy for his former guests.

The pilot's eyes widened as he watched the half-sunken *Caligula* and *Billion* slowly get caught up in the water funnel's torrent. The massive ships angled forward and began to rotate with increased velocity around the funnel the closer they approached.

Another large wave rocked the stratoskimmer. Though strapped in, Jules held on to the armchair. He could hear cries of pain and moans from the hull.

Suicide, the pilot mentally reiterated. Not daring to question Jules, he followed the man's orders despite his better judgment. With his eyes on the yachts, he angled the stratoskimmer directly towards the funnel until the air ship was caught in its unbreakable grip.

"Hold on," Jules said as if he were a schoolboy at the top of a roller coaster waiting for it to drop.

The pilot could do nothing at this point to control the ship; they were now at the mercy of the ocean. As they spun around the funnel, he watched the two massive yachts lurch out of the water and ascend the massive vortex.

The faster the stratoskimmer spun around the funnel the louder the laments stemmed from the hull. The crew were at their physical and mental breaking point. Many wished they could die to end the pain.

The nose of the stratoskimmer then lurched upward toward the sky as the ship began to ascend the massive funnel in a clockwise rotation. Screams of anguish along with the sounds of furniture and glass breaking echoed from the ship's hull. The pilot clung to his seat as he watched them rapidly approach the two massive yachts above.

Though Jules had complete confidence in his pilot, he knew there was one person who would be able to pull off such an aerial stunt with absolute surety—Alex Pella.

Alex Pella. Jules let himself linger on the thought for a brief second. The name still aggravated. An intellectual equal. A greater thinker. And more importantly, a superb strategist. Jules knew the world was too small to accommodate both of them. Though he attempted never to dwell on the past, the knowledge that Alex's body was never recovered continued to make Jules uneasy.

"We're going to crash!" the pilot yelled; impact with the yachts seemed inevitable.

Wide-eyed, Jules clung on to this seat. "Wait for it," he exclaimed. "Wait for it!"

The lights in the cockpit began to flicker on as the dashboard and steering wheel lit up in a grand display of light.

"Depolarize the engine," Jules commanded. "Now!"

The pilot ran his hand across the dashboard. In the process, a sudden jolt and hum of the engines let him know that they were ready to fly. The impending collision with one of the ships directly above them still seemed inevitable.

"Concentrate," Jules implored.

The pilot watched as the two ships were thrown from the funnel as if they were weightless ephemeral structures blown by the winds. The yachts erupted with the sound of destruction as their metal hulls grinded and collapsed in on themselves.

Just as they were being flung out of the air, the pilot noted a small, yet hopefully navigable space between the ships. *Our father…*, he began to pray as he then further depolarized the engines for maximum acceleration.

Everything grew dark as the yachts blocked all outside illumination. *…who art in heaven!* the pilot continued to utter after being thrown back on his seat with the mounting G-forces.

Hallowed be thy name, he chanted louder as he attempted to keep his eyes open and not flinch. Even a millimeter of a miscalculation, he knew, would plummet them to their deaths.

The ship rocked back and forth until the blackness in front of them opened to a view of blue skies. Like a gift from heaven, they were now above the maelstrom.

"Good show, my boy!" Jules applauded, laughing with pure joy. He clapped his hands together. "Now that was a ride!"

CHAPTER 5

"MR. WINDSOR," Drew said, relieved at the sight, "you are alive."

"And why wouldn't I be?" Jules responded almost indignantly. "You don't think that little nuisance you caused out there on the high seas was going to undo me, did you?"

Wearing a new dark blue suit with a fresh black shirt underneath, Jules entered the lab. New Reality emblem cufflinks added to the attire's overall air of style and power.

"So, this is what caused all that ruckus?" he said, pointing at the shield.

"But what happened to your yacht," Drew questioned, "and all her guests? As soon as I increased the electromagnetic pulses in the shield, I lost contact with you. Plus," he sputtered, appearing more exasperated with the situation, "drastic weather and seismic activity was recorded over the entire planet."

"So, what did you learn from your little experiment?" Jules asked nonchalantly, unconcerned about the material or humanitarian losses.

Drew was taken aback by the response. After noting the massive seismic and weather changes he had caused by increasing the electromagnetic field around the shield, he could only speculate as to how much destruction and loss of human lives it must have caused. He felt sickened by the experience and was shocked by Jules' indifferent attitude.

"I'm sorry, Mr. Windsor," Drew apologized. "When I finally realized what was occurring in the Atlantic, I immediately cut the electromagnetic field around the shield. I could only imagine what you and the guests on your ship must have endured."

Jules conceded, "It was certainly too bad what happened. The Atlantic took *The Caligula* to the bottom of the sea. With regard to the guests who were on her, let's just say you did me a favor by trimming some of The New Reality's fat."

Drew gasped at the admission. Holding on to the side of the table, he tried not to collapse under the weight of his guilt.

"Chin up," Jules commanded, looking the man almost a foot smaller than him in the eye. "This is not some pity party. Must I remind you of the values inscribed on the pillars around which this great Georgian complex was built?"

Drew was well aware of the pillars to which Jules alluded. Created from six large slabs of stone with one positioned in the center, four arranged around it, and a final capstone on top, the monument stood boldly at over nineteen feet tall.

Inscribed in eight languages including English, Spanish, Swahili, Hindi, Hebrew, Arabic, Chinese and Russian, the Guidestones each conveyed the same New World Order message. Ranging from population control and social duties all the way to reproductive responsibilities, the pillars outlined the crux of The New Reality governing philosophy. Commissioned in 1980 by a secret society known as the Illuminati, the pillars had been painstakingly rebuilt after they were destroyed in an attack on the headquarters. Using the original pieces, hundreds of laborers pieced the monument back together as if it were the world's most complicated jigsaw puzzle.

Serving as the centerpiece to their main headquarters in Elbert, Georgia, the Guidestones stood in the epicenter of the enormous thirty-story structure built as a precise replica of the company's logo—a diamond with a golden circle in the center. With shimmering windows representing the diamond positioned around the perimeter and a large golden dome covering the vast courtyard in the center, the building was an unequivocal testament to modern architecture.

Though Drew did not completely agree with all The New World Order's philosophies, he certainly believed in Jules Windsor. The man had proven a great inspiration ever since he first met him while working in England. Jules' charisma motivated Drew to be a better scientist and expand his mental horizons beyond all he had previously thought possible.

Be more than the sum of your parts, he recalled Jules saying when they first met. *You can do more than you ever expected. The only confines to your successes are the limits you place on them.*

Though he was just an intern in The New Reality at the time, Drew aspired to work his way up the company chain until he became its lead scientist. Long nights, endless work, and hours of studying had paid off. After multiple promotions and accolades, Jules personally commissioned Drew and his team to oversee the lab at the massive Georgian headquarters.

"Yes, Mr. Windsor," Drew capitulated, regretting his doubts. "Always look forward and not backwards, as you say."

"Good show," Jules said as he patted the man on the shoulder. He then looked at the shield in the glass case with great anticipation. "So, have we uncovered any of its secrets after that little diversion you put me through?"

Drew looked with awe on the shield. Despite the enormous achievements of modern science, this artifact dating back well over 10,000 years possessed mysteries that were beyond what he could explain. He remembered the ancient Greek myth from *The Iliad* of how the blacksmith god of metallurgy known as Hephaestus had constructed it for Achilles. Hephaestus was also believed to have manufactured the Greek god Hermes' winged helmet and sandals, Aegis' breastplate, Helio's chariot, and Eros' bow and arrows.

The composite metals used in fashioning the shield were so strong that not even a high-powered laser could cut through them. Also, as described in *The Iliad*, the shield was made of five separate layers with its innermost one being pure liquid mercury as evidenced by indirect methods of analysis using low coherence interferometry, spectral analysis, and magnetic-particle resonance.

Drew walked over to the shield and placed his hands on the rectangular glass console protruding from the clear encasement. The console rose a few inches in response.

"What you experienced was a bloch wall effect," Drew explained as a holographic globe encased in intersecting lines forming a triangular grid appeared between them, "As I mentioned before, the Earth is surrounded by a massive electromagnetic grid forming these lines you see right here."

Drew touched the globe and a separate two-dimensional scene with three lines intersecting in its center appeared. "Where these electromagnetic lines cross is figuratively known as a bloch wall."

"And as you can see," he continued as the scene zoomed in until a three-dimensional view of *The Caligula* came into view, "this is where the electromagnetic waves cancel out each other, producing a negative gravity effect. It works just like the engines on the stratoskimmer, but on a global scale. In effect, non-spin energy in a polarized universe is rejected, weakening gravity at that exact point."

"As you intensified and fluctuated the field around the shield," Jules surmised, "it somehow directly influenced the grid and intensified it accordingly. But why don't we notice this negative gravity effect at that point all the time?"

"It's too weak to be of any significance. But," Drew elaborated, "if there is a shift in the Earth's crust, if the magma underground moves a certain direction, or if the liquid iron core in the center of the Earth changes its rotational velocity, it can transiently enhance this bloch wall effect at certain places and cause local anomalies."

The image zoomed out back to a holograph of the Earth surrounded by grid lines. Drew then pointed at the Atlantic where Jules was sailing. With a grin on his face he said, "And some areas are given particularly ominous names—like the Bermuda Triangle."

Jules raised an eyebrow with increased interest.

"What is more interesting," Drew explained, "is that where these bloch walls occur we find megalithic structures such as the Giza pyramids in Egypt, Easter Island in the Pacific, Stonehenge in Ireland, Baalbek in Lebanon, and Mohenjo-Daro in Pakistan, among many others."

Red dots appeared across the globe as he spoke.

"Somehow the great builders must have known about the grid," Jules concluded, "and utilized this bloch wall effect to their benefit, creating such magnificent structures." He looked at the shield. "And this shield here must be somehow connected to that lost knowledge and to the people who created it."

The globe rotated and turned slightly to the side, highlighting South America.

"However," Drew said with a little more gusto, "nowhere on Earth was this Bloch wall effect more noticeable than in Bolivia.

The more I turned up the electromagnetic field around the shield, the more spectacular its effect became. You can see how the grid lines blur and curve around this one particular red dot at 16 degrees, 33 minutes, 42 seconds North by 68 degrees, 40 minutes, 48 seconds South."

"And what, pray tell, is located at this God-forsaken spot besides a desert?" Jules asked.

"An ancient site known as Pumapunku," Drew noted. "Inca tradition believes it to be the birthplace of the world."

"And I would bet it is no mere coincidence that this is where these grid lines intersect," Jules contemplated aloud while looking at the shield. Implications, options, and counter options ran through his mind as his lead scientist continued speaking.

"Located 12,800 feet above sea level," Drew continued as a holographic of the ancient site appeared, "Pumapunku hosts some of the largest and most intricately cut red sandstone blocks in the world with some weighing over 100 tons. Archeologists today still marvel at the stonework. With highly complex geometry, perfect right angles, and faces that are as smooth as glass, one wonders what type of technology created such a structure."

The more Drew explained, the more he was memorized by the ancient ruin. "It is almost like some advanced lost civilization built it and—"

Drew abruptly stopped speaking as he watched Jules place his hand on the clear encasement surrounding the shield. Quantumly coded for only his and Jules' specific subatomic neurally-generated quantum field, the clear façade on that side faded away with Jules' mere touch.

"What—" Drew stammered in concern. "What are you doing?"

He then watched Jules walk up to the levitating shield and place his hands around it.

"I don't think," Drew said. "No, I don't think it would be a good idea."

Jules yanked the shield out of place and walked confidently out of the encasement with his prize in hand. When Drew saw the grin on his boss' face, he knew what Jules was thinking.

"Let me humbly recommend," Drew implored, "that the best place for the shield would be exactly where you took it from."

Jules smirked. "My boy. Life's too short to stand on your heels all day."

"But—" Drew started before he was cut off by Jules.

"Reflexivity!" Jules boasted. "We are looking at a most perfect opportunity where cause and effect meet at the precise time. Both the shield and Pumapunku are somehow tied together so closely that they are directly affecting one another. We must discover how—with haste."

"I don't think it's a good idea," Drew sheepishly responded.

Jules began to walk out of the room.

"Let us not dilly dally here any longer," Jules turned back and said. "We have a most urgent appointment to keep at Pumapunku."

CHAPTER 6

CHRISTINE'S BODY JOLTED as her subconscious mind willed herself to awaken. She uttered, "Benjamin." A trickle of light shining through the debris and dust next to her were the only indication that she was alive.

"Benjamin," she attempted to yell but began to gag in the process. The air seemed to burn her throat with every breath. Her body also ached as she started to slip from her safe haven under the desk.

"Christine?" a feeble voice echoed from the rubble next to her.

"Murph?" she answered, suddenly forgetting about the pain. "Murph!" Christine yelled. "Are you alright?"

The rubble began to move, and a hand reached out from underneath and grabbed her knee. "I got you," Christine uttered, putting her hand over his."

As the rubble shifted, more light shone down. What was once a cool morning had turned into a bright, humid afternoon. The heat and sun soothed her body, providing it with the needed strength to continue.

Christine rose to her knees and began to push some of the rubble and debris to the side, creating a narrow passage for her escape. Hoping also to get some of it off Murph, she threw pieces of wood to the side, freeing up some of his body in the process.

"Try to stand," Christine implored her friend as she made her way out from underneath the desk. Grabbing Murph's hand, she attempted to pull him to his feet.

She noted how bloodied his arm looked now in the light and hoped the rest of him had fared better. Because the collapse of the building was so sudden, she was surprised that both of them had managed to survive the destruction.

"A little more," she willed aloud, seeing more and more of his body appear from underneath the rubble.

Murph pushed a piece of wood off his torso. The relief it provided was instantaneous. As more light trickled through the debris, he saw two long support beams that had fallen during the earthquake about a half-foot above him. Instead of crushing him, Murph concluded that they must have created a small safe space for him to escape the brunt of the building's collapse, thus saving his life.

"That's it!" Christine coached as she helped Murphy climb out of the debris.

Though battered and covered with white dust, he looked much better than expected. A few dried-up patches of blood on the side of his neck were the only other noticeable injuries.

Taking off his badly torn and ripped jacket, he threw it on the ground and looked towards the door where he had entered the room. It was no longer standing; only a pile of debris remained in its place. The more Murph surveyed the area, the more he realized that the entire museum was leveled. Nothing had survived.

The once great edifice with priceless works of antiquity had been destroyed. Only support beams and concrete poles stood as silent witnesses of the past. What shocked Murph even more was that he and Christine appeared to be the sole survivors left standing among the ruins.

"Benjamin!" Christine cried aloud, reaching the same conclusion. "Anyone!" she yelled while touching her auricular chip, hoping for any answer. Instead, only the roaring sound of the Susquehanna below and the chirp of a lone bird responded to her calls.

Stumbling on the rubble, Christine retraced her steps. She also continued to yell Benjamin's name as if it would make him and everyone else suddenly appear.

To her distress, the room where they were once barricaded was completely gone.

"Murph!" she yelled in horror. "What happened?"

Standing at the edge of the rubble, Christine saw that half the building, including the ground underneath it, must have collapsed into the earth. Looking straight down she noted how the Susquehanna River, which previously flowed a quarter of a mile away from the museum, now ran directly below her.

Its torrents were ruff and billowed with foam and debris. With revulsion, Christine observed dead bodies floating in the mix. The small river now looked like a large bay, sprawling for miles.

Christine dropped to one knee and began to cry. Though she was relieved to be alive, her victory over death now felt hollow. She had lost so much over the past few years. What The New Reality had not stolen, Mother Nature had taken. Christine's body shook with grief.

Murph placed his hand on her shoulder. He wished there was something he could say to console her, but he knew he would only make things worse by putting the unspeakable into words.

His gruff, blunt attitude would certainly not provide Christine with the solace she needed. Plus, he, too, felt an overwhelming sense of dread, as if death was waiting at the next turn.

Murph turned back and looked out into the heart of Philadelphia. In their haste to locate their colleagues, the true devastating consequences of the earthquake had been lost on him. The city, like the museum, lay in complete ruin. The once beautiful skyline which only hours before had risen out of the earth as if attempting to touch heaven itself had been destroyed much like that of the Tower of Babel.

Water flowed through the street while cars, debris, and dead bodies lay in piles along the side of the once great buildings. From atop the mound on which the museum once stood, Murph felt like a castaway on a remote island.

Murph pondered a moment, wondering if any civilized society still existed. From generations of economic debt, unscrupulous scientific exploitation, embracing false leaders, and blurring the lines between right and wrong, humanity was collapsing, just like the buildings around him. Despite the evidence at hand, he still held out hope that Jules Windsor would change everything and bring back stability to the planet. Murph believed the media's portrayal of his leader and truly wanted to trust him.

As he turned back to console Christine, Murph noted a faint golden glow emanating at the far edge of the rubble where it dropped down into the Susquehanna. *What is that?* he wondered, walking over to the area.

Maybe someone is still alive? Murph hoped as his pace quickened.

Now at the edge of the debris, he noted the light emanated from a hole in the face of the newly-created cliff abutting the river.

Was someone down there? Is that where Benjamin and the rest of his friends were now hiding?

Murph cautiously scaled the side of the cliff, holding on to the protruding rocks for support. Luckily, the drop off was not sheer and sloped at enough of an angle to make the descent manageable. Plus, with years of heavy weight lifting, his well-toned muscles made the journey relatively easy.

Grabbing a stone slab overhead, Murph lowered himself into the cave. "Benjamin?" he said while holding his auricular chip. He continued to call out his name a few more times as he walked.

Murph wound his way down steps carved with precision from solid granite; faintly glimmering walls of the same stone illuminated his path.

"Kate?" Murph said louder, hoping anyone would answer his plea. He then ran through ten more names, but each one was answered with silence.

"Benjamin?" Murph said one more time before he abruptly stopped walking.

He knew what stood before him was certainly not part of the Art Museum. Though he was admittedly not the most cultured man on the planet, Murph recognized that what he was looking at was no modern construction.

"Christine!" Murph yelled into the auricular chip as he ran back up the steps.

"Christine!" he beckoned. Reaching the top of the cave and now looking towards his only surviving friend, kneeling at the edge of the debris, Murph yelled, "You've got to see this!"

CHAPTER 7

Pumapunku, Bolivia

"AMAZING, SIMPLY AMAZING," said a thin brunette with her long hair wrapped up in an unkempt bun on her head. "Charles," she said with a soft and soothing Australian accent, "you must have a look here at the exquisiteness of the stone work."

Wearing a thick silver glove with fluctuating, multicolored lights on the fingertips known as a *latumscreen*, she waved her hand slowly over a massive sandstone block. With perfectly cut edges creating a multilayered H-shape, she marveled how these blocks fit so precisely together that she could not run even a strand of her own hair between them.

"You found something?" Charles asked. Wearing long, thick boots and a tan jacket and hat to match, he walked over to her. An elderly gentleman at least in his early eighties, he used a long metal stick to balance his way.

"Yes, Cindy?" he responded.

"Charles," she said, "though our archeology team has scoured the two square miles of this hilltop for the past month,

I still don't understand; in fact, the more I look the less I understand."

"What has peaked your curiosity this time?"

Cindy waved her hand over a fallen H-shaped block next to her, causing holographic numbers and figures to appear above it. "After surveying most of the stone blocks in this area, I've determined that they all originated from the same quarry five miles from here. But a few things strike me as odd." She lifted up her head and pointed to the geographical area surrounding them. "What do you see?"

Charles chuckled to himself, encouraged by her youthful enthusiasm.

"Barren mountains," she answered herself. "There are no trees. There is no water. How were these people who created this place able to move 100-ton blocks of stone? What is even more interesting is that all these H-shaped blocks are of the same exact dimensions."

As more numbers began to appear above the stone block, she added, "It's as if they were made from the same mold."

Charles poked his metal stick at a different block of sandstone with an intricately cut curved hole in it. A holographic image of the stone enlarged above the stick and began to zoom in until it became visible on a microscopic level.

"Nor can I explain what the people who created this place used to cut the stone," Charles added. "Just look at this. Not even modern lasers could create such a smooth surface."

Their conversation unexpectedly ended as a World Order Guard also known as a WOG landed with a hiss followed by a bang ten feet from their position. The gravitational concussion knocked them both to the ground as if they had been punched in the stomach.

Dressed in a pure black uniform with a New Reality diamond and gold emblem on each shoulder, a gray helmet, and a crimson visor, this anonymous soldier wore a gravity-wing on his back. Colloquially named after their cherub-like appearance, these jet-black wings were certainly not from heaven. Used as a gravity decelerator, gravity-wings replaced parachutes and modernized the art of aerial assault.

Cindy crept backwards, inching herself away from this menace. As she looked around, more and more of the WOGs began to descend upon them and surround the entire Pumapunku mound. She estimated that there were at least fifty of them, with increasing numbers dropping in by the second.

"What do you think they want?" she asked.

"I don't know," Charles said, "but I'm aiming to find out."

Cindy placed her hand on his knee, as if to say *keep still.*

Charles complied. His thoughts now were solely on his team of archeologists at the site and the other tourists examining the area.

The WOG closest to them dropped his gravity-wing and grabbed a metal cylinder attached to his thigh. With both hands, he held it directly in front of him and turned, now with his back to them.

The cylinder expanded directly into the ground with a loud crunch as it embedded itself in the rock. The top of the cylinder also rose another two feet, and its tip began to glow red once secured into the earth. The WOG then began to slowly walk backwards, approaching the position of the two archaeologists without a care to their existence.

"Don't move," Charles warned as the WOG stopped only a foot away from their boots.

Cindy looked around the area and noted that the other WOGs had deployed the same cylinder. She quickly recognized these instruments. Called bioshields, they create an electromagnetic barrier around an area that repelled all life ten feet in front and behind and thirty feet above and below.

Four striker crafts then appeared from above and rapidly descended onto a flat landing area in the center of Pumapunku. The long cylindrical-shaped ships with four tail fins equidistantly positioned around its rear side and two slender wings running down its entire length made no sound as they touched down. Fine dirt picked up from the ground spun around the ships in a vortex-like motion for a few seconds before dissipating into the wind.

As the back doors of these enormous ships opened, WOGs flying silver, chariot-like crafts known as heliocrafts, after the Greek God of flight Helios, flew out of them like an angry swarm of wasps. WOGs controlling hover-rams followed close behind. The hover-ram featured a circular base floating about a foot off the ground, a single seat for a driver, and was surrounded with multiple weapons and devices along its exoskeleton. The vehicle proved an effective, quickly portable, and powerful deterrent.

The WOG in front of Cindy and Charles turned and grabbed a rifle-shaped weapon from his side and pointed it at them.

"On your stomachs!" bellowed the ominous voice, echoing throughout the Pumapunku site.

Cindy and Charles complied without hesitation.

Now looking towards the center of the site, Cindy noted a single stratoskimmer enter the ancient ruin. With a large New Reality emblem along its side, the aircraft began to land without making a sound. The site of the stratoskimmer piqued her interest as she wondered who was inside and why they were coming to this location.

As the ship touched down, she felt an eerie sickness overtake her, and her insides felt as if they were being ripped apart.

"We're too close to the bioshields," she said.

Cindy grabbed Charles's hand, hoping not to be shot in the process. The two crawled away slowly, not making any sudden movements until the sickness subsided. The WOG behind them followed, most likely also nauseated by the field's strength.

The side of the stratoskimmer in front of them opened and then descended to the ground, unfolding a set of stairs in the process. Recognizing the man standing in the doorway, Cindy now understood the need for so much security.

***

Jules walked out of the stratoskimmer and down the steps; he stood proudly at the base of the ship. A WOG with the Achilles Shield secured in both hands stood by his side.

"Sir," the WOG alerted with some alarm in his voice, "we have a problem."

Jules turned and saw the shield begin to glow and levitate by itself into the air. The WOG instinctively let go of it and took a step backward.

"Reflexivity!" Jules applauded. "Grab hold," he then commanded. "This is not a show. Secure your property, soldier!"

The WOG grabbed the shield without further hesitation. With both hands, he glided the ancient artifact effortlessly in the air. It was as if the shield were weightless and all he needed to do was provide a slight nudge for it to move.

"We are certainly in the right spot," Jules commented on his auricular chip, communicating with Drew.

Now where to look? Jules contemplated assessing the entire area while eyeing each megalithic stone. *Where is this shield leading us?*

Unlike his uncle, Albert Rosenberg, Jules had no interest in antiquity. As he looked at the massive stone blocks, he could care less about the people who built them or why. His gaze was always towards the future.

An explosion suddenly rocked their position. The concussive blast caused a nearby hover-ram to flip over and crash violently into a low-flying heliocraft. Both vehicles fell to the ground in a ball of fire and smoke.

Jules stood tall and smiled at the distraction. Touching his ear, he yelled, "Hostiles behind two large stones in front of us. Surround and attack!"

Another projectile landed twenty feet from him and detonated upon impact. Four WOGs around its blast perimeter fell to the ground; their bodies sizzled while their suits oozed around them. "Lethal force only," Jules commanded as he grabbed a rail gun from one of the WOGs standing next to him. Taking cover, he threw himself on the ground as the soldier behind him, still grasping the Achilles Shield, did the same.

A barrage of projectiles erupted from the large megalithic stone directly in front of them. Like popcorn spewing from a kettle, they began to pepper the area.

Jules took aim with his rail gun, sending a bullet propelled by alternating magnetic currents at mock 3 towards the granite stone. The impact obliterated the corner of the rock and blew apart the chest of the hostile who was crouched next to it. His shoulder-mounted projectile launcher fell to the ground. Upon impact, the weapon discharged, sending a concussive shell into the megalithic rock next to him. The explosion obliterated every person within a twenty-foot perimeter, both WOG and hostile alike.

The large, beautifully carved 100-ton stone began to explode in multiple puffs of rocky smoke as a barrage of rail gun projectiles pelted it. Its once smooth surface was now riddled with large holes.

"Charge!" Jules commanded.

Just as he rose to his knees, a circular projectile began to descend in front of him. As if in slow motion, he watched it approach and knew it was already too late to react. The silver ordinance with a single red stripe barreling his way meant only one thing: instant death.

CHAPTER 8

CHRISTINE FELT IT SACRILEGIOUS how quickly Murph seemed to have forgotten about their friends. If it weren't for the fact that this cave he was ranting about might provide some form of shelter, she would have simply left and gone on her own again like she had so many other times in the past.

Though she deeply appreciated Murph for saving her in the museum, she would have preferred to get as far away from this place as possible and forget everything and everyone there; it would be much easier that way. She also knew there was no place to go. The city was flooded and in ruins. Her home and all her possessions were lost.

Christine rubbed her eyes, which were still red and blurry from crying; she wiped away a few last tears so that she could safely lower herself into the cave.

"What?" Murph said gruffly, feeling that Christine was somehow angry at him for their predicament.

"Don't you have any remorse?" she finally said, letting down her guard. "Our friends are all gone, and all you care about is this cave."

Murph attempted to respond but was interrupted.

"I don't really give a damn about this cave," Christine lashed out as she attempted to hold back the tears.

"We must move on," Murph said as compassionately as possible. "Just like we all needed to do when *The Disease* and nanosplicers decimated our loved ones."

Neither said a word as the graveness of the situation sank in a little deeper.

"Trust me," Murph said cautiously as they both climbed into the cave, "I am truly sorry for the loss of Benjamin and the rest of our friends. However, I know they all wouldn't want us crying over their deaths. They would want us to find food and shelter and most importantly, to survive."

Christine knew Murph was right.

"Regardless of what's in this cave," Murph said, "it will at least provide us with some accommodations until the water hopefully recedes. Plus, there may be something we can use down here. Benjamin always said you were the smart one. Maybe you can figure out what any of this is in here."

Murph then pointed into the cave and said, "Plus, I think there are a few things that you may find interesting down here. Maybe it will take your mind off of what's happened over the last few days."

The two began to descend the steps without another word. After going about halfway down, Christine stopped walking; a map on the wall had caught her attention. She had seen something like it before but could not recall where.

"Odd, huh?" Murph said, pulling out a flashlight. "There are a few more along the way. I don't know who etched them into the walls or what planet they even represent. But it doesn't look like it was from any exhibit at the museum."

Murph shined his flashlight on the map so that they could get a better view: greens and blues radiated in the light.

Christine ran her fingers around the circular map's contours. She inspected the single large landmass and smaller masses in its center and the three other partially-visible pieces of land around the map's perimeter.

"Phillipe Bauche," she said. "This looks like a map I once saw. I don't know how I remembered the name, but I do remember how mesmerized I was with the drawing."

"Science fiction writer or something?" Murph asked.

"Not science fiction," Christine said, allowing her curiosity to temporarily usurp her sadness. "He was an eighteenth-century cartographer." She then pointed to the landmass in the center of the map. "Do you know what this is?"

"A map," Murph answered glibly.

"I believe it's supposed to be Antarctica without the massive ice cap," she responded, as if not hearing his comment. "And these three other areas around the perimeter are South America, Africa, and Australia."

Murph shined his flashlight on the map but still could not see what she was attempting to explain. "Oh," he then said, acting as if it all suddenly became clear, "there it is."

She stared back at him. "You don't see it, do you?"

"Not at all," he said. "But I can tell you there are a few more of these maps along the walls."

Christine then looked at a different map as she descended down the steps further into the cave. Murph attempted to shine his light on them but had noticed the further they walked, the dimmer it grew until the flashlight was rendered completely useless.

"Is this supposed to be Antarctica, too?" Murph asked, looking at the rectangular etching.

"I don't think so," Christine said. "However, these lass masses along each side look similar to North America and

Europe. The large island in the center isn't anything I can identify."

Murph shook his head. "If those shapes look like North America and Europe to you, I'm wondering how hard you were hit on the head when the museum collapsed."

Maybe it was her imagination, but surely their contours were more than just a coincidence. Though such features as The Great Lakes and Mediterranean Sea were not visible, the similarities could not be denied.

Christine went to another map and shook her head in disbelief. There was a different landmass in the middle of what looked like the Pacific Ocean between North America and Asia.

"I think these are supposed to be ancient maps of the Earth," she then concluded. "I mean, what else would they be?"

"I don't know," Murph acknowledged. "What I do know is that this place is giving me the creeps. The further we walk, the more I feel as if bugs are crawling all over me. Plus, I can't figure where this light is coming from. It seems as if the rocks simply glow in the dark."

The two continued to walk, examining the etched maps as they passed. Murph's interest in them quickly dwindled as each one looked similar to the last.

The stairwell ended, and they both walked into a large circular room with a dome at the top. Their bodies tingled and their hair stood on end when they entered. Christine was in awe at the sight. *This is amazing!*

"It sure is," Murph responded.

"But I didn't say anything," Christine responded.

"I heard you say 'This is amazing.'"

Christine turned her head away from him and thought, *Can you hear me?*

"Of course, I can hear you," Murph said. "You are right next to me."

Wide-eyed, Christine turned back to him and explained that they were somehow connected telepathically. After a few attempts at communicating with only his mind, Murph's disbelief vanished.

"Who do you think made this room?" Murph asked.

"And why?" Christine added.

The two were almost afraid to walk any further. Instead, they both stood at the entrance, taking in the entire area before proceeding.

In the center of the room, silver liquid slowly spiraled clockwise in a large circular pool in the floor. It made no sound, swirling as if in perpetual motion.

"What is that?" Murph asked, looking at the pool. "This whole place gets spookier the further we go."

Christine cautiously walked into the room and approached the pool of silver liquid. The closer she drew, the lighter she felt. It was almost like an out-of-body experience, as if her soul was about to escape its mortal confines.

Before she reached the pool, Christine noted writing etched around it on the marble floor. The silver liquid filled grooves of the characters and seemed to undulate as if it had a mind of its own. Though she had seen both cuneiform and hieroglyphics, this writing seemed to be a hybrid of the two.

Was this some sort of prototype language? she thought. *Or maybe the writing of a lost civilization?*

"I don't know," Murph responded, now exploring on his own.

Christine was amused by their telepathic link and for the first time in days let out a small chuckle. She remembered how the Egyptian culture and writing seemed to spring out of nowhere; no precursor society or any ancestors could ever be identified in the archeological record. Maybe this writing was a clue.

Christine then knelt down and slowly lowered her hand to the pool. The liquid seemed to respond to her presence and gently swirled around her fingers, picking up speed the closer they approached.

Murph walked around the room. Along its perimeter, pedestals in the shape of bulls' heads each supported a baseball-sized crystal slightly levitating and rotating in the air. As he approached one, the crystal spun faster and its glow radiated brighter.

Along the walls there were other maps etched into the stone. These, however, displayed more topographical information and were confined to smaller localities as opposed to the entire planet. Murph looked at each one, attempting to make sense out of any of them.

As he continued to walk, one crystal in particular reacted to his presence. Its glow outshined all the others in the room and seemed to draw him closer. Placing his hand nearer to it, the crystal levitated higher and sparkled with amazing brilliance as if it were a massive, perfectly carved diamond. Its radiance seemed to hypnotize him as light flickered off it in a methodical and soothing manner.

With both hands, Murph reached out for the crystal.

"Don't touch it!" Christine yelled, telepathically realizing what he was about to do.

Just as she stood up and began to run towards him, Murph grabbed the crystal. It was as if everything began to slow down. The crystals along the walls decelerated their rotational spin to a stop while her own movements diminished in speed until she was frozen in the air.

Christine tried to scream but nothing came out. It was like a dream, but she knew that she was awake.

Her mind began to fade as all sensation within her body slowly dwindled away.

CHAPTER 9

INSTINCTIVELY, JULES THRUST HIMSELF to the side. His survival skills enabled him to act almost without thought. Subconsciously, he somehow knew that his only possible means of further existence would be to hide behind the Achilles Shield. Though most of what his lead scientist Drew had discussed about this artifact up to this moment was inconsequential, he suddenly remembered the fact that this shield was supposedly indestructible.

With his eyes still intently focused on the projectile, Jules took cover behind the shield and in doing so landed on the WOG holding it out in front of him on the ground. The shock wave of the blast struck before the sound. The soldiers next to him died upon impact.

Jules could both hear their bodies sizzle and smell the odor of rotting leather exuding from their corpses.

Bio-ordinances, Jules concluded.

One of the most lethal weapons in combat, upon detonation this weapon could instantaneously denature all proteins within a lethal radius. Plus, it would leave no collateral damage, preventing the area from being otherwise marred by the destruction of war.

Other bio-ordinances and explosions rocked the entire Pumapunku area. Heliocrafts came crashing down to earth while hover-rams burst into flames. Bodies of dead WOGs, archeologists, hostiles, and even tourists now littered the area.

Jules rolled off the WOG and took aim at the hostiles around the megalithic stone. He then fired out a few more shots towards the giant sandstone slab in front of him as his WOG attack force descended upon their aggressors.

Despite the massive barrage of fire, the megalithic stone block barely seemed to shrink in the process.

A loud, monotonous hum could be heard over the battlefield. Jules knew that it was not one of their weapons or anything else that he could have ordered. It was almost as if a band of monks had begun to chant, and the chant slowly increased in volume and intensity.

Jules sprang to his feet and began to run towards the stone block, but its appearance began to blur as it started to levitate. At first Jules thought it may simply be an illusion or even a possible side effect of the bio-ordinance that had detonated next to him; however, the closer he and the WOGs around him approached, the more undeniably obvious the fact became that the stone block was rising in the air.

Just before it came crashing to the ground, Jules noted a few of the aggressors leaping underneath it. Four were shot either by a rail gun round or an atomic disruptor blast and never made it to the stone. Two managed to find safety.

Jules reached the stone just as it came crashing back to the earth with a massive thud. The loud humming sound ceased in the process, leaving his ears ringing. The brown earth around the megalithic stone was soaked in blood. Dead and dismembered bodies cluttered the area and piled up on top of each other in certain places.

"Mr. Windsor," a voiced sounded in his auricular chip, "we have secured our position and subdued the enemy."

"Hold your fire!" Jules announced. "Inspect the hostiles to see if they hold a clue about what just happened here." He then placed his hands on the side of his ear. "Colonel Manfry, I want a full casualty report. And make sure the wounded are tended to ASAP."

"Yes, sir!"

Jules walked over to the rock and placed his hands on it. Making sure it was not some makeshift façade, he pushed the massive stone, testing to see if it would actually move.

"What are you doing?" a voice asked from behind him. He turned back and saw that Drew had emerged from the stratoskimmer. Now personally holding the shield, Drew said, "That stone block weighs over 100 tons."

"Well then, it should be no surprise that I couldn't move it," Jules said. Appreciative of Drew's help and the valuable information he had already provided, Jules added, "Glad you decided to join me on my little adventure here in South America."

It's not like I really had an option, Drew thought.

"Colonel," Jules said. "I want this stone block moved, immediately. I need to see what's under here."

"We have nothing to move it, Mr. Windsor," the colonel responded. "No heavy machinery was brought on this assault. Plus, even if I attached the biggest electromagnetic decoupling engine we have, I am sure we could still not budge it."

Jules stared at the stone block in amazement. *What a magnificent bit of lost technology!*

"I can certainly blow it to smithereens," the colonel commented. "But it would create one hell of a crater in its wake!"

"That won't do," Jules responded. He took a deep breath, assessing his options. After replaying the battle scenario over and over in his head, one thing about it stuck out the longer he thought.

"That hum," Jules said aloud. "There was this hum sound I certainly heard as the rock began to levitate. It must be of some significance."

"Tibetan monks," Drew said, "have been rumored to levitate heavy objects through chant and prayer."

"We don't have monks," Jules noted, "but we can most certainly replicate the frequency of the sound." He placed his hand on his ear, "Colonel, bring over the amplifier you use for crowd control."

"Yes, sir. Right away."

He looked at Drew, "Check our stratoskimmer's logs, and have that sound's frequency and waveforms replicated. We must be precise with this."

"Already completed," Drew responded, as his fingers swirled through a holograph above his wrist. "I've also transferred the sound bite directly to the amplifier."

The colonel brought over the amplifier. Shaped no larger than the palm of the hand, this rectangular device was as light as it was small. Jules placed the speaker portion directly onto the rock and took two steps backwards. Drew then touched a button on the holographic readout to activate it.

The sound and clarity of the amplifier were both crisp and robust even though it directly faced the rock. "That's it," Jules said with great anticipation. "Now slowly increase the volume."

The hum echoed throughout the area. Jules felt the sound pulsate throughout his whole body; even his teeth were vibrating. "Keep going... a little more."

Nothing.

The rock did not move or even vibrate. "Enough," Jules finally said, waving his hand in the air. "This is simply not going to work. There had to be more than just sound that levitated the rock." *But what?*

Jules scratched his chin, attempting to solve the millennia-old mystery.

"There is a theory I've been working on," Drew spoke up while examining the digital holographic readouts in front of him, "of how the Achilles Shield was able to levitate, and it may apply here."

"Go on," Jules said.

"Have you ever heard of the Heisenberg uncertainty principle?"

"Have I?" Jules scoffed. "My boy, the theory of reflexivity is based upon this principle. The more you observe a given situation, the more you can directly influence its outcome. Just like in stocks. The more you advertise and publicize a business, the more its price will theoretically rise. I've made a fortune off of good old Heisenberg."

"Yes," Drew agreed, "but on a mathematical level the formula itself theoretically quantitates the fundamental energy which creates the basic fabric of the universe. It's what makes atoms spin. It creates the entirety of all space-time. It's also the energy that allows helium to remain in liquid form at absolute zero when theoretically all elements should be solid at this temperature."

"The point of this is?" Jules said impatiently.

"Zero-point energy," Drew responded. "When you take Heisenberg's uncertainty principle and plug in the temperature at absolute zero, there is still energy in any given system. We call this energy zero-point energy, and it directly equals half Plank's constant times the frequency."

"Can you harness this zero-point energy?" Jules asked.

"Just like how the shield levitates in certain electromagnetic fields," Drew conjectured, "somehow we have to replicate the process on this rock." He thought a second. "But the process might prove painstakingly long as there are so many different variables here to consider."

"Think simple," Jules implored. "What could the Tibetan monks of today use? What could have been a simple method, God only knows how long ago, to move thousands of these massive stone blocks all around the world?"

A holographic image of a ceramic pot appeared above Drew's wrist.

"This may be the answer," Drew said.

Jules looked closer, unable to determine the significance of the simple clay jar.

"It's called the Bagdad battery," Drew explained, "and can generate an electric charge of two Volts. To this day, no one knows its purpose, and many speculate as to its previous use. Maybe the quartz in this sandstone block requires an electrical charge in order to extract its zero-point energy and create a negative gravitational field?"

"I like the way you think," Jules applauded.

Drew grabbed a handheld rectangular gadget from his lab coat pocket and pulled out a small, silver, circular disc. He then placed it on the rock and took a few steps back. Turning towards Jules, he asked, "Are you ready?"

"Colonel," Jules said, "if Drew somehow manages to levitate this stone block, I want you and two of your finest to accompany me down to wherever the hostiles are hiding. On my command."

"Yes, Mr. Windsor," he responded, signaling two WOGS to his side.

"I'll take that," Jules said to Drew, grabbing the shield levitating next to him. "On three," he went on to say before Drew could offer a rebuttal.

"One, two, three."

Drew pressed a button in the holographic display. Slowly, a humming tone began to reverberate throughout the area, intensifying by the second. At first nothing occurred. But as the scientist manipulated the electric field and increased its intensity, the rock began to visibly vibrate.

"Good show!" Jules said.

Gradually the stone began to levitate. The ancient megalithic mystery had been solved. Placing his hand once again on the rock, Jules set the shield to the side and gave the stone one large shove. As if pushing a two-pound baby carriage, the massive rock moved with little effort, revealing a stairwell underneath it.

"Now," Jules said, commanding his men into action.

With their weapons drawn, the colonel and two WOGs stormed down the stairs. With the shield in one hand and a rail gun in the other, Jules followed. Anticipation pulsed through his veins.

Upon reaching the bottom of the stairs, three men holding spears blocked their path. The two who were dressed in dark pants and long overcoats, Jules surmised, must have been the ones who escaped the fire fight. The third, wearing a more ceremonial gown embroidered with ancient symbols and writing, must have already been hiding under the stone.

The WOGs and colonel took aim and began to fire, but, when they pulled the trigger there was no response. Their weapons were useless. Jules also attempted to fire a few shots to no avail. *Just like out in the Atlantic,* he thought, *our modern technology is rendered useless.*

The three men with spears charged their position. The colonel dodged the first hostile's attack while his two companions were not as lucky. One was pierced through the throat by one of the hostiles, while the other took a weapon directly to the chest; his protective body armor fortunately prevented the tip from entering.

Jules grabbed the shaft of the spear the colonel had dodged and used his foe's momentum to his own advantage. Yanking the spear to his left, the hostile lost his balance and fell forward. As he collapsed, Jules delivered a powerful roundhouse kick to the side of the man's head. The metal-tipped boot smashed into his skull, rendering him unconscious on the floor. Blood pooled out of his ear.

The colonel grabbed a knife from his belt and thrust it up below the center of a different attacker's rib cage. The weapon tore through his ceremonial gown and punctured the man's heart. As the man gasped for air, the colonel then punched him squarely between the eyes. The hostile dropped flat onto his back with a thud. He lay unconscious, gasping instinctively for air, life draining from him.

The colonel then bent down and removed the knife from his attacker's chest and hurled it towards the one remaining foe. Before the hostile could remove the spear from the WOG's neck, the knife pierced his back.

Still with a spear in hand, Jules reversed its direction and rammed it through the front of the man's chest and out his back. The hostile's eye's opened widely as he coughed up blood. Feebly attempting to remove the spear, he fell to the ground and slowly stopped moving. Jules then placed his foot on the hostile's chest and yanked the spear from it.

The colonel quickly knelt at the fallen soldier's side. Blood gushed from his throat as the man lay motionless on the ground. The colonel then detached the man's helmet and removed it from his head.

Blank, cold eyes stared upward in an undeniable gaze of death; a look the colonel recognized all too well. Without another option, the colonel placed a white handkerchief over the soldier's face. There was nothing further he could do.

Jules went up to the golden door the three men had been guarding. Not taking any chances, he held the shield in one hand and the spear in the other. Like an ancient Roman preparing for battle, he pushed open the door, expecting a fight.

His eyes merely met with beauty and not war. Standing with her arms to the side, a stunning Tibetan-looking woman stood at the room's entrance. Dressed in a flowing white gown with similar emblems and writings as the men outside the door, she held up her hands and began to plead with them in a foreign language.

"Who are you?" Jules asked.

Before she could answer, the woman was taken aback at the sight of the shield. "Please," she attempted to say now in English, unable to keep her eyes off of it. "We mean you no harm here."

"We meant you no harm either," Jules said, entering the circular room, "until your people began opening fire on us."

"Where did you get that?" she asked, pointing to the shield. "The key," she uttered in hushed breath.

"It was a little present from my dear old uncle," Jules said. "A most magnificent object, isn't it? Now if you could kindly tell me what it has to do with this place here, I will bid you a good day."

"Nothing," she responded indignantly as the remaining WOG grabbed her hands and pulled them behind her. "It has nothing to do with this place—and neither do you."

"You are mistaken. There is a secret here, and I must find it." Jules looked over to her and offered a friendly smile." Your help would be greatly appreciated."

The woman spat on the ground and cursed him in her native tongue. Before she could continue her rant, the WOG behind her placed his gloved hand across her mouth, curtailing further admonishments.

"Well then," Jules commented, "I can see that your accommodations are just as inviting as your friends. Let's hope that you don't meet their same end."

Jules then took his eyes off the woman and appraised the room. Around its perimeter hung elegant tapestries, each of a separate design and color. It almost reminded him of different countries' flags or a family's coat of arms. But it was the center of the room that captured his main attention. There, a magnificent football-shaped crystal levitated in the air. Surrounded by four smaller crystals rotating around it, the site brought him a calming feeling and made all aggression leave his body.

As if being called by an ancient Siren, Jules walked methodically over to the crystal. Handing the shield to the colonel, he said not another word.

"Don't go any further!" pleaded the woman, shaking her head violently to free her mouth. "Get out! You don't know what you're doing."

Jules smiled. He knew what he was doing. This crystal in front of him was somehow connected to the shield, and more importantly, it tied directly into the Earth's electromagnetic grid—with power strong enough to neuter modern technology. He knew that he must have it.

Below the crystals, Jules noted the outline of a bull's head with undecipherable cuneiform writing etched in the floor around it. A silvery fluid flowed within the crevices and undulated more vigorously upon his approach.

As Jules reached out for the main crystal, the woman's pleas grew in intensity. Her words fell on deaf ears as he grabbed the large crystal in the center.

"No!" the woman screamed.

The four other crystals surrounding it fell to the ground, smashing into pieces upon impact. The same silver fluid in the floor's crevices began to ooze down the walls and seep into the beautiful tapestries. The room then began to shake, and a large crack formed through the direct center of the floor.

"Let's get to the surface," Jules commanded while walking over to the room's entrance. "And take her."

A piece of the ceiling came crashing down next to where he had been standing only an instant before. The ambient light illuminating the room flickered and slowly dimmed, eventually leaving the area engulfed in blackness.

Jules could hear what sounded like the walls collapsing and felt a few rocks pelt his head and body. He knew this entire room was about to collapse and realized that the entirety of Pumapunku might do the same.

CHAPTER 10

JULES INSTINCTIVELY REACHED for his auricular chip. "Evacuate. All evacuate."

Nothing but static and the faint sound of distant voices answered his command.

Still dead down here, he surmised.

Jules continued walking towards the door as if nothing unusual was happening. Though the room was completely dark, he adeptly kept his bearings despite the violent tremors around him. "Colonel," he yelled, "follow the sound of my voice."

The Tibetan woman continued to curse them. Despite not understanding the language, Jules comprehended her meaning. Whatever he did had upset some planetary balance; now they all were paying the consequences.

A rock crashed down on Jules' shoulder, almost dislodging the crystal from his hands. Knife-like pain shot down his arm in response as a burning heat momentarily overwhelmed the appendage.

"You have the shield and our guest!" Jules yelled, ignoring the pain. He knew that he needed to continue to talk so that his men and their captive could follow. Pain or no pain, they all needed to escape.

Both men acknowledged him with an affirmative.

A glimmer of light in front of him let Jules know he was heading in the correct direction. "Avoid the bodies on the ground. Keep moving... moving."

Jules reiterated the words over and over, turning himself into a verbal beacon for his men to track. He then began to ascend the staircase at full speed. Looking back, he saw the two men and their captive not far behind.

Upon exiting the cave, Jules noted the outside had fared no better. The earth violently shook as deep cracks opened in numerous places along its surface. In the distance, he could see one of the striker crafts on its side rapidly being swallowed up by the earth.

The heliocrafts were no longer flying, and the hover-rams lay dormant. WOGs stumbled along the ground, abandoning their equipment. All were attempting to take shelter in one of the available striker crafts. The archeologists and tourists visiting the area made their way to the ships but were denied entry. With either the butt of a rifle or elbow to the face, the WOGs let them know they weren't welcome.

"Into the stratoskimmer," Jules turned and yelled as he again touched his auricular chip and gave the order for all to evacuate.

Drew stood at the ship's doorway. With the stairs halfway retracted, he made sure no unwanted guest would board the ship.

The area began to shake more violently. One of the striker craft began to sputter as it attempted to take flight. Despite its initial ascent, gravity won the battle and sent it crashing back down to the ground. It struck with a massive thud, twisting the ship in the process and disfiguring its once sleek façade.

The stairs to the stratoskimmer slowly descended upon Jules' approach. Behind him, he could see that an enormous crevice now occupied the space where the boulder and cave once stood; unfortunately for all of them, its size was widening and heading directly towards his ships.

Jules jumped onto the steps behind the colonel, WOG soldier, and Tibetan woman. Upon entering the hull, he ran up to the cockpit. "Let's go, George!" he said. "Time's not a luxury we currently possess."

"The electromagnetic dipoles won't align," the pilot said frantically, while attempting to make adjustments on the flickering dashboard. "There is some fluctuating electromagnetic field that is interrupting our equipment."

The ship rocked back and forth as Jules tumbled back into the ship's hull.

"Retract that door," Jules said. "We are about to take flight."

"It's stuck," announced one of the two WOGs who were manually attempting to close it.

The stratoskimmer then jerked violently to the side as it took flight, sending one of the soldiers headfirst out of the doorway. Jules instinctively ran over to the door, hoping the man might somehow be holding on to the stairs.

Instead of finding a WOG when Jules looked out of the ship, he saw the land west of Pumapunku collapsing into the ocean. What was once over 12,000 feet above sea level now resided under the great Pacific. Jules stood at the doorway, impressed with the raw power of Mother Nature.

More ocean to sail, Jules thought wryly.

"Mr. Windsor," said one of the WOGs. "Sir, the shield is secured." The soldier then presented the ancient artifact to Jules.

"Good work," Jules responded, taking the shield. Now staring at it and the young woman that they had commandeered in Pumapunku, he could only fathom what further secrets they would both reveal.

The ship rocked slightly back and forth, hurling one of the WOGs against the hull's wall.

"Somehow," Drew conjectured, while analyzing a fuzzy, blinking holograph above his wrist, "taking the crystal from Bolivia has completely disrupted the world grid. The whole thing is in flux and appears to be growing more unstable by the minute."

Jules walked over the woman. Pure hatred shone in her eyes. With his free hand, he placed it on her chin, and she responded by attempting to bite him.

"No worries," Jules said, tightening his grip on the much smaller woman. "We may have the solution right here."

Before she could answer, the ship dropped violently. Jules could barely hold onto the shield as he was thrown over one of the white couches. Moans and screams rang out throughout the hull as the stratoskimmer attempted to stabilize.

A WOG, still with his visor in place, ran over to Jules and held out a helping hand. Jules reached up and grabbed it. "That's the way to do it," he commended. "However, instead of bringing him to his feet, the WOG slammed his elbow violently down on Jules' face.

Jules' head thumped onto the floor as the plush rug did little to lessen the blow.

The WOG then took the shield from Jules' hand. "Expectation, Julius," the helmeted soldier said. "Expectation."

Stunned, Jules laid on his back as if staring at a ghost. Though the man's face was covered, his identity was not hidden. His old nemesis had somehow survived. The fear that had been haunting him for over a year was now being fully realized. The only man in the world with the cunning, intellect, and bravado to threaten both him and The New Reality was alive.

"Alexander Pella," Jules groaned as blood sputtered out of his badly bruised lip.

The WOG then ran over to the hull's doorway and jumped out of the ship. The rest of the soldiers in the stratoskimmer never knew what happened. In the commotion, they just assumed he had accidentally fallen to his death.

Seeing an opportunity, however remote, the Tibetan woman grabbed the crystal which had fallen free and followed Alex. Without hesitation, she jumped out of the ship a brief second after he made the plunge.

Jules leapt to his feet and ran to the cockpit. "The electromagnetic dipoles are continuing to fluctuate," the pilot frantically said. "It's almost impossible to keep this ship in the air."

Strapping himself into the copilot's chair, Jules waved his hands along the ship's dashboard. He no longer cared if he and the stratoskimmer plummeted to the ground; if he took Alex with him, it would be worth the loss.

"There he is!" Jules said, pulling up a holographic picture of a stratoskimmer on the windshield. Unlike the ship they were flying, this one appeared to be modified with larger engines along the side and two smaller ones under its wider wings.

"Let's blast it out of the sky," Jules said as the steering wheel he grasped expanded along the sides and a red bullseye appeared on the stratoskimmer displayed on the windshield.

CHAPTER 11

ALEX THREW OFF HIS MASK and ran to the ship's cockpit. Still with a very youthful appearance, he looked easily ten years younger than his actual age of forty-six. He was a handsome man with olive skin, thick, black curly hair, broad shoulders and strong facial features.

"Tom, deploy electrostatic fog," he ordered. "They must have a lock on us by now."

"I'm trying," the pilot responded. "It's just not working. Nothing's working. You're lucky I was even able to stabilize the ship long enough for you to dock with us. Another second longer and you would have missed us completely."

"Don't interrupt the pilot when he's trying to fly the ship," blurted a man built like a linebacker, sitting in the copilot's seat. Wearing a dirty, red hat with only the letters *G* and *R* visible above the brim and a crumpled outfit, he looked as if he had been sleeping in his clothes for months. Grabbing onto the chair while attempting not to hyperventilate, the man sputtered, "We're not going to make it."

"Deep breath, William," Alex soothed while looking at the electrostatic smog readiness readout on the dashboard.

Sizzling smoke then began to encase their entire ship, obscuring all visibility outside the windshield as the readout flashed green on the dashboard. "That should jam their sensors long enough for us to get out of here," Tom said confidently.

"I was sure we were going to die," William gasped.

Alex smiled. His old friend had been there for him from the first day they met. Except for a few extra pounds and a little less hair, William had not changed much at all. The two of them had been college roommates, and they remained in close contact ever since. While Alex went for his PhDs in bioengineering and neuroscience, William pursued his medical interests and became a virologist. Although appearing as if he could cultivate many new strains of viruses or bacteria simply by allowing them to thrive on his unkempt clothing, he was an extremely successful scientist and had provided invaluable help to Alex on multiple occasions.

"Please tell me you at least got the shield," William said, wiping the sweat off his forehead.

How times have changed, William thought. Back in college, he was the one getting Alex in trouble. Whether it was joining a crazy fraternity, staying out all night partying, or engaging in something of questionable legality, he always found a way to have a good time. In fact, it was his personal mission to pull Alex's head away from the computer screen or out of the robotics lab long enough for them to have some fun together.

"We must take The Mark to Nan Madol," the Tibetan woman pleaded as she also entered the back of the cockpit. "It's our only hope."

"That does not look like the shield," William commented, cocking his head. "In fact, I would conjecture that looks more like a person than a shield."

And a certainly beautiful person.

"It's not a shield," Alex commented, "it's a key."

"She'll be traced," interrupted an equally lovely and sophisticated woman unstrapping herself from the seat behind William. With her vibrant green eyes, long, brown hair, fair skin, and athletic figure, Alex could not help but smile every time he looked at her.

"You're right, Marissa," Alex said to his fiancée. "You better administer her a dose of the biotag ablator."

"One step ahead of you," she commented. As a physician and past member of the National Institutes of Health medical team, she was well equipped to handle most emergent medical situations. Grabbing a half-dollar sized sphere, she twisted it once and pulled it apart into two halves.

"Hold still," Marissa said gently, putting each half up to the Tibetan's woman's neck and pressing them against her skin. "In a few moments, The New Reality won't be able to track you."

"But I don't have these—what did you call them—biotags," she protested.

"We all have biotags," Marissa said, "unless we've been inoculated against them. The New Reality dispersed them throughout the atmosphere and into the world's water supply. Once inside your body, they divide and attach to your nascent red blood cell's DNA. The biotags are then able to transmit a unique, personalized quantum signal that The New Reality can utilize to track the entirety of the world's population."

Marissa then grabbed an IV bag from a drawer in the ship's hull and slapped the end of the IV line on the top of the woman's chest. Taking a few other vials from the drawer, she pressed them against the bag so that their crimson, gold, and violet contents mixed together with the fluid inside of it. "Lay down on the couch in the ship's hull," she instructed, watching the woman grow weak in the knees as the biotag ablator went to work.

"But we must get the Mark," she said, holding onto the crystal.

"Rest," Marissa responded with compassion. "I'm going to strap you in for your safety."

The woman wanted to oppose, but her weakness made her capitulate.

Marissa then turned to Alex and gave him a huge hug; she didn't want to let go. Every time Alex left, she feared she would never see him again. Though it was over a year since she thought she'd lost him forever, the fear still lingered.

Marissa remembered how her fiancé Alex Pella and Jules Windsor once teamed up together to destroy The New Reality and remove its crooked leader, Myra Keres, from office.

Marissa cringed at the thought of how Jules double-crossed Alex; instead of bringing down The New Reality, Jules had usurped control of the entire company and tried to kill Alex. Though he put an end to Myra's tyrannical reign and her life, he attempted to do the same for Alex.

Jules could not have gained control of The New Reality without Alex. In addition to being one of the greatest scientific minds and inventors on the planet, Alex was also as shrewd and cunning as Jules. Plus, unlike anyone else on the planet, Alex possessed the precise genetic code that could potentially bring down his entire empire.

Only the correct genetic key would allow someone to infiltrate The New Reality's main computer system and access the entire global network. And this unique genetic key was forged from one of the most prestigious men who ever walked the planet: Alexander the Great. Cloned from this DNA by The New Reality, Alex never learned of his true heritage until Jules revealed it to him. Jules also willingly failed to mention that he, too, was a clone from just as prestigious and ever more sinister a heritage: Jules Windsor was an exact genetic replica of Julius Caesar.

If it were not for the help of Dr. Harding, a physician under Jules' employment, Alex would have perished in a deep underground genetics facility covertly run by The New Reality. Now, he and those he loved were all wanted by The New Reality as threats to the global state. Forced into hiding for over a year, Alex and his team used the time to plan and prepare.

The stratoskimmer trembled, ending Marissa's embrace.

"We're losing the fog," Tom bellowed out from the cockpit. "It's destabilizing in the erratic electromagnetic field."

Alex leaned into the cockpit; to his surprise only a few sparks glimmered in front of the windshield. The fog had almost completely disintegrated. The ship continued to shake and weave as the electromagnetic field grew more unstable by the minute.

We're sitting ducks! Alex realized. "Evasive maneuvers."

The ship then rocked violently to the side as a sizzling sound emanated throughout the stratoskimmer.

"I'm losing control!" Tom yelled. "We've been hit by an electric blast. Shields losing power."

Alex ran to the copilot's seat as William unbuckled himself and moved to the back of the cockpit. He knew Alex was one of the most accomplished pilots he had ever met and had watched him annihilate multiple competitors in the racing arena. If anyone could get them out alive, it would be him.

"What are you doing?" Tom asked as the stratoskimmer took a dive. "You just turned off the engines."

"It's difficult to lock onto the ship without the dipoles in alignment," Alex commented, grasping the steering wheel. "Plus, with this electromagnetic interference pattern, they're becoming more useless by the second."

Alex turned his head to the side. "Strap in everyone! This isn't going to be easy."

CHAPTER 12

CHRISTINE FELT HELPLESS as she attempted to move her body. Though her mind willed her to do so, she could no longer feel her limbs, let alone move them. She noted that Murph, too, stood motionless. The crystal in his hand glowed brightly and emitted an angelic light that bathed her friend with a soft glow.

Put the crystal back, she thought, hoping to telepathically communicate with Murph.

Murph, nevertheless, remained immobile and failed to respond.

She attempted to communicate with him once again; however, her focus began to diminish, and it was increasingly difficult to concentrate.

Christine's mind began to slowly drift as the image of the room faded away into a white haze. When her eyes focused once more, there was no longer a pool of silver liquid in the center of the room, nor did she see Murph standing motionless with a brilliant crystal clutched between his hands. Instead, she found herself present in mind only, in a much larger chamber filled with people. No longer confined to her body, she felt as if her consciousness had drifted somewhere else altogether.

She did not recognize the people in the room but could feel their presence. Her mind felt more connected to theirs by the second. At first, they began to speak in a foreign tongue unlike anything she'd ever heard in the past; the more her mind became at one with them, the easier it was to understand. Before long, she began to decipher what they were saying.

Christine could feel their tension in the room. She somehow knew that there were two distinct factions at odds with one another. Their tempers were at an elevated level, and their patience dwindled.

"We must consider the consequences," pleaded a distinguished Indian gentleman with a short, wispy white beard, standing in the center of the room adjacent to a clear, circular table sitting atop a waist-high, clear pedestal.

Christine felt as if she knew the man as their consciousness merged; she understood that his name was Rhukma, leader of the Katholes and head of this council. Like the other six members of his faction, he wore a long, white robe. While his ended above the ankles, his female counterparts flowed gently on the marble floor. These other six sophisticated women, each with sharp features donned a red scarf and wore their long, black hair in a perfect bun.

A much gruffer voice echoed throughout the hall in an angry rebuttal. Wearing a shin-long leather tunic at the waist and white and red shawl tied at the right shoulder to cover his chest, he was in loud disagreement.

"This is completely unacceptable," he demanded. "We must not turn back on what we have accomplished. To do so would be counterproductive!"

Christine recognized him as the lead representative of the other group known as the Phrees. A much more matter-of-fact person, this man of probable European descent was dogmatic in his thoughts. The other two men accompanying him donned similar garments while the three females in his faction wore long silken white dresses with a red stripe down the sides, tied with a ribbon around their waists. Each also donned golden necklaces and multi-jeweled earrings. Though these women seemed outwardly harmless, Christine could tell they were just as fierce as their male counterparts.

Zorian, the gruff Phrees leader spoke up once again before any rebuttal could be made. "Our outposts have stabilized the situation for over a century. Must you continue to deny their success?"

His cadre of Phrees representatives ardently agreed. Some clenched their fists while others pointed an accusatory finger. They were the pragmatists and came from a long lineage of manual laborers. Christine could feel that it was these people who built the outposts and took great pride in their accomplishments.

"Please," pleaded Rhukma, "do not let your emotions blind you from the facts."

A much more intellectual person, he and the rest of the Katholes were spiritual in nature and were the thinkers in their land.

"We have tended the outposts for over a century," Zorian bellowed, "not you nor your fellow Kathole countrymen. You act as if you are too good for such a lowly task. Remember, if it were not for us Phrees, our lands by now would be in ruins."

"The ground continues to quake," Rhukma noted. "Many of our homes have turned to rubble. The Earth has rejected us—we must stop before it's too late."

"More outposts then!" bellowed one of the Phrees, while the others cheered his suggestion.

Zorian waited for the banter to end. He then placed his hands together and looked at each of the twelve present. After a deep breath, he uttered as if in despair, "What I am saying is that time has run out. There are no further options. The Earth will be destroyed unless we act now."

CHAPTER 13

"IS JULES STILL FOLLOWING US?" Alex asked as he clenched the stratoskimmer's steering wheel.

A faint holograph of two nondescript ships flickered on the windshield as the dashboard's lights dimmed and brightened at random.

"I can't tell," Tom bellowed as the ship began to shake. "Our instruments aren't working correctly, and the ship's not responding properly. We're slowly losing control."

Then so is he, Alex conjectured.

"Time to go manual," Alex said, reaching under the dashboard. He then yanked a lever, creating an enormous roar in response.

"What's that?" yelled William over the enormous racket.

"Old school," Alex said, smiling.

The ground rapidly approached. Alex knew that if his ship was having this much difficulty in the fluctuating and unsteady electromagnetic field, then so was Jules'. And that was the advantage he was hoping to exploit for his escape.

"Alex!" William frantically pointed towards the windshield, "Turn on the engines or do something. We're going to crash!"

William's nihilistic banter always managed to calm Alex's nerves. Whether he was amused at his old friend's pessimistic outlook or whether it just kept him more observant, he wasn't sure. He, however, understood one thing: If William were not complaining about something, they would be in serious trouble.

Alex then pushed the pedal on the floor and pulled back on the steering wheel. Under manual control, the ship proved enormously more difficult to operate. It felt as if he were physically lifting the entire stratoskimmer by himself. Slowly, the ship ended its dive and attempted to level.

An enormous roar reverberated from the engines. It was a sound that William had never heard on board a stratoskimmer before, and with its intensity, he felt as if his entire body was vibrating.

The lights on the dashboards flickered until the entire panel went dead. The shrinking holographic images of the striker crafts also disappeared in the processes. The stratoskimmer then sputtered and began to descend despite Alex's best attempts to pull back on the steering wheel.

As the ship began to rock side to side, Alex struggled to regain control of the stratoskimmer. Sweat poured from his brow as the vehicle slowly approached the ground. Stone terraced mountain cliffs with a grassy plain below rapidly came into view.

Though an expert pilot and competitive aeronautical racer, Alex had never landed under such circumstances. In fact, he wished he could depolarize the engines in order to make the landing safer. But with all controls now on manual, he needed to bring the ship safely down without a single guiding instrument—and he had to do it before crashing into the mountainside.

"Hold on!" Alex shouted over the loud roar of the engines. He then pulled a second lever; to his delight, he felt the wheels descend from underneath the ship.

"This is going to get rough!" he bellowed.

Somehow avoiding the mountaintop, Alex steered the stratoskimmer toward an open grassy field. He could hear William behind him yelling something to the point that he hoped people recognized his corpse after it was all over.

"Here we go," Alex said as the ship's wheels smashed down on the grassy earth. "Hold," he then said to himself pleading that the wheels did not break and send them into a death spiral.

Ever observant, William yelled, "Mountain!" as Alex cut the engines.

To their delight, the enormous noise ceased, though the ominous approach of the mountain ahead brought them no further solace. Alex then pulled a final lever hidden under the dashboard, deploying a parachute from behind the ship and bringing the stratoskimmer to a halt.

The team sat motionless as their ears continued to ring. The gravity of the situation slowly subsided as they all caught their breath. As usual, William was the first to speak. "Are we dead yet?" he groaned.

Alex unstrapped himself and looked to the back of the cockpit. "Everyone alright?"

The faces of pure exhaustion told him everything he needed to know. After taking a direct hit by an electric blast and having to land the ship manually, he was just glad to see that everyone was alive and in one piece.

"I've got to see how my patient is doing," Marissa said. Stumbling to her feet after unstrapping herself, she proceeded back towards the hull. Before doing so, she gave Alex a little wink and attempted a smile to let him know she was proud of him.

That was all Alex needed.

"Tom," Alex said, "I think that blast from the striker craft damaged the jet engines. They responded much better during the test flights."

"We better have a look before we venture out of here," Tom acknowledged.

Alex felt vindicated for all the time he had spent preparing for the electromagnetic disturbances they had just encountered. Since the world's entire grid had been in fluctuation for over a year, he knew a backup means of flight would be necessary. Consequently, he added newer versions of an old jet engine design to his stratoskimmer. Because these types of engines were not as sensitive to fluctuations in the world grid as the modern electromagnetic dipole versions, it was the perfect addition.

"Where *is* here?" William asked.

"Before the dashboard went dead," Tom answered, "it showed that we were flying above Peru at an ancient place known as Ollantaytambo."

"Never heard of it," William grumbled.

"I better fix the engines before Julius or any of his cronies arrive," Alex said, getting out of his seat. "Tom, could you give me a hand?"

They had to manually lower the heavy door in the stratoskimmer's hull to exit the ship.

Marissa brought their guest outside for some fresh air. She felt it would be much healthier than being confined inside the ship's hull.

William gawked at the ruins of the ancient city upon exiting the ship. Staring up at the stone-terraced mountains and plateaus of massive monolithic stones, he could not but help ask himself who built such an enormous site. He surmised by looking at the smaller stones on top of the much more massive ones, that a newer city must have been erected on an older one. Though he wasn't willing to admit it out loud, this place certainly piqued his interest as a scientist and researcher.

Alex walked up to the engine underneath the stratoskimmer's right wing. Reaching above his head, he turned a knob and lowered a mechanical panel along its side.

"You bring the tool box?" Alex turned and asked.

"One step ahead of you," Tom responded, holding a duffle bag around his shoulder.

Alex reached down and activated the gravity dampeners on his specially-engineered black boots. Disguised to appear as if they were New Reality standard WOG issue, he had designed them for his free fall out of Jules' stratoskimmer. They also allowed him to levitate a few feet in the air if necessary.

"Looks like the electromagnetic field may be finally stabilizing," Tom commented, noting how well the levitation boots were working. He then reached over his head and handed Alex the bag.

"For now," Alex noted. "With the chaotic way the field has been fluctuating, things could change any second." He patted the engine along its side. "And this right here is our safety net."

Taking pride in his work, Alex was pleased with the engine's success. Despite taking a direct hit from the striker craft, it continued to function and land them safely on the ground. His former robotics teacher would have certainly been proud of him. *If he's still alive...*

"It seemed as if the blast fused a few of the blades here together and slightly melted a couple other parts," Alex commented.

Light projected from his forehead into the engine. Utilizing what he designed and coined a "light-aid," Alex had placed a small rectangular sticker above his eyes. Once activated, it emanated a tremendous amount of continuous light, which would last for almost four hours.

Alex then grabbed his trusted pocketeer out of the bag. Taking this pocketknife-like device, he deployed a screwdriver-like appendage that clicked out from the tool's top end. Alex began to fix the engine once its tip started to glow a bright red.

"Will that do?" Tom asked. "It's not like we have any spare parts around here."

"We have rocks," William chimed in sarcastically, "plenty of rocks. As far as the eye can see, there are rocks."

"Being that rocks will not be of much help," Alex responded, amused by his friend's banter, "this will have to do."

After five minutes of fiddling, Alex lowered himself to the ground while taking the light-aid off his forehead.

"Alex," Marissa commented with a little smirk, "I must say, that WOG uniform is very becoming on you."

Alex laughed. After the stressful situation he'd endured, the chuckle was much needed. Looking down at his attire, he then said, "I've been so caught up with everything, I must have forgotten to take it off."

He looked over towards the Tibetan woman lying on the ground covered in a silver blanket with her head propped up on a similarly colored pillow. She held a sparkling crystal tightly against her bosom as if carefully carrying a child. William knelt by her side and dabbed a wet rag along her forehead.

"She'll be fine," Marissa said. "I think she is more air sick than anything else right now. Her body took to the biotag antidote rather quickly."

The Tibetan woman suddenly sat up and turned to William. "We must get there," she implored with a weak voice. "There is no more time."

"Take it easy," Marissa comfortingly assured, overhearing the conversation. She then walked over to her patient. "We will be leaving soon."

"We must get there," the woman reiterated with a little more strength to her voice.

"She says her name is Terzin and that she is the keeper of the Mark," William said as he continued to dab her forehead. "And the crystal she is holding is what she refers to as *the Mark*."

"What do you mean *the Mark*?" Alex asked her.

Terzin held out the crystal in response. "It will all happen again if we don't stop it." She looked Alex directly in the eyes. "You are all so naïve. Just like the elders. You know not what you are doing."

"So, you say this crystal," Alex commented, thinking aloud, "I mean, *the Mark*, has something to do with all the electromagnetic disturbances and seismic changes?"

"We must stop it before it happens again," Terzin said, growing more anxious and beginning to sweat.

"Take a deep breath," Marissa implored. "Rest, and you can tell us more about it when we're safely in our hideout."

Terzin became more frantic, "No, no!"

William continued to pat her on the forehead. Forever a bachelor, he was at a total loss of words when dealing with a woman.

Her agitation mounted. "The Mark," Terzin insisted. "We cannot wait. Things will only get worse."

Marissa reached in her bag for a tranquilizer just in case she needed to administer one to Terzin for her own safety.

"What will happen again?" Alex asked. "Why is this Mark so important?"

"Nan Madol," Terzin insisted. "Nan Madal. It's our last hope. We must get to Nan Madol."

William shrugged his shoulders. "What's Nan Madol?" he mouthed.

"It's an ancient city off the eastern shore of the Pacific Island Pohnpei, somewhere between Hawaii and the Philippines," Marissa answered.

William furrowed his eyebrow as if to say, "How did you know that?"

"When I worked with the NIH," she said, "my team was assigned to examine an outbreak of typhoid on a few of the Pacific Islands."

As the ground began to rumble, Alex looked at the stratoskimmer with urgency, "Let me finish fixing the engines."

Looking in Terzin's eyes, Alex somehow trusted her and believed in the authenticity of her story. He sensed that he needed to trust her. Something was definitely awry with the electromagnetic grid, and he feared that what just happened in Bolivia could occur anywhere on the planet.

"Then it's off to Nan Madol," Alex commented.

Terzin smiled as a sense of relief fell across her face.

"I hope you do a better job flying this time," William responded.

CHAPTER 14

"ASSESSMENT," Jules barked after exiting the ship.

"We have totally lost contact with three of the striker crafts, but the forth touched down successfully less than a mile from here," responded a WOG with a red stripe across the shoulder.

"Any word on what happened to them?" asked Jules.

"Presumed destroyed," the WOG answered. "An SOS signal was sent moments before contact was lost with each of them."

"I saw one of the striker crafts consumed by the earth at Pumapunku while a second crashed moments after takeoff," chimed in another WOG.

Jules understood. Because of the rapidly shifting electromagnetic field, it created an unstable situation whereby flying, let alone landing safely, was almost impossible; their faltering engines had fortuitously provided just enough antigravity to prevent them from crashing.

Under his breath, Jules wished the brave men and women lost at his command a peaceful journey as they became one with the Grand Architect of the Universe, GAOTU.

"Agreed. All three ships must have been destroyed," Drew interjected, exiting the stratoskimmer, which had landed on top of the rocky landscape. "If the ships were at all intact, we would still be receiving a homing signal pinging from their engines."

"Drew, any further word on what occurred back at Pumapunku?" Jules asked, presuming the answer.

A flickering holograph appeared above his wrist. "It looks as if the western coasts of Bolivia, Peru, and all of Chile sunk directly into the Pacific." He looked up at Jules. "The entire west coast of South America is now under water!"

"Be not a cancer on earth," Jules responded rather smugly.

"I know the Ten Commandments of the Georgian Guidestones," Drew said, "but this massive loss of humanity is just so senseless."

"Maintain humanity under 500,000,000," Jules recited. "The commandments of the New World Order are rather specific in nature."

Jules walked over to Drew and placed his arm around him while looking at the barren landscape. "Do you know how many people still inhabit this great Earth despite the recent plague and the destruction caused by *The Disease* and the nanosplicers?" He paused a brief second. "About 4.5 billion. And after the recent mishap here in South America, maybe we're fortunate enough to have reached the four billion mark."

Though Drew certainly respected Jules enormously, he could not embrace all The New World Order beliefs. To him, they were much too dogmatic and ideological—and most importantly, they dehumanized the Earth's population.

"When you think truly about it," Jules further postulated, "are we not but a cancer on this Earth, spreading indiscriminately and metastasizing all over the globe? Where has humanity not gone that we have not destroyed everything in our path?"

Drew dared not contradict him. Though he agreed with some of Jules' beliefs, mass human extinction was certainly not a view he wished to entertain.

"Machines do most of the work now, my boy," Jules commented in triumph. "They have rendered mankind mostly useless. What was once accomplished through sweat and muscle can be done in a fraction of the time and a pittance of the cost with the touch of a button. Machines have made most of humanity obsolete."

He held his hands wide. "What machines cannot accomplish, the remaining 500,000,000 humans left on the planet will do. Plus, how exquisitely simple will it be to rule over a mere half-billion people inhabiting the globe as opposed to the blistering eight billion that once suffocated our planet?"

Jules patted Drew on the back. "Let us not dawdle any longer in such conversation. Off with you. We must destroy our stratoskimmer and rendezvous with our neighboring striker craft."

"What?" Drew asked.

"Was I not clear? We must destroy the stratoskimmer. Lord only knows what surprises Alexander has left behind for us in that ship. I, for one, will not be waiting for an answer. You heard me," he pointed towards the ship. "You have the codes."

"Should I remove anything first?"

"Leave it as is," Jules said. "Though I will miss the old girl, what must be done, must be done."

"How about the shield?" Drew finally mustered up the courage to ask.

"And what about it?" Jules asked with a sly smirk on his face.

"The shield is undoubtedly in Alex's possession."

"Absolutely," Jules responded. "Remember what William Thomas wrote, 'The situation that men define as true will become true to them.'"

"The truth is Alex has found the shield," Drew reiterated, not understanding Jules' point.

"No, my boy," Jules answered. "What Alexander has found is far from the truth."

Jules smiled in confidence.

A glow began to shine through his white button-down shirt. Its heat bathed Jules' chest in warmth, and sent tingles throughout his entire body.

Jules took a deep breath, marveling at its power. He unbuttoned the top few buttons of his shirt, revealing a shining Achilles Shield replica medallion hanging from his neck.

"Before we say good bye to the old girl, I have one last thing to do," Jules commented as he tightly embraced the medallion.

The key, Drew thought, impressed at the site.

Though rumored to exist, he never knew for sure its authenticity or whereabouts until now. It was regarded as almost a mythical device the former leader of their company, Albert Rosenberg, had utilized to unlock the entire New Reality computer system, providing him with full and instant control over anything and everything owned, run, or manufactured by the company.

Heat rushed through Jules' body as his mind connected to The New Reality's computer systems around the globe. It was as if he were mentally connected with each and every single one of them simultaneously. The boundaries of his mind melted away as his consciousness spread effortlessly between New York, Paris, and Hong Kong. Everywhere The New Reality's computer tentacles reached, so did his mind. He now had complete control over the global grid.

Jules' body shuddered as his breathing grew shallow.

"Mr. Windsor?" Drew asked. "Are you alright?"

It almost appeared as if his boss were possessed. Watching his eyes roll back and body stiffen, Drew all but wondered if his head were about to spin.

Before he could ask again, Jules popped out of the trance. A trickle of sweat ran down his brow as he released the Achilles Shield replica. Its glow slowly faded.

As if nothing occurred, Jules touched his ear. "Let's assemble our team and be off to our sister striker craft."

"Yes, Mr. Windsor," a voice echoed in his ear. "Right away."

He turned to Drew while buttoning his shirt. "Can one of these elite striker crafts float?"

"I'm not sure," Drew answered. "But I assume these ships were designed only for flight."

"We may have to find out for ourselves then," Jules said, almost excited about the prospect.

"I know what you're thinking," Drew cautioned. "But the world grid is still too unstable. Let's wait a little longer for it to stabilize."

"If it stabilizes," Jules countered. "The entire grid may in fact do the opposite and become more unstable, nullifying any chance we have of getting out of here. No, we must take flight now and not lose our opportunity."

"Back to Georgia then?" Drew hoped.

The smile he received in response only let him know that this little expedition had just begun.

CHAPTER 15

"NAN MADOL," Marissa explained as the island came into view, "is on the eastern shore of the Island of Pohnpei and was once part of the former States of Micronesia before their autonomy was usurped by The New Reality."

As their stratoskimmer descended upon the area, the ancient megalithic structure came into view. It looked like a large lagoon with multiple man-made islands separated by canals. However, these islands were constructed from massive stone pillars crisscrossing as they rose out of the water and towered into the sky.

"Its original name was *Soun Nan-leng,* or as translated into English, *Reef of Heaven,*" Marissa went on to describe while pointing to the site. "Because of the man-made canals you see there, it is also referred to as the *Venice of the Pacific.* Island legend says that the whole area is haunted and taboo to enter. Local inhabitants believe ghosts and evil spirits inhabit the area. Therefore, virtually no one has explored Nan Madol for centuries, leaving it essentially untouched."

The jet engines cut in and out during their decent, creating a bumpy landing.

"Can you make those engines any louder?" William said, shaking his head. "I really enjoy not hearing myself think."

Alex smirked. The jet engines were vital for their safety during the flight. With each fluctuation of the grid, they would kick in whenever the native depolarizing electromagnetic engines faltered. Without this noisy addition to the ship, they would have assuredly crashed by now.

"We must get *the Mark* to the other Keepers," Terzin explained once again. Holding the crystal out in front of her, she reiterated the precariousness of the world's situation.

Alex could only surmise that this crystal, or Mark, was involved in the stabilization of the world grid and tectonic plates. Somehow the two were intricately connected by a sophisticated lost technology, foreign to modern science.

"And who are these Keepers?" Marissa asked.

"The world will once again be engulfed by the ocean unless the Marks are in proper alignment." Terzin said, ignoring the question.

She bit her lip, contemplating if she should reveal any further information. Secrecy had been the cornerstone of her and her ancestors' beliefs. It was the main reason they could oversee the Marks for so long, unhindered by war, governments, or other global conflicts.

Terzin realized the gravity of their situation. There was no other option but to win the trust of her fellow travelers, and to do that she must tell them the truth. "I come from a long line of Keepers believed to span millennia, all with one designated task—to ensure the safety of the Mark."

"Millennia?" Alex questioned.

She nodded her head. "Humanity has thrived much longer and is far older than you believe. Much has been lost."

"What has been lost?" Alex asked quickly.

She shook her head. "I can say no more." She embraced the crystal and placed her chin on it. "We must return this to the other Keepers before it is too late."

Marissa placed her hand on Alex's shoulder as if to say, *She's had enough.*

The door to the stratoskimmer descended after the ship landed without incident. Before they exited, Alex turned to Tom. "Place the ship in a geostationary orbit around this island. Try to maintain it in stealth the best you can and be ready for a rapid pick-up."

"This isn't my first rodeo," Tom responded. Wearing his vintage black leather bomber's jacket and brown flight pants with multiple pockets, he sat back confidently in his seat, awaiting, if not hoping for, any excitement. After being cooped up with Alex and the rest of their colleagues for over a year hiding from Jules and The New Reality, Tom reveled in the thought of some action.

Alex and the rest of his colleagues marveled at the ancient megalithic site as they exited the ship.

"Impressive," William commented, staring at the massive basalt towers of crisscrossing stonework. "These walls must be at least forty to fifty feet tall. It's one thing to actually transport one of those massive pillars, yet another to raise it another few stories. I wonder how they accomplished such a task?"

Not having ventured to this part of the island during the previous stay, Marissa, too, was amazed at the architecture. "The natives also state that twin magicians from a lost place known as Katau built this place using an ancient form of sorcery."

"Or a little lost ancient technology," William rebutted.

With shield in hand, Alex asked, "Terzin, where to now?"

Though Alex trusted her superficially, he definitely harbored some healthy skepticism towards their new guest. He had been double-crossed before. As a result, his friend Guri Bergmann's death still stung.

"Follow me," she responded, leading them deeper into the maze of buildings.

Alex attempted to focus on the entirety of the island using his left contact lens known as a vedere lens. However, the satellite feed directly linked to it became fuzzy the moment they landed. Something in or about the island was obscuring the aerial reconnaissance feed. However, a clearer infrared image revealed what appeared to be a person or possibly even an animal approaching their position.

Alex turned and saw that it was not one but two men heading towards them. Taking the shield and placing it under his arm to hide its identity, he greeted them both with a friendly nod and smile. With his free hand, he moved it slowly towards the pulse gun in his back pocket, just in case he had to defend himself and the group.

The scowl-faced men continued to approach. Both wore red wetsuits covering their entire body and had fish hanging from a rope over their shoulder.

With a stern look on his face, the taller of the two Polynesian-appearing men pointed accusingly to the group and said, "Be out of here by nightfall. The darkness only brings death."

The other nodded while pointing them back towards the direction of their ship.

Before Alex could answer, Terzin approached the men.

Both islanders were taken aback by the site. Still wearing her silken, yet wrinkled and dirty, dress, she held the Mark in front of her for them both to view.

"Planeta da nive serreran zain," Terzin then uttered.

"Zara eta jokaldi bat," one responded.

Terzin held the crystal above her and stated, "Planetako nive atezainada."

Upon her words, both men knelt on one knee and bowed in unison with respect. After the gesture, they humbly stood and asked her and the rest of them to follow.

Now leading the way, the two men took them down a long path heading towards one of the largest stone structures in the complex. Both its massive height and width suggested that it must have once been the centerpiece of this manmade island.

Ever cautious, Alex continued to reconnoiter the area via his vedere lens, making sure there were no other unexpected guests. *Bergmann*, Alex perseverated.

Both men placed their hands on either side of the same long basaltic pillar lying horizontal to them at eye level. Where their hands touched, the rock appeared artificial and not part of the natural pillar.

The two men then pressed forward in unison. In response, a hum began to echo throughout the complex. At first low and barely audible, it began to intensify, sending the island's native red parrots known as lorikeets flying above them in a chaotic frenzy.

A large rectangular area of the wall encompassing the pillar the men were pressing began to vibrate. As the hum reached a maximum intensity, the rectangular area spontaneously swiveled along a vertical axis at one end and opened as if the door were weightless.

One of the Polynesian-appearing men turned to them. "Come," he invited. "Our leader Orisihpa will be honored to meet you."

William looked over to Alex and raised a suspicious eyebrow.

His friend need not say a word to know what he was thinking. William was also present when they were taken hostage by a supposed monk at the monastery on the Island of Patmos.

William, too, remembered how their blind faith nearly cost them both their lives—and claimed that of Guri Bergmann.

Alex nodded as if to say, *Be ready*.

CHAPTER 16

ALEX SAT ON THE FLOOR next to Marissa. The warmth of the rock surprised him. Though far below ground, the stone radiated a soothing, ambient heat.

He was amazed at the complexity of the underground basaltic tunnels hidden under Nan Madol. The further and deeper he descended, the more he was astounded by what an enormous undertaking it must have been to erect such a complex. He felt what they saw above ground was just the tip of a proverbial iceberg concealing the true mysteries of the island underneath.

"I hope they didn't bring us down here to kill us," William whispered in Alex's ear as he leaned over to his friend.

"Drink," offered a wise looking, older woman with long white, braided hair and a flowered tiara on her brow. She was sitting in the center of their half circle arrangement. Wearing no more than a grass skirt and brown top strapped around her bosom, she held up a half coconut with both hands and offered it to Terzin.

Other island natives in the room also began sitting around them. Many were in traditional island attire while a few donned more modern clothing.

Terzin walked over to the elder woman and bowed. "Thank you, Orisihpa." Already well aware of this sacred ceremony, she tilted her head back and closed her eyes. Taking a sip, she then inhaled through her nose to intensify the flavor.

William could not help but stare at her beauty. He appreciated her feminine silhouette as it cast a slight shadow in the torch-lit room. The violet flower behind her ear, which she must have taken from one of the many floral arrangements that decorated the room, accentuated her blue eyes.

"Close your eyes when you drink it." Terzin said as she handed William the coconut. "And let your mind drift away in the process."

William gently took the coconut, barely able to take his attention away from her. All concern about his safety and the authenticity of their hosts quickly dissipated. With a smile on his face, he closed his eyes and brought the drink to his lips.

The sense of serenity abruptly ended as he swallowed. The syrupy mixture tasted like a combination of mud and grass mixed together. With grainy bits of this chalk-like concoction clinging to his throat, William attempted not to gag. His only solace after drinking this mixture was that he would have the pleasure of handing it to his friend Alex.

Finally regaining his composure, William turned to Alex and said, "Drink up. Make sure you take a big gulp."

From the bits of grass and brown substance stuck between William's teeth, Alex could only surmise the taste. Acting as if he were taking a sip, he feigned a swallow before handing the coconut to Marissa. With a wink, he attempted to forewarn her of what she was about to drink.

However, after having stayed on the island previously, she was painfully aware of this brown concoction even before she brought it to her lips. She'd already had the misfortune of sampling what was known as sakau. Marissa certainly would not make that error again. Also feigning a sip, she passed the coconut to the islander next to her.

"I can sense that you are still worried about the Mark," Orisihpa said, staring into Terzin's eyes.

Terzin felt ashamed that she had somehow offended their host, and bowed her head as if asking for mercy.

"Be not afraid." Orisihpa assured. "The Mark is in its proper place in the Mukulian Hall with the others that have fallen astray. All is well now. The world is at peace—for the moment."

Terzin smiled, needing extra assurance. The elders had repeatedly taught her that if the Mark's place at Pumapunku were at all compromised, it should be immediately brought to Nan Madol. However, she understood that time may have distorted the truth behind these old stories told to her at bedtime.

Alex wished he understood how the crystal worked. The knowledge that could be gleaned from this lost science seemed limitless. Plus, if these Marks stabilized the Earth's electromagnetic field and tectonic plates, he would like to understand them more in case there was ever again a problem with the tectonic plates or the Earth's electromagnetic grid. Hoping for at least some clue, he asked, "Who created the Marks?"

"One of the unenlightened," Orisihpa responded with a smile. "You see," she explained while holding her hand in front of her, "Pohnpei and Nan Madol were once part of a vast Pacific continent we referred to as Mu. Also known by other Pacific Islanders as Hiva, Ka-hoopo-kane, and Kumari Kandam, this great land was lost; only its highest mountaintops remain.

Pohnpei, Hawaii, Fiji, Midway, Tonga, and Easter Island, to name a few, are all that are left of this once massive landmass."

"What happened?" Marissa asked. "What could have caused such massive destruction?"

"Legend says Mu was lost in the great disaster." she explained. "Swallowed up by the sea.

"The biblical flood?" Marissa conjectured. "As mentioned in the Christian and Hebrew Bibles?"

William looked at her skeptically. "I thought all of that was folktale or old stories created to make a point."

"That's not exactly true," Marissa rebutted. "There are over 350 flood stories spanning the entire globe. Because my work took me around the world, I personally heard a few of these myths from the Berber in Africa, the Hopi tribe of North America, and the indigenous people of Australia. Not only in the Bible can you find these flood stories, but tales of a great deluge are also located in Mayan writing, the Babylonian story of Gilgamesh, the Ingorot tale of the Philippines, and the story of Nügua in China."

Orisihpa added, "The flood story is the common theme among all of them. Every culture seems to parrot the same story. Though the names are different, the story remains the same."

"The Greek myth of Phileman and Baucis," Alex added, "also tells the tale of how Zeus brought the brothers to the mountaintop as the water inundated the Earth."

"The sea, too, arose, and in a stupendous catastrophe of nature the land sank into the sea. The new Earth arose out of the womb of the last Earth," Orisihpa said, "to quote the Samoan."

"Where is the proof?" William asked, still unconvinced. "Maybe it's a coincidence. Flooding is a common natural disaster that has occurred since the dawn of humanity. I'm sure every civilization has somehow been affected by it."

"There is," Alex said, "but we've ignored the evidence in the dogmatic pursuit of a uniformitarian version of history. Geologists abandoned such theories of catastrophism in the early nineteenth century."

Alex took a small, black card out of his pocket and placed it on the stone floor in front of him. A holograph appeared above it. "I've always been intrigued by what geologists call Alaskan muck. As you can see on this image, there are bones, plants, trees, and mud crushed together and frozen as if created in some great cataclysmic event."

Different holographic scenes displayed above the card, activated by Alex's narration.

"This muck can also be found in Siberia," Alex added, "and is full of insects, plants, and bones from various animals such as bison, mammoth, and other large mammals. Plus, there are caves and crevices all over the world that appear as if they were suddenly inundated with the same material. Not a single continent is without one of them. In addition, hundreds of sunken ancient cities have been found under the Mediterranean Sea, as if inundated by a mass deluge."

"There are also these massive boulders," the holograph changed as Marissa spoke, "found haphazardly in the Saharan desert. Geologists call them erratics because they have no explanation about how such massive rocks could be found in desolate areas. It is as if they purposely want to ignore the fact that the rocks appear to have been carried by raging waters before reaching their final destination."

"So, if this biblical flood already occurred," William asked, "what are you trying to stop now with these Marks of yours? Hasn't the destruction already happened?

William looked around at his friends and host. "Did any of you ever think that these Marks may have somehow triggered this biblical flood, and by tinkering with them again, we may cause another one? Just look at what happened when Terzin's Mark was removed from Bolivia."

Despite his friend's skepticism, Alex agreed that William made an astute point.

"My word is all that I can provide," Orisihpa humbly responded. "It is all I have to give you."

"Maybe the Marks are preventing something even more catastrophic from occurring," Marissa added. "Maybe something worse is in store for the planet."

"Legend has it—" Orisihpa began to say.

The room began to rumble, knocking down a few bowls and causing the potted plants in the room to sway.

Terzin looked suspiciously at the ground and placed her head on it. "The Earth remains unpleased."

William jumped to his feet, "Orisihpa, I thought you said all is well since *the Mark* is in its proper place in the Mukulian Hall?"

Orisihpa appeared just as surprised as William. "Check the hall!" she bellowed to one of the men in traditional island attire. "Find out what has happened."

"Don't bother," Alex said. Taking the shield and turning it over, he revealed his ancient treasure to Orisihpa. "The Earth is not the one displeased with us. Peering directly into his vedere lens, Alex realized the problem was coming from above and not below.

"We must leave now!" Alex insisted. Looking at his shield, he realized his error too late. "We've been discovered."

CHAPTER 17

CHRISTINE CONTINUED TO WATCH the members of the council argue. She could feel their tensions mounting as the frustration level in the room escalated rapidly. The two factions vehemently disagreed. However, she sensed the Phrees' emotions transcended mere discontentment and ventured into the realm of hatred. More spiritual in nature, the Katholes refused to allow such basic emotions to overwhelm their conscious.

"The outposts will assuredly protect the planet," insisted Zorian as he slammed his fist on the glass table in the center of the room.

The reverberation from the strike echoed throughout the hall but did little to curtail the argument. Instead, it acted as if it were a bell, signaling the next round of the fight.

"My people have harvested more Marks," Zorian maintained, "and have strategically built more outposts throughout the entire globe. It will be only a short matter of time before we have them all fully operational."

"Plus," one of his female counterparts interjected, "we have plans for another hundred more. Do not let your fear continue to blind you."

"How may outposts will it take?" questioned a calm and sophisticated Kathole representative. Her strong voice engulfed the hall, overpowering the minor bickering that interfered with the conversation. "Will 100 work? Will 1,000 work? Will there ever be enough?"

"Bhadra is correct," bellowed Rhukma, the leader of the Katholes. "The more outposts we erect, the less effect each one provides." He looked up at the Phrees standing opposite the table. "Let us not fool ourselves into the blind belief that these outposts will prevent the inevitable."

Before the Phrees could amount a rebuttal, Rhukma waved his hand over the top of the clear table. Its surface began to shimmer in translucent colors as a three-dimensional image became visible under its surface.

The other twelve members of the council aggregated around the table's perimeter, waiting for the image to come into focus.

"As you all can clearly see," Rhukma explained as a three-dimensional representation of the Earth became visible, "the problem lies here at the northern icecap."

Christine peered at the image. It was as if she had become one with the council members and was in the room standing around the table. However, the planet she saw was far different than the one she recognized today. Instead, it appeared much like the etchings of the maps she observed under the Art Museum. Though the planet looked foreign, she could clearly recognize the basic outline of the modern-day world. In this image, North America was far closer to the north while Africa boasted large lakes and streams, without the massive desert currently engulfing it.

The ice cap located at the Earth's northern pole was larger than she had ever seen. Encroaching far into North America, Asia and Europe, its size was immense. Christine wondered if these people were living sometime during the last ice age.

That has to be at least 10,000 years ago! she concluded, remembering her history. Dumbfounded, she was amazed that such technology, or even any technology, existed at that time. She thought humanity was still hunting wooly mammoths and rummaging for food.

"The increasing weight of the Earth's asymmetric northern ice cap," Rhukma explained, "is being accentuated by the planet's rotation and inherent wobble, creating an enormous instability within the Earth's fragile crust."

"The outposts," Zorian insisted, "will correct this instability and neutralize the problem for the next hundred generations. It's success in undeniable."

Zorian then held out his hand to remove the image. However, Rhukma firmly pushed it aside, denying him the opportunity. The act only infuriated Zorian, who felt as if it brought dishonor to him and his council members.

Calmly, Rhukma continued speaking as Zorian's gaze bore down upon him. "Zorian, you and the Phrees must remember: The Earth's crust is but a thin layer floating atop a massive ball of hot, flowing magma."

With a clenched fist, Zorian shook, "No, it is you and the rest of the Katholes who must remember the outposts have brought us all great prosperity. Without the toil and labor of my people, you would still be living in the dirt from which you came."

The Katholes were aghast at such an inflammatory comment. Many gasped in disgust.

Red dots sprung up all along the globe as Rhukma waved his hand over the table once again. Unaffected by mere words, his mind was clear, and his thoughts remained coherent. Spiritual in nature, he turned inward and upward for self-control and motivation.

"The Earth's crust is slipping," Rhukma continued, "and continues to slip as the weight of the ice cap grows. As you can see Zorian, despite the outposts, these places here have already been destroyed as a result of minor crust slippages. As the weight of the ice cap grows, it will eventually destabilize the crust enough to potentially destroy the entire planet."

The image in the table shifted to that of rubble with another wave of the hand. With H-shaped blocks and shattered wooden boats, the area was completely razed to the ground. "Our port city of Svastra," Rhukma explained, "is now over 10,000 feet above sea level. As you can see, what once was a magnificent harbor is now lost high in the mountains, never to witness a sailing ship again."

"This, you blame on these ice caps?" Zorian exclaimed indignantly. "Could this not be of natural causes? We have records dating back thousands of years. Who says things such as this could not have occurred millions if not hundreds of millions of years previously?"

"Listen to reason Zorian," Rhukma pleaded. "Don't you see how the Earth's crust buckled at this location? While Svastra rose, other parts of the continent sank, lost to the depths of the ocean."

"What you see here is just a precursor of more to come," Bhadra interjected. "The Earth's crust barely shifted during this incident. Imagine what will happen if it shifts an entire degree—or even a few degrees? There will be mass destruction unlike that described in even our most ancient texts."

"So, what is your solution?" Zorian heckled. Joined by the rest of the Phrees, they taunted Rhukma and his companions, hurling disparaging remarks.

"Shut down the cradle," Rhukma insisted, bringing an instant hush to the room. "Before any further ice forms on the northern cap."

"You surely gest!" Zorian rebutted. "What you speak of is blasphemy. We will all be lost without the cradle."

Tired of further discussion, Rhukma wanted to end the conversation. "As leader of the council, I call for a vote."

Zorian walked with a huff away from the table, indignant at such a request. With his hands folded, he could only utter, "You old fool."

"All those for not shutting down the cradle," Rhukma stated succinctly.

Instead of a show of hands, Zorian's fellow councilmembers protested the vote and pounded on the glass table as a boisterous display of their discontent.

"Those for shutting down the cradle," Rhukma then voiced above the commotion. He and the other six Katholes raised their hands in defiance of their detractors. Their voices would not be silenced by the Phrees' disobedience.

"Bhadra," Rhukma stated solemnly, "bring me the key."

The room went silent. Rhukma's words struck all present like a bolt of lightning. With the gravity of the situation now bearing down on all of them, each understood the far-reaching consequences of their decision.

Bhadra slowly walked to the far wall and waved her hands over two brilliantly shining rubies along its face. Attempting to suppress her fear of humanity's future, she knew what must be done. A portion of the wall next to the precious stones slowly descended in response, revealing a sacred object secured for centuries behind it. All those in the room gazed upon the artifact. Though many had heard of its existence, few believed it actually existed. Even Zorian was at a loss of words at the sight.

"Proceed," Rhukma commanded.

With trembling hands, Bhadra secured the object in her grip and slowly brought it to Rhukma. Mesmerized, the councilmembers watched in amazement. The artifact was long conjectured to be more myth than reality. Now, with it in front of them, each stood in awe.

Christine's only thought was that the object looked nothing like a key. Instead, it reminded her of something she read in the ancient Greek poem, *The Iliad*. To her, it looked more like the shield described in its pages.

"Thank you," Rhukma stated as he went to take the key. Before he had an opportunity to grasp it, a sharp, piercing pain seared straight through his back, knocking him down upon his knees. No longer able to support himself, Rhukma fell flat on his face.

Bhadra stepped forward, attempting to help her fallen leader. Zorian waved the bloody dagger that he had just thrust through Rhukma's back in her direction, deterring any sudden movements.

"Now, give me the key," Zorian insisted, brandishing his bejeweled weapon.

"Never!" Bhadra yelled as she turned and sprinted out of the room. Though priding herself in her spiritual prowess, Bhadra also took great pride in keeping her body as fit as her mind.

Before Zorian could follow, a finely dressed Kathole councilwoman pulled a slender, half-hourglass-shaped golden object from her shin and belted him across the side of his head with it. Zorian dropped the dagger and staggered backwards from the blow. Before he could react, the rest of the Katholes joined the fight.

Blood splattered onto the floor as the two groups clashed. Christine could hear and see the breaking of bones and the smashing of skulls as each defended themselves with different weapons they had stashed on their bodies. Helpless, she just wanted to reach out and bring an end to the fight.

Even so, she knew this fight foreshadowed a much more dire confrontation soon to follow.

CHAPTER 18

THE ROOM CONTINUED TO RUMBLE as the floor shook in response. Water began to trickle through walls and the potted plants hanging from the ceiling fell to the ground. A decorative stone pillar against the wall crashed down, barely missing two islanders as it tumbled.

The whole room reverberated as shock waves continued to assault the area. Chips of stone began to crumble and fall on Alex along with the others. Fine stone grit created a fuzzy haze that was slowly engulfing the room.

"What's going on?" William asked. Standing up and looking all around the area, he anxiously searched for any viable means of escape.

Other islanders in the room were just as terrified. Looking nervously towards their leader, each awaited her next command.

"It's Julius Windsor," Alex replied. "He's found us."

Alex shook his head in disgust. As he placed the shield over his fiancée's head for protection, he realized that it was his fault they had been found. Jules obviously had a lock on the shield and was able to use it to determine their location. Whether it was a ploy to let him steal the shield or just a stroke of good luck for Jules that he had stolen it, Alex could not decide. However, he realized one thing: The shield was both a detriment and an advantage.

"What do you mean he found us?" William asked. "We were under stealth. Even the fumes from the jet engine were supposed to be untraceable. How could he possibly..."

Marissa realized the answer was above her head. "It's the shield," she said, trying to keep her footing. Jules must be able to track it. Unless Alex can cloak it, Jules will know our exact location as long as it's in our possession."

Alex knew that cloaking the shield would not be possible at the moment. Somehow, he needed to distance himself from the rest of them so that he did not jeopardize all their lives. His friends were his family. They were with him throughout The Disease and Jules' takeover of The New Reality. They all had risked so much and suffered just as much as a consequence. As fugitives to The New Reality, they were forced to hide from not only Jules but also from their friends and family. Sequestered for over a year, they plotted to restore their names and rescue humanity from The New Reality's tyrannical oppression.

While peering into his vedere contact lens, Alex watched as Jules exited an elite striker craft that had landed on one of Nan Madol's manmade islands. Another striker craft soon accompanied it.

It was a third ship, hovering overhead, that was causing the commotion. Sending electric shock pulses above their location, it demolished more and more of the stony island with each burst. The intensity of the blasts was great enough to obliterate the once forty foot stone structure above them and create at least another ten foot hole in the ground. With each new pulse, more destruction ensued. Alex grasped that it was a short matter of time before this entire area would be destroyed.

"Follow me!" Orisihpa said hastily. "We will be safe in the Mukulian Hall."

The island natives along with Alex, William, Terzin, and Marissa followed the island leader.

"The hallway is beyond that fallen rock!" Orisihpa shouted as the rumbling in the room grew louder and more intense.

Climbing over a large fallen stone deterring their progress, the group splashed down on the other side and ran into the open hallway.

Orisihpa's agility surprised Marissa. As they followed, she commented, "Spry for such an old lady." "Maybe it's the mud that she drinks!" William bellowed over the noise while still attempting to get that earthy taste out of his mouth.

The further they followed, the cooler it became and the less they could feel any sort of rumbling. There was no longer any water trickling through the floor, nor were the walls or ceiling cracking. Only a distant reverberation could be heard far off down the hall.

Alex watched on his vedere lens the action unfolding above ground. While the pummeling continued, he noted the increasing numbers of WOGs pouring out of the ships. Nan Madol was under full assault.

The elite striker craft overhead appeared to be changing weapons. The black satellite-dish appearing armament that had already reaped so much destruction on the island retracted into the ship's underbelly while a more sinister cannon-like device appeared in its wake.

The momentary cease-fire provided Alex with no relief. Realizing the arsenal of weapons aboard the ship, he knew something more destructive was in store for them.

Alex tapped on his auricular chip, signaling to his pilot Tom their circumstances. Specifically tuned into his cerebral frequencies, Alex had specially designed this chip to translate his thoughts into words.

As he followed Orisihpa further down the passage, the image on his lens disappeared. He blinked a few times and even tapped it to ensure that it still functioned. Additionally, the signal on his auricular chip went silent. His only hope was that Tom received his full message before it was too late.

As Alex entered the great hall, he understood why the transmissions had been lost.

Terzin dropped to her knees upon entering. The site was too great for her to handle. She had heard tales of this place from her mother and even great grandmother but never expected to behold its magnificence in person.

Orisihpa proudly stood at the edge of the large circular room. It was as if the room breathed both life and vitality back into her. "Behold," she announced, "the great Mukulian Hall."

Terzin marveled at its magnificence. In the center stood a large white marble pedestal with a stunning bull's head ornately engraved at the top. Along its side were intricate scenes ranging from the mundane such as farming or fishing to the more intense scenes of man to man combat and siege warfare. Pregnant woman with bulbous bellies fluted out from the pedestal's base, creating a ring around its perimeter.

A massive, sparkling crystal floated above. Unlike that which she had kept watch over since her initiation as a Keeper, this massive stone dwarfed anything she had ever seen. It stood at least five feet tall and glimmered in the light. Crystals, similar to the one she had kept watch over, rotated around this central stone like planets orbiting a mother sun. There must have been at least fifty of them, each moving in harmony with the other.

Alex felt the shield in his arms suddenly become weightless. He instinctively let go of it as a fine white light sparkled around its perimeter.

"Do you see that?" William asked, pointing at the ceiling. "Those are the same as the constellations on the shield."

"I knew bringing you would prove useful," Alex jested to his longtime friend.

"I'll give you useful," William rebutted.

Alex smirked while looking up at the ceiling. Just like the shield, the constellations of Orion, Taurus, and Ursa Major spanned from left to right. The V-shaped cluster of five stars making the bull's head in Taurus were much larger and more brilliant above them than on the shield. Additionally, they were prominently located in the center of the ceiling.

"What do you make of the Hyades star cluster in Taurus?" Marissa asked, also making note of the V-shaped display.

"It represents the cradle of civilization," Terzin explained, now standing next to them.

Still in awe, Terzin continued to marvel at the room as she spoke. Highly polished marble formed the floors, walls, and ceiling. Along the room's circular perimeter were twelve separate ornately engraved and intricately colored scenes with a unique emblem above each one. The chiseled emblems sparkled and glimmered in the light.

"That is why the bull is so revered in our ancient legends," Terzin continued explaining. "My grandmother told me on many occasions that all life sprang forth from the cradle and populated the Earth."

That sounds like a bunch of bull, William grumbled to himself. But out of his growing affection for Terzin, he nodded his head as if truly interested in her legend.

Alex wished he could inspect the area further. But he was unsure if this room could sustain further assaults by the elite striker craft. "Orisihpa," he asked, "is there a secure way to get out of here and back to our ship?"

"Relax," she responded with a smile. "We are secure enough down here, protected by the ancient power of the Marks."

Skeptical, Alex noted two well-lit hallways at the other end of the room. But without any of his gadgets functioning at the moment, he could only fathom their destinations.

"Let me show you the magnificence of the Maternal Mark," she said, gesturing to the largest crystal in the center of the room.

Terzin gasped and brought her hand to her mouth. The first of the group, she followed Orisihpa across the floor.

As they walked closer to the Maternal Mark, Alex felt increasingly weightless with each step. His bodily aches and pains slowly dissipated in the process. While grasping the shield, he took a deep breath as his lungs rejoiced at the incoming air.

"I feel great," Marissa said. "It is like these crystals are rejuvenating my entire body."

"Don't touch that," Orisihpa scolded as William attempted to poke one of the crystals floating by him.

He quickly retracted his hand as if he had been scolded by his mother for sneaking a cookie. "You are not going to believe this," he then blurted. "My mother—her face is in the crystal. The way I remember her from when I was a child."

Orisihpa smiled. "You have made a connection with this Mark. It can see what's on your mind. Only a good and pure soul can make such a union."

Alex stopped walking as an image of his own mother then appeared in the crystal next to him. William's revelation must have triggered an inner memory. Alex was struck by her beauty and once again wished she was still living. Since losing both his mother and father as a child, he never went a day without thinking about either of them.

"Stay focused," Marissa nudged. After having long conversations with Alex, she knew the sight of his mother could distract him. It was certainly his weak point, and she did not need for his mind to wander at this critical moment.

The image vanished and was replaced by that of Jules Windsor. Alex clenched his teeth and continued walking, focusing on the two hallways at the other end of the room. "Thank you," he responded to Marissa.

The only other person Alex felt as much love for besides his mother and father was his fiancée. The bond between the two grew even stronger during their time together isolated from the world. Though Alex spent endless hours tinkering on his inventions, he always made time for her and the rest of his colleagues-in-hiding.

As they walked closer to the Maternal Mark, an image of the Earth came into focus. Located in the center of the crystal, the three-dimensional representation became much crisper until its brilliance matched that of the Mark itself.

Sparkling white dots blotted each continent, creating a large maze that had an interlocking triangular configuration. The majority of these dots blinked while but a small few remained solid.

"Take a gander at South America," William said. "Looks like half of it's gone."

Terzin held back the tears. Her home and her people were all gone. The momentary feeling of bliss was lost. Not even the positive power of the crystals could negate the mounting sensation of remorse building inside her.

As a few of the crystals floated by her, they each turned black and cloudy until they moved past her position.

"I know you hurt," Orisihpa consoled. "But you did the right thing by bringing the Mark home. You have saved the planet."

Marissa placed a comforting hand on Terzin's shoulder. As the crystals passed by the two of them, they soon no longer darkened in Terzin's presence.

"The single red dot," Alex pointed at the globe. "What does that represent?"

Orisihpa peered closer. Never had she'd seen such a sight. "I do not know," she admitted. "The blinking white dots represent the location of where Marks used to be located across the globe while those not blinking are the ones still maintained by an active Keeper. But the red dot?"

"Looks like it's somewhere in Pennsylvania," Alex commented.

"Philadelphia," Marissa chimed in.

"I think we must go investigate this spot next," Alex said. "It may represent a problem."

"What about getting safely to our hideout?" William implored. "Wasn't that the goal all along, after we acquired the shield?"

Alex pointed to Bolivia. "Don't you see what happened to South America? What if the same thing is about to occur in Philadelphia, or worse? Who knows what could potentially happen? The entire East Coast of the United States could be heading for a watery grave under the Atlantic if we don't do anything about it. Think of your family, your friends."

William bit his lip. "Ok," he capitulated. "You win."

The entire room suddenly shook with one massive thud. A few of the crystals fell to the ground and broke into countless pieces in the process.

Orisihpa cried out, "This can't be!" She looked up at the ceiling, pleading, "You will destroy us all!"

A faint sight flickered into Alex's vedere lens for a brief second. No longer on Nan Madol, Jules now stood on the Island of Pohnpei's shore facing the manmade island situated in a lagoon adjacent to it. The immense stones once intricately stacked upon one another all lay in ruin. The entire site had been transformed to rubble.

Alex lost sight of the image before he could examine it any further. "We have to get out of here."

"What's going on?" Marissa asked.

"Jules completely decimated the island," Alex explained, "and there is much more to come. I caught a glimpse of it on my lens." He turned to Orisihpa. "Where do those two hallways at the far end of the room lead?"

"They all lead to death," Orisihpa lamented.

Definitely not taking one of them, William thought.

"But do they lead out of here?" Alex insisted.

"Yes," Orisihpa responded. "But where will you go? If the Maternal Mark is destroyed, so will be the entire planet."

CHAPTER 19

JULES LET GO of the small Achilles Shield medallion hanging from his neck. Its glow faded as Jules buttoned it behind his well-ironed starched, white shirt. Though the temperature was now almost ninety-five degrees, Jules barely had any sweat on his brow.

"I can't seem to find it anymore," Jules said.

"It's highly unlikely that it was destroyed," Drew concluded.

"Agreed," Jules said, "the location of the Achilles Shield is somehow being blocked, and the key can no longer identify its location."

"Do you think this is Alex's doing?" Drew asked.

"I sincerely doubt it," Jules answered. "Though my sly foe is mentally equipped for just such an endeavor, I believe that we took him off guard with this attack. There must be something deep under Nan Madol that is cloaking the shield."

"Probably the same thing that disabled your weapons under Pumapunku," Drew concluded.

"Right again," Jules noted.

Standing on the Island of Pohnpei, they examined the decimated ruins of Nan Madol. The once towering stone edifices were now but a pile of fragmented stones—it's architectural glory lost forever.

WOGs surrounded Jules and Drew. Brandishing their weapons in full battle regalia, they stood alert for any sign of trouble.

"Do you think Alex and his friends are still alive?" Drew asked. "That was an intense pummeling the island took."

"Surely you don't believe that these mere stones represent the entirety of Nan Madol?" Jules scoffed. "What you see before us is just the proverbial tip of the iceberg. The true magnificence of the city lies far below its aboveground facade. I have no doubt that Alexander is somewhere down there hiding, plotting his next move."

Jules slammed his hand into his fist. "Let us therefore not provide him the opportunity to make the next move." He turned to Drew. "If you could do the honors?"

Drew placed his hand against the auricular chip in his ear. Speaking to the striker craft hovering within eyesight above the island, he instructed, "Captain, I believe the sonic burst we used was the correct frequency." A holographic depiction of a stone from Nan Madol appeared above his wrist along with a readout of numbers and figures around it. "However," he said after further analyzing the schematics, "increasing the intensity of the electrostatic pulse by 24.5 percent while maintaining it at full capacity the entire time would maximize the zero-point energy effect I discovered at Pumapunku."

"Yes, sir," a voice echoed in his ear.

"On my signal," Drew commanded, scanning the analytics once more.

He waited a few seconds, correcting his calculations. "Start the sonic burst at twenty-five percent and escalate it to full power, increasing it at a gradual intensity over twenty seconds. At that point discharge the electrostatic charge at full capacity for ten seconds before terminating."

"Yes, sir," the captain responded.

"Three, two, one," Drew counted down. "Now!"

A low hum reverberated throughout the entire area. As it increased in intensity, the sound made not only the stones on Nan Madol but also the bones in Drew's body vibrate in response. When it reached its maximal intensity, a faint visual distortion on the island let Drew know the striker craft discharged the electrostatic charge.

The entire aboveground stony edifice of Nan Madol arose from the ground and levitated over 200 feet above sea level. Water dripped from the stones as they hung weightless in the air.

"Good show!" Jules applauded. "This is by far much better than your prior attempt."

Drew agreed. Previously, the stones only levitated a mere ten feet into the air. Now, the zero-point antigravity effect was significantly stronger.

The hum ended, sending the enormous stones pummeling back to Earth. With a loud roar, they struck the lagoon, creating an enormous splash in its wake. As the water subsided, Jules noted that the rocks remaining were pulverized and that large portions of the island were now submerged. Luckily, the WOGS standing at attention in front of him took the brunt of the deluge.

Within a few seconds, a significant portion of Nan Madol collapsed into the water, sending an enormous amount of bubbles up to the surface in response. It was as if the lagoon had suddenly swallowed it up, leaving nothing behind.

Impressed with the results, Jules looked out at the remaining island and said, "Let us continue."

Drew placed his hand against his auricular chip as he again analyzed the holographic readouts. "Same parameters, but let's increase the sonic pulse's intensity by five percent this time."

✳✳✳

Orisihpa fell to her knees as the Mukulian Hall shook violently for a few seconds. Multiple crystals fell to the ground in response, shattering into pieces. The remaining crystals all turned dark as if feeding off of Orisihpa's emotions.

Alex took her by the arm. "You've got to get out of here. This whole place is about to collapse."

Orisihpa spryly got back on her feet. She smiled towards Alex. "Young man," she said as if a loving mother. "This is where I belong. I was entrusted with the care of the hall, and here I shall stay."

Part of the ceiling collapsed, crushing a few of the islanders. Screams of terror echoed throughout the hall.

"Now, *go*," Orisihpa insisted. "Both passageways will lead you to the surface."

In her heart, she knew that no matter which passageway they chose, no one would be safe if this hall were destroyed. Just like the stories foretold to her by her mother, grandmother, and great grandmother, if the Mukulian Hall was destroyed, so would go the entire planet—what began many millennia ago would not be able to be stopped.

Their dire warnings echoed throughout her mind as she watched more and more of the crystals crash to their destruction. Those remaining continued to darken and grow ashen in color.

A large crack in the ceiling suddenly opened, sending a torrent of water into the room. A wave of rock and debris propelled Orisihpa against the wall. Alex, his colleagues, and the rest of the islanders in the hall fared no better. Thrashed by the water, they all did their best to stay afloat and not get hit by any rocky debris.

"Get to the passageway," Alex yelled, pointing to the left exit. "Go now!"

Having to swim, Alex, Marissa, William, and Terzin fought the debris and waves until they were safely out of the hall. They could hear the room behind them rumble as more of it continued to collapse by the second.

The remaining island natives refused to leave their sacred hall. Surrounding Orisihpa, they all treaded water and began to pray in unison.

"Come with us," Alex insisted, pointing to Orisihpa and the islanders around her.

Orisihpa turned to Alex. With a solemn look on her face, she could only utter, "We must stay."

In her heart, she felt running would be futile. If death did not overtake her now, she knew her demise and that of her companions was but a few more moments away. The end would soon come as the oceans reclaimed the Earth, unabated by the protection once granted to the planet by the Marks.

More water began to pour into the room as the ceiling in the Mukulian Hall continued to collapse.

Realizing they could not change Orisihpa's mind, Alex and his colleagues turned away from the hall and swam down the long passageway until they reached a flight of steps, slowly inclining up a lengthy tunnel. As they scurried forward, they were able to reach ankle-high water.

After spitting out some water, Alex addressed his friends. "Tom will be waiting for you when you get out of here." Gazing into his vedere lens, which was now working again, he continued, "This tunnel will lead you about a mile away along the shore of Pohnpei. Get out of here as soon as you can and see what's happening in Philadelphia. I'll meet you there."

"What?" Marissa asked, flabbergasted. "You're not coming with us?"

Alex held up the shield. "Not with this. And I'm certainly not going to leave it behind. This is the key."

"So?" Marissa said. "Take it with you."

"I can't," Alex said. "Jules can track it. He'll be able to find us wherever we go."

"Can you do something to cloak the shield?" she asked.

"Not at this moment," Alex admitted. "Now go. The longer Tom waits, the more chance he will be discovered."

"Then I'm going with you," William insisted. "I'm not leaving you behind."

Alex placed his hand on William's shoulder. "You've always been a good friend, but now is not the time for heroics. Trust me. This is something I need to do alone. I can't risk your lives any further. You all have sacrificed enough."

Before he left, Alex gave Marissa a kiss on the cheek and descended the steps without another word. He could hear his colleagues beckoning for him to reconsider.

After inhaling deeply, he then dove into the water and began to swim under its surface. With one hand holding the shield, he managed to swim in one breath to where the passageway met the great hall.

Peering his head above the water, Alex noted that most of the hall was submerged. He could also hear a few screams echoing towards him from the hall. Sounds of agony were intermixed with a few groans of the remaining islanders' gurgling prayers.

Alex swam into the room. He could see Orisihpa's body floating next to the Maternal Mark. Blood trickled down her wet hair as one of the island's natives fought to keep her afloat. Bodies of other natives floated face down in the water while other rock and debris cluttered the once magnificent hall. A dim light continued to illumine the area, and only five stars were left shimmering on the roof—the V-shaped Hyades.

The Maternal Mark's glow faded by the second.

Will this mean the end of the planet? Were Orisihpa's predictions true?

Alex did not have the answer, but with such commitment by Orisihpa and her colleagues, he had no reason to doubt her word. Alex looked at the shield and pondered its significance to this whole predicament. The further he delved into this mystery, the more questions arose.

A loud rumble abruptly echoed throughout the room as the roof completely collapsed. Rocks came crashing down, engulfing the entire area. Alex had barely enough time to take a breath and submerge himself before being pounded by a barrage of debris.

All went dark in the room except for a faint glimmer scarcely radiating from the Maternal Mark. Alex could barely see his hand in front of him because of the dark, hazy mist and bubbles that obscured his vision. Stones surrounded him, and neither exit was in sight.

His chest felt tight as his rapidly beating heart quickly began usurping most of the oxygen in his blood.

Relax, Alex thought, *and concentrate.*

Letting his muscles go limp, Alex calmed both his mind and body before making any further movements. Floundering under water would prove counterproductive. He had only one opportunity to escape from this room without drowning. If he acted too rashly, his prospect for survival would be lost.

Let's hope this works in here, Alex prayed. He hoped that the electrical interference once caused by the crystals would no longer be present as most of them had been destroyed.

Reaching into one of his pockets, Alex grabbed his weatherometer. Designed to withstand harsh climate conditions, this instrument was also waterproof.

Taking out the weatherometer, Alex held it close to his face in an attempt to discern the holograph displayed above it. Fortunately, the image was not only visible in the murky water but it also helped shed some light in the dim surroundings. He then pressed his thumb on the pen-like device and the holographic image of clouds once projected above it changed to small arrows pointing in certain directions.

Fantastic, Alex thought. Using the instrument's parameters originally designed to measure wind speeds and directions, he instead switched its settings so that it now assessed the water current in the room.

Alex noted that despite the turbulence, the general direction of water flowed in three directions. Alex surmised that these were the two exits and the initial hallway of the other room from which they had entered.

Alex took the shield and placed it under his left arm while still holding the weatherometer. With the instrument now about a foot from his face, he used its light to help guide him towards where the arrows pointed. Rocks significantly impeded his retreat. Swimming around, and even under these boulders, he slowly made his way to the exit that had not been used by his friends.

The closer he approached, the more the arrows unified in the same direction. Alex's lungs began to burn as if he had inhaled sulfuric acid vapors. Fighting the urge to breath, he removed a few small rocks blocking his path and popped his head through the exit.

Fortunately, no further obstacles infringed the path ahead of him. However, with his head already touching the top of the passageway, there was still no air in sight. His muscles began to ache as their lactic acid levels rose precipitously.

Every movement felt like an enormous chore. His vision began to blur and his head pounded. There were but moments left before consciousness would evade him.

With one final thought Alex grabbed an electromagnetic pulse stun gun from a pocket while dropping the weatherometer. He then placed the shield firmly against his chest, securing it between his arms. Taking the gun, he maneuvered it in front of the shield and grabbed it with both hands.

With barely enough power to even hold the shield or gun, Alex pressed its muzzle on the shield and fired. Pain radiated through his body as if he had stuck his finger into an electrical outlet. Again and again he pulled the trigger, jettisoning him through the water and further up the hallway.

As his consciousness faded, Alex could feel cool air wisp over his back. With his muscles now frozen, the buoyancy of the shield managed to turn his face up as the world around him went black.

CHAPTER 20

MARISSA CONTINUED TO WORRY about Alex's safety. She thought she had lost him once before, over a year ago. The memories of the event came back now to haunt her: The sight of him laying dead in her arms. The holographic readouts of total organ shut down. His cold, ashen face. It was like it was all happening again. She turned back, hoping to see him running up the steps.

William, too, carried with him a sense of remorse. He could not stop feeling that he had abandoned his friend. He knew Alex would never do the same to him. William recalled how Alex helped him pass his organic chemistry class in college and somehow also managed to tutor him to high-honors in calculus. He couldn't forget how Alex funded his original research project on retroviruses. The research was an overwhelming success, spring boarding his career upwards and his reputation internationally.

Overwhelmed with guilt, Terzin fell to her knees and began to weep uncontrollably. "I have failed," she cried. "Humanity will perish, and it's all because of me."

"There was nothing you could've done differently," Marissa assured. "You are not the one to blame."

"My mother guarded the Mark," she continued though pouring tears. "My grandmother guarded the Mark. For hundreds of generations my ancestors did the same." She looked up at Marissa, "They all successfully guarded the Mark, no matter what happened. All but me."

William pondered how many years a few hundred generations must be. He fathomed that it had to be over 10,000.

How old is humanity? he contemplated. *Maybe Alex and Marissa were right about that flood thousands of years ago*? The sincerity in Terzin's voice made him believe the authenticity of her claims.

"This is not your fault," Marissa said firmly. "The blame lies directly on Jules Windsor's shoulders. You saved the Mark. You brought the Mark to Nan Madol. What could you have done differently?"

Terzin stopped crying and attempted to compose herself. Dripping wet from the water, with her long hair strewn across half her face, she looked physically and mentally beaten.

"Let's keep moving," William insisted, knowing that was exactly what Alex would say right now under these circumstances. The longer they delayed, the more they risked their lives—and Tom's life.

"It looks like the tunnel comes to an end just ahead," he pointed.

"Almost out of here," Marissa said to Terzin. "Maybe there's something we can still do in Philadelphia."

This prospect provided Terzin the hope she needed to continue. As they walked further up the hallway, William nudged in front of them and ran the rest of the way, seeing what appeared to be a major obstacle ahead of them.

"This is not good!" he yelled back towards his companions.

"What is it?" Marissa asked, losing sight of William as he ascended the stair's sharp incline at the end of the tunnel.

"There's no way to get out," he exclaimed frantically. "We're trapped. This tunnel leads to nothing but a rock ceiling. What moron designed such a thing?"

Marissa ran up the steps behind William only to discover the validity of his words. There was no exit. She was met only with the same slightly glowing whitish-brown stones that created this passageway.

William pounded on the ceiling, hoping he could find some means of escape. Marissa took a much gentler approach and began to dig her fingernails along the rock, attempting to uncover a crack or crevice indicating a door.

"This is it," William said. "The is literally the end."

He pounded his palms against the rock a few more times. "I wish Alex were here," William finally blurted.

So do I, Marissa thought.

William rethought his words for a second. "It's not that I want him here trapped and destined to die with us in this tunnel. What I was trying to say is that—"

"I know what you meant William," Marissa responded. "Say no more."

"I doubt Alex would have been much help," Terzin commented as she seemed to glide up the steps.

Despite his despair, William again noted how beautiful she looked with her hair gently strewn across her face. For a moment, he almost forgot about rotting to death in the tunnel.

Terzin joined Marissa and William at the top of the steps. Slowly, she placed her right palm against the ceiling and began rubbing its underbelly. "Think of these rocks as living and breathing entities."

William's infatuation with their new friend slowly began to fade. *I'm not in with any rock-loving hippy*, he thought. *Doesn't matter how beautiful or mysterious she is.*

"These rocks resonate at an inherent frequency derived from the crystals inside them," Terzin explained. "Every rock is different based upon its composition."

She now put her other palm on the ceiling and ran them both across its smooth face. "Your mind also resonates at certain frequencies and projects an aura around you. However, unlike the rock you can change your mind's frequency at will."

Maybe Terzin is not that much of a hippy, William conceded. He remembered that Alex had mentioned on numerous occasions that human consciousness lies at a subatomic, quantum level. And at that level it generates a quantum field corresponding to one's own thoughts and emotions.

The rock above them began to vibrate and then slowly slide to the side. Sunshine beamed into the tunnel as clear, fresh air filled their lungs.

"You did it," William said in amazement. "You actually moved the rock." He paused a second while he peered into her eyes. "You're amazing."

Moving the rock had provided Terzin a brief sense of purpose. She smiled back at him, amused by his boyish attitude. "You learn a few tricks as a Keeper."

William blushed.

I hope Alex is all right, Marissa thought, feeling a bit guilty that she survived while his very existence remained in question.

As the three exited the tunnel, they found themselves at the far end of Pohnpei, near the beach. Surrounded by jungle, they peered through the trees, wondering when Tom and the stratoskimmer would arrive.

A cool breeze floated through the jungle as the scenery next to them began to blur. The further distorted it became, the more in focus became the image of a stratoskimmer with its stairs descended.

"Let's go," Marissa whispered, as all three dashed towards the ship. As they ran, each had the same eerie feeling that they would be struck down by a striker craft overhead before they were even on the beach. Each felt a great sense of relief upon finally entering the stratoskimmer.

"Strap in," Tom said, as the three scurried into the cockpit. "I'm going to bring us fully out of stealth so that I can depolarize the engines at maximum capacity." A cowboy at heart, he relished the thrill.

"Have you done this before?" William asked hesitantly.

"Once," Tom said, adjusting the readout on the dashboard.

"When?"

"Today!" Tom responded enthusiastically as he pushed the two side buttons on the edge of the steering wheel.

The ship violently jettisoned forwards, sending all their heads directly against the seat behind them. The G-force was overwhelming and made breathing an enormous effort.

"Yes!" Tom yelled at the adrenaline rush.

The blue skies instantly disappeared as the blackness of the outer atmosphere filled their windshield.

"What about Alex?" Marissa insisted as the G-force on her body diminished. "We left him on the island. We've got to go back!"

"Don't worry," Tom assured. "He told me to open a secure line once we are in stealth. Pressing his thumb on the steering wheel, he said, "Alex. Mission successful. All safe and secure. Status report."

They all impatiently waited for a response. Any response. After a few seconds, Tom repeated the message once again, but they received the same absent reply.

"Alex, do you read me?" he then said slowly and distinctly.

The bitter silence let them each know: Alex did not read him.

CHAPTER 21

"I HAVE A LOCK ON THE SHIELD," Jules said self-assuredly. Dropping the Achilles Shield emblem from his hand, he pointed towards the forest behind them. "Alexander naively believes he would be able to sneak right under our noses."

Jules slipped out a playing card-shaped digitizer from his lapel jacket and placed it on his palm. A holographic black and white image appeared above it, displaying everything around them for about a mile radius. In the center of the holograph were tiny representations of both him and Drew along with the forty WOGs surrounding their position. Two elite striker crafts were visualized adjacent to them with a distinct red figure deep in the jungle.

"I've locked on his position," Jules announced. Examining the holographic numbers that appeared above the image, he noted, "Our dear friend Alexander is but a mere 500 feet from us right now. Poor unfortunate boy."

The red figure moved side to side, not making any headway. *Maybe he's stuck*, Jules thought, zooming in on the image. *Or possibly attempting to hide himself.*

"Surround target's designated position and deploy the biogrounders," Jules commanded into his auricular chip, while providing his men with the proper coordinates.

About half the WOGS dispersed into the woods while the remaining ones stood with Jules along the shore. As the WOGs ran, two of them grabbed a small cylinder from their back along with a hockey puck-shaped ordinance from their belt. In unison, both got down on one knee and pointed their weapons high into the air.

"Launch biogrounders," Jules commanded while looking at the holograph still above his hand. With great anticipation, he sprinted into the forest as two projectiles pierced through the forest canopy in front of him.

Drew and the remaining WOGs had great difficulty keeping pace with Jules. His agility was better than the best-conditioned soldier among them.

"Wait for it," Jules said as he stopped running at the line of WOGs encircling Alex's position.

A moment later a loud thud reverberated through the area. Birds fell from the sky in front of him, and he could hear the wildlife in the immediate vicinity collapse from the trees to the ground like raindrops on a rooftop.

Alex's holographic image fell—just like the wild beasts surrounding him.

"Got you!" Jules celebrated.

He then touched his ear, "Let me do the honors. Close in behind me."

The closer Jules walked towards Alex, the tighter the circle of WOGs around his position became. As Jules traversed the forest, he stepped over different birds, a few deer, and a wild pig.

"Are they all dead?" Drew asked one of the WOGs.

"No," he responded. "It's a no collateral damage weapon. The biogrounders just momentarily paralyze all animal life in the impact vicinity, rendering it helpless for up to ten minutes."

Jules held up his hand, curtailing any further approach. Putting away his digitizer, he proceeded to his target alone. As he closed in on his prey, Jules noted that both Alex and the shield at to his side looked gray in color.

"Your silly little stealth technique has certainly failed you here," Jules said as he grabbed the shield. Immediately, he noted its texture and feel were different than he remembered. However, what truly disturbed him was a small, intensely black cube on the ground, which had been hidden by the shield

Before Jules could react, Alex jumped to his knees and punched him square in the chest. The force of the blow propelled him to the ground. Barely able to breath, Jules leaned forward awaiting the next attack.

Alex simply winked at him as his image—and that of the shield—dissipated.

"What was that?" Drew asked, running to Jules' side. "What just happened?" Though a well-versed scientist, he was completely astonished by what he had just witnessed.

"It's one of those quantum entanglement cubes Alexander somehow made," Jules coughed, catching his breath.

"How does it work?" Drew said. Taking one of his hands, he pulled Jules to his feet.

"I don't know how the damn thing works," Jules responded. Frustrated at the situation, he sputtered, "It uses some scientific principle which Alexander refers to as quantum entanglement. It's when atoms are inextricably linked through some process that Lord knows I don't understand."

Drew decided not to inquire any further. He surmised that Alex must have another sister cube, and somehow they interacted through this process of quantum entanglement, whereby solid, three-dimensional images could be transmitted from cube to cube. *Amazing*!

Brushing off his sleeves, Jules smiled at the challenge Alex presented to him. Never before had he ever come across such brashness, intelligence, and overall bravado as he had with Alex. Though he knew the man must be terminated, he admired him as a worthy foe.

Jules went to grab the Achilles Shield medallion around his neck once again but the sudden shaking of the island knocked him to the side.

"Not Pumapunku again!" Drew lamented.

The island shook for a second time, sending a WOG next to him tumbling onto the ground. A few trees fell and birds in the far distance scattered in the sky. It was as if they knew something grave was about to occur but could do nothing to stop it.

"Evacuate," Jules commanded on his auricular chip. "Evacuate."

This is insanity! Drew thought. *What are we doing? The more we meddle with these ancient ruins and shield, the more destruction we cause.*

Jules walked through the forest as if he were taking a morning stroll; though the earth rumbled around him, he seemed little inconvenienced by the wrath of Mother Nature.

"Let's go, Mr. Windsor," urged one of the WOGs retreating behind him.

"Can you swim, my boy?" Jules asked.

"Well, yes," he replied, confused by the question.

"Then you can survive," Jules responded.

He stopped and looked at the man directly in the helmet. "Be the master of your life," Jules admonished. "Don't let your surroundings or circumstances rule you. You rule them."

Jules relinquished his reprimanding gaze and continued walking through the forest. Though the WOG simply wanted to flee for his life, his fear of Jules exceeded his fear of death. Instead, he nervously walked by Jules while attempting to stay afoot on the shaky land.

"Mr. Windsor, we—" reported a WOG commander as the communication abruptly ended.

"Come again," Jules requested as he neared the closest striker craft on the beach.

WOGs clamored up the two ships' steps as the island behind them began to crumble in their wake.

"Blasted auricular chip," Jules said aloud.

"I don't think it's the chip." Drew responded. Also fighting the urge to run, he tensely walked by Jules' side as his heart pounded in terror.

Jules needed to hear no more. He understood Drew's insinuation. Somehow the destruction of Nan Madol was causing a destabilization in the world grid, interfering with communications.

"Let's get out of here before it's too late," Drew pleaded, realizing that this latest fluctuation in the grid would also most likely affect their ships' engines.

Jules held up both arms and pointed directly to the ships. Between the rumbling of the island and ineffectiveness of the auricular chip, it was his only means to convey a more urgent order. "Double time!" he shouted.

The WOGs boarded the ships in as orderly a fashion as they could muster. Attempting to maintain the strict discipline that Jules had instilled, they marched in line as the earth shook beneath them.

A shriek in the sky caught all of their attention. Looking up, Jules saw the striker craft that had been hovering above the island fall like a brick. The high-pitched sound was the pilot's attempt to manually override the engine and hyper-magnetize the entire ship in order to generate an antigravity effect. As Jules watched it helplessly plummet to Earth, he realized the pilot's attempt was painfully futile.

With a monstrous explosion, the striker craft struck the ground about a mile from their position. Flames and black smoke bellowed up from the site.

Those that witnessed the event shuddered in fear. Instead of running, they stood motionless, as if paralyzed by the realization that they were no safer on board the ship than they would be on the sandy beach.

"Go, go!" Jules ordered the last of the WOGs up the stairs into the remaining two ships. After the last soldier finally entered, Jules followed. Straightening his jacket, he walked to the cockpit with his head held high.

"Chins up," Jules demanded. "Discipline!"

The soldiers in the hull instantly obeyed. With their heads held high and chests puffed out, they all sat in attention on the benches along the walls.

"Mr. Windsor," the WOG pilot said rapidly. "Striker Craft number eight. It simply fell from the sky."

Jules strapped himself in the copilot's chair in front of Drew. Without much overt concern, he looked forward and said, "Sir, be not concerned about striker craft number eight. Let us bring our full attention to this ship and striker craft number ten, which are both still in one piece."

"But the dashboard?" the pilot responded. "Everything's going crazy. The engine's depolarization is waxing and waning, and the flight control is spotty at best.

A sharp jolt hit the ship. As the earth moved underneath them, it became impossible to sit without rocking back and forth.

"Improvise my boy," Jules insisted. "Improvise."

"Sir?"

"Have you ever flown instrument-free before?" Jules asked.

"No," the pilot replied.

"This island's about to sink," Drew's concerned voice chimed in from behind them.

"You heard the man," Jules responded. "We all will assuredly die if we remain grounded on this beach." He pointed to the sky. "Now's the time to take a chance."

The ship lifted off the ground. On its ascent, the striker craft randomly dipped and swayed.

"Stay low and head east," Jules instructed.

"Yes, sir," the pilot responded as sweat rolled from his brow down his beat-red face.

Touching a button on the steering wheel, Jules asked the other striker craft accompanying them on a secure line, "What are you waiting for?"

"It's not safe to fly," replied the pilot from the ship still on the island. The communication was choppy, but the message was clear.

"Get out of there," Jules insisted.

"It's not safe," the pilot again reiterated. "Poor flying conditions."

"Think, man," Jules chastised. "Don't be a blind fool."

As Jules admonished the pilot, Drew looked out the window. Though only about 100 feet above the sea, it still felt too high. The further and faster they flew away from Pohnpei, the more apparent it became the island was sinking piecemeal into the ocean.

"Get off the island!" Jules reiterated.

"Mr. Windsor," Drew interrupted, "it's too late. Pohnpei has completely sunk. The striker craft is lost—sucked down into the ocean by the vacuum effect."

"Fools," Jules muttered. "Utter fools!"

The ship dipped violently and shuddered back and forth.

"I'm losing her," announced the pilot.

The dashboard lights flickered on and off.

"She's not responding," the pilot bellowed.

"Take us down over there," Jules said, pointing to a barren landmass rising along the horizon. "Just a little further, my boy. Concentrate. Be more than the sum of your parts."

The pilot grasped the steering wheel, holding on for dear life. It seemed as if the ship were flying itself as his control slipped by the second. *Just a little further,* he willed. He wiped his brow.

As the ship reached the landmass, the pilot pressed one of the only two remaining lights still lit on the dashboard. Holding his breath, he hoped the ship would properly respond.

With a thud, the striker craft struck the ground and began to skid along the uneven terrain. Without wheels, the ship's smooth underbelly spewed sparks as it bulldozed its way along the crusted land, leaving a deep, long crevice in its wake.

"Steady," Jules said calmly.

Drowned out by the earsplitting roar, Jules' calm words were lost in the commotion. The pilot pulled up on the steering wheeling, attempting to stabilize the ship so that it did not flip.

The striker craft skidded for another fifty feet before coming to a complete stop. The pilot took a deep breath and put his head between his legs. Totally exhausted, he uttered, "Successful landing."

Jules patted him on the shoulder. "That's the way to do it!" He then unstrapped himself and stretched his aching muscles. "Drew," he said, "let's get some fresh air."

"Yes, sir," his lead scientist replied. Though sick to his stomach, he was glad they were safely on the ground.

Jules walked back into the hull. The soldiers there fared no better than his lead scientist. Most appeared sick, and vomit was splattered along both the floor and walls. "Exit ship," he then ordered.

Relieved, the soldiers all stood and staggered out of the striker craft onto stable land. Many fell to the ground and simply laid there, looking blankly up to the sky.

"Which island is this?" Jules asked as he exited onto the crusty, coral filled landscape. As he gazed along the vast, monotonous scenery, he wondered why he had not noticed such a massive landmass previously.

A holographic imaged flickered above Drew's wrist. "Mr. Windsor," Drew noted with astonishment. "This isn't an island at all."

CHAPTER 22

RUN BHADRA, RUN, Christine thought, watching the young, beautiful woman flee for her life.

Though Christine wanted to look away, she was engulfed in the entire scene. Unable to interfere, she watched helplessly. With the key in hand, Bhadra athletically sprinted out the open doorway. Her tan leather moccasin-like shoes flew off in the process.

Now out on an open grassy field, Bhadra headed straight towards a golden beehive-shaped ship. With four small propellers around the base and four circling the top, the ship was at least thirty feet in height and glimmered in the sunlight.

Two pillars stood adjacent to the vehicle. Each boasted a wing at its top and two snake-like coils wrap around its entire length. Between them was a golden carpet leading up to the ship. A symbol similar to that of the pillars was emblazed above the ship's door, ten feet above ground.

Bhadra ran to the ladder at the base of the ship and began climbing, holding the key under one arm and pulling herself higher with the other. She refused to look back, fearing someone was just behind her. After her last step, she bent down and yanked the ladder up and into the ship.

"Close the door!" she ordered a crewman who was standing next to one of the four huge cylindrical shafts in the center of the room.

The man, who was wearing a long tan robe tied at the waist and similarly colored pants, complied without hesitation.

"Start the boilers," Bhadra ordered. "Set the hydrargyrum engines into motion. We must take flight this instant! There is no time to spare."

The two other crewmen present rushed down the steps onto the lower level. "Set the hydrargyrum engines into motion!" they shouted while descending. Pointing towards large boilers at the base of each of the four cylindrical, metal shafts, they signaled the other crewmen on this level to immediately get to work.

Bhadra then ran up the steps to the upper level. At the helm were two men sitting at opposite ends of the conical room. "Fly," she ordered holding the key prominently out in front of her.

"Fly!" she repeated.

Both men were in disbelief as they stared at the legendary relic. The beauty and radiance of this shield-like artifact exceeded their expectations. Both were unsure whether to bow down and give grace or follow their consulate's orders. Doing both would be inappropriate. However, doing one seemed just as unfitting.

"Take me to Dilmun at once," Bhadra commanded as the men continued to sit motionless as if in a trance. "I need to return the key to the cradle."

Hesitantly, the pilot to her right responded while bowing his head, "Consulate Bhadra, that area is forbidden by the council, and all flights there have been grounded due to geographic instability."

"I am the council," she demanded. "Now do as I say!"

The other pilot waved his hand over a red crystal on the dashboard. The cylinders in the center of the room began to hum as heat radiated from each, raising the room's temperature in response.

"The mercury is almost at a boil," he then stated. "One more minute, and we can set the engines into motion."

"Very good," she commented while nervously looking out the window. Because she was facing away from the council hall, she could only surmise how the brawl there had ended.

Christine watched as the magnificent ship began to glow and float up into the sky. It looked like a giant orb radiating a brilliant white light. *What technology*, she thought.

The ship then took flight like a dart shot out of a gun. Accompanied by a gentle hum, it zipped through the sky.

Though Christine knew nothing about engineering, she felt as if she understood everything about this ship. Her mind was inundated with the most amazing information explaining its technology, construction, and means of flight. It was almost like she had known the information all along but had forgotten it until just now.

Rhukma Vimana, Christine thought. *It's the name of this type of ship. And there are many more of these vehicles, many with different shapes, designs, and sizes.*

She also came to realize that unlike combustion or the magnetic dipole engines of her day, these ships flew by the nascent energy within the element mercury. By heating this liquid metal to its boiling point and subjecting it to alternating electromagnetic currents, the mercury became ionized and released the zero-point energy stored within it. Because this energy has anti-gravitational, ultrasonic properties, flight became a possibility.

Christine watched as the Vimana touched down in the center of a large and open city complex surrounded by a thriving jungle. Beautiful gardens full of colorful flowers, trees laden with fruit, and green vines adorned the landscape.

A large, white dome stood prominently in the center of this lush city. Attached to it at the Northern, Eastern, and Western poles were three white, cylindrical shafts projecting out along the ground as far as the eye could see. They radiated in the sunlight and appeared to pulsate in sync with the dome to which they were attached.

Young women with silken dresses and flowers in their hair tended the gardens. Upon the site of Bhadra exiting the ship, they all bowed with respect.

Bhadra looked towards the brilliant dome in the center of the city. Because it was surrounded by gardens and flowering trees, this portion of the city was the closest open area her Vimana could set down without destroying anything sacred in its descent.

With great urgency, she sprinted down a grassy path leading directly towards the dome. Adorned on both sides by abundant peach and pear trees, they provided shade from the midday sun. As she approached the dome, Bhadra noted a beautiful depiction of a pregnant woman holding her expectant belly engraved at the entrance. In her womb was an upside-down triangle punctuated by five large, red dots.

The cradle. Bhadra thought.

As she ran, Bhadra stumbled onto the ground, landing on her chest and abdomen. A sudden quiver along the earth knocked her off balance. The key thrusted out of her arms upon impact. As she lay face down on the grassy path, she could hear a distant roar. Her palms also felt the earth rumble.

A white glow caused her to squint, obscuring the dome. As the light faded, an unmistakable sight came into view. A cigar-shaped ship known as a valix now blocked her path to the cradle and destroyed the flower garden on which it landed. Piloted by the Phrees, she knew they were here for only one thing.

The key.

The rumbling in the distance grew louder as she scuttled on her hands and knees over to the key. Grasping it in both hands, she jumped to her feet and attempted to run. However, two strong men wearing white tunics tied at the waste and long kilts made of strips of brown leather grabbed her. Pulling her by the elbows, they turned her to face their leader, Zorian.

"Why such haste?" he asked. "Were you planning to carry out an unsanctioned action?"

"The council of thirteen already decided, Zorian," she indignantly responded.

Bhadra's arms were forced behind her, causing her to drop the key.

"The council is no more," Zorian stated as he sauntered over to grab the key. "The Phrees are now in charge. That means you and the rest of your pitiful Kathole clan must submit to our will."

Taking the key, he placed it under his arm and said, "There will be more outposts, and the cradle will continue to function at full capacity."

"Stop it now—before it's too late," Bhadra insisted. "No matter how many outposts you create, as long as the cradle remains functional, you can't stop the inevitable. Do the right thing!"

Before he could answer, Zorian became distracted by the distant rumble. Pausing for just a second, he turned and walked into his ship.

"You will kill us all!" Bhadra yelled feverishly. "The death of our planet and all her inhabitants will be on your shoulders!"

His soldiers boarded the ship after throwing Bhadra to her knees. Pleading outside the vehicle, she said as the door closed, "You are to blame! It is your fault!"

"Take us out of here," Zorian ordered. "And let us never return."

He then walked to the back of the ship and laid down on a hammock stretched between two glass poles. Other hammocks also bordered the periphery of the room. Each were accompanied by a large circular window to their side.

Nonsense, he thought, resting the shield on top of his stomach. *Utter nonsense. If it were up to the Katholes, we would be left fending for ourselves using stone tools and our bare hands. Turning off the cradle would be like turning back time.*

With his body sore from the recent scuffle, he wanted to rest before returning home. Once there, he planned to finish the remaining outposts and put forth a global initiative to create hundreds more.

Zorian could feel the ship slowly levitate into the air until the cradle's dome descended out of view.

His eyes began to close as he let the urge to sleep overtake him. Zorian's worries dwindled as quickly as his consciousness. In what seemed like a mere second, one of his countrymen ran frantically into the room and startled him out of his slumber.

"Consulate Zorian!" the man said. Wide-eyed and completely white with fear, he pointed out the window. "Sorry to disturb you sir, but—"

The man was left speechless, unable to finish his thought.

Zorian jumped out of the hammock and peered through an enormous, adjacent window. His arrogance quickly dissipated at the sight. A massive tidal wave at least 100 feet tall was overtaking all the land as far as he could see and heading directly towards Dilmun.

"This can't be," he said as his voice cracked. "This isn't happening. The outposts. They were supposed to hold."

He muttered the same words over and over as he watched the colossal wave submerge Dilmun in the far distance as it continued its path of destruction. Bhadra's last words echoed throughout his head and stung like a thousand bees.

You will kill us all...

CHAPTER 23

"MAYBE THIS IS JUST an isolated event?" Zorian stated, grasping for hope.

In haste, he pushed his fellow countryman to the side and ran up the stairs onto the ship's observation deck. There, a pedestal not unlike that located in the council hall, stood under a domed glass window on the ceiling.

Zorian waved his hand over the pedestal. His palm trembled in the process.

A hazy, three-dimensional image began to form. Grabbing both sides of the pedestal, Zorian dropped the key, watching in complete horror and disbelief the sight unfold before him. His face turned white while his legs quivered.

Blue, foamy water engulfed the entire planet.

Christine, too, was aghast at the site. While Zorian observed the disaster unfold on the pedestal, her mind filled with the details of this great flood.

She could hear, *The trouble began in 9600 BC, modern time, when the growing northern icecap's asymmetric weight destabilized the Earth's thin, fragile crust overlying a massive, viscous ball of magma underneath it.*

The image in the pedestal zoomed in on the North American ice cap.

The Earth's wobble and rotation accentuated the force of this asymmetric weight and caused the Hudson Bay area, originally located at the North Pole, to slip fifteen degrees southward. Like a domino effect, other massive tectonic plates also shifted as a result, creating massive destabilization of the Earth's crust.

Volcanoes erupted around the globe as large plumes of smoke and ash filled the atmosphere from every continent.

The image in the pedestal shifted to Europe as Christine watched an enormous tidal wave crush the continent. Italy and Sicily, which had been connected, both became small dot-like islands on the globe. The same occurred with the British Isles and Ireland.

As the globe rotated, Christine observed how the vast Russian and Chinese landmasses were washed under the sea. The deluge also pummeled India, causing this once large landmass stretching far into the Pacific beyond its modern-day borders to become but a small island isolated from the entire planet.

The great landmass known as Mu on the Pacific continental shelf sunk precipitously into the ocean, leaving but a few scattered islands in its wake. These were the remnants of a once mighty continent lost into the ocean.

Christine could not bear to watch any longer. The carnage and massive loss of life was too immense. She tried to tune out the voice, but it continued, explaining in detail the destruction that ensued throughout the planet.

Zorian fell to his knees. No longer able to support himself, he simply collapsed under the weight of his own guilt.

"What have I done?" he wept.

Zorian knew he was at fault. He and the Phrees had been fighting the Katholes for decades about minimizing or even temporarily halting the use of the cradle. Though they clearly understood its adverse effect on the polar ice caps, pride and the blind belief in their own technology overshadowed reason.

"Consulate Zorian," a concerned voice inquired.

Too distraught to answer, Zorian continued to weep.

"The captain wants to know where to land," the voice again intruded.

"There's nowhere to land," Zorian muttered with his head down. "It's all gone, swallowed up by the oceans."

"There must be somewhere we can go," the soldier asked, also shaken by the recent events. "We cannot fly forever."

Grasping the podium, Zorian finally stood. His bones and muscles ached with each laborious movement. "No, we can't fly forever," Zorian commented. "Nor can we live forever either."

Finally having the courage to look into the young man's eyes, Zorian saw the same fear and distress that he, too, felt. Everything was gone. His friends, family, and home had all been swept away by the ocean. He was alone.

They all were alone. Orphaned by Mother Nature.

Zorian felt a slight sense of urgency jolt through his body. *Now is not the time for self-pity*, he thought. *I have failed the entire planet, but I'm not going to fail this crew. If there's one last thing I need to do, it is to bring them all down safely. Anywhere—.*

Black smoke and soot began to cloud the windows, making it more difficult to see outside the ship. However, the crystal network that created the image in the pedestal was not subject to atmospheric conditions. Looking at the image, Zorian saw a tiny island projecting out of the blues seas surrounding it.

Taking his finger, he pressed on its exact location. "Go," Zorian said, "tell the pilot to plot a course for this place. The coordinates have been sent."

"What is it?" the soldier asked.

"Your salvation," Zorian answered. "Now, go before there is zero visibility outside."

The man turned and ran out of the room.

Zorian looked blankly out the ship. As if in a trance, he stood unmoving for the entirety of the trip.

Through the smoke, Zorian slowly saw land come into focus as the ship approached. Recognizing the architecture of the temples, he knew that they arrived on the mountaintop fort of Athens.

Zorian bent down and grabbed the key with one hand as the ship landed. Since it no longer served any purpose, he was unsure what to do with the useless relic.

"Consulate Zorian," asked one of the soldiers aboard the vessel as he and a group of Phrees entered the ship's upper deck, "what do we do now?'

Zorian had no answer to give. Though his fellow countrymen repeated themselves and pleaded with their leader, he stood still, blankly staring ahead. He was simply at a loss of words.

After a few more futile attempts to garner his attention, the Phrees left the room, mumbling amongst themselves. Zorian soon followed, exiting the ship while in a continued trance-like state.

The area was in complete chaos as people clamored everywhere for safety. Choking on the smoke, they ran haphazardly. Many had nothing while others clenched onto whatever meager belongings they could carry. Some families huddled together and sobbed. Others moaned wildly and screamed in horror.

Zorian walked through the crowd with the key in hand. He knew not where he was going, nor did he care. His face was cold and pale. His eyes were wide open, and he stared blankly into the distance. All was lost for him.

A holy man wearing a long red and white robe prayed on his knees to a chiseled marble statue in front of him. As if lamenting, the priest cried out for mercy and begged for forgiveness.

"Take this," Zorian insisted, handing the man the key. "I have no further need for this relic."

The priest took the key and grasped it under his arms. Before he could ask any questions, Zorian turned and walked away from the holy man. He then blended into the frantic crowd and became one with the mass of humanity.

The vision slowly began to fade as Christine felt her mind once again enter her body. A tingling sensation ran through her body as the two once again united. The room gradually came into focus.

"Murph," she blurted after a few failed attempts. "Murph?"

Before Christine called out again to her friend, she suddenly noted that they were no longer alone.

"Who are you?" she asked defiantly, assuming they were Lopers.

Still uneasy on his feet, Murph looked at the trio of uninvited guests and said, "Why don't you all leave now before there is any trouble."

"We mean you no harm," Terzin responded warmly. Carefully grasping the crystal in Murph's hands, she tenderly placed it above the pedestal in its rightful place.

"I see you must have stumbled into one of our lost hall of records," Terzin said, pleased that some relic of her past remained. Surprised that any of these rumored places still existed, she went on to ask, "What did the crystal reveal to you?"

"I don't know what you're talking about," Murph responded curtly. Still eying them with caution, he, too, suspected they were most likely hostile.

"That is unfortunate," she responded, with disappointment in her voice. "Regardless, you must not touch the crystals unless you understand what you're doing."

"So, this is just a hall of records?" William came up from behind and asked. "Are any of these crystals around here one of those Marks that will stop this seismic catastrophe that has overtaken the planet?"

Christine shuddered at his words. *Is it happening again?* she thought. *Was the great flood in my vision just a precursor for something far greater that is occurring now?*

Images of the planetary destruction haunted her. She could still see the entire planet engulfed by the ocean and hear the cries of agony.

Christine looked over to her friend Murph to see if he had a similar reaction. His usual gruff exterior concealed what he was thinking—if anything at all.

"No," Terzin stated. "These crystals harbor stories from long ago, like a modern-day library."

William went over to grab a crystal, but Terzin held out her hand in response. "One day I'll show you how it all works."

William certainly liked the sound of that and complied without debate.

"But what does this place have to do with the red dot on the Maternal Mark?" Marissa asked. "And why didn't Orisihpa recognized its significance?"

"It has long been believed that these halls of records were lost to time or destroyed." Terzin explained. "When our friends here stumbled into this room and activated one of the crystals, it must have relayed back to the Maternal Mark their unauthorized entry. I can only assume that even Orisihpa had not known of the continued existence of such places."

"You all OK down here?" echoed a voice down the stairwell.

"Alex!" Marissa exclaimed as she turned and ran over to her fiancé who was entering the room. Embracing him with a firm hug, she placed her head up against his chest and held him tightly. "I thought I'd lost you again."

"I thought I'd lost you," Alex responded as he rubbed her back with his free hand.

William walked over and gave Alex a small punch in the arm. Trying to hide his overwhelming sense of relief, he nonchalantly said, "I'd knew you'd get out of there."

That makes one of us, Alex thought, recalling the narrow escape.

"How'd you find us?" Marissa asked.

"I have my jet-engine enhanced aero-bike and our stratoskimmer quantumly linked," Alex answered. "Like a beacon, the ship led me directly to you."

Alex then looked around the room and noted all the crystals levitating above the pedestals, "This is where the red circle on Maternal Mark lead us? How did you figure out the exact location of this area?"

"The fluctuating magnetic fields converged directly on this spot," William explained. "So, that's where Tom landed the ship. When we exited, this cave's what we found."

"Are all these crystals Marks?" Alex asked.

"None of them," Terzin said, disappointed. "We are in a hall of records. Legend has it that they are scattered across the globe. When one of the crystals was removed from the pedestal here, it must have somehow alerted the Maternal Mark."

Christine slowly walked over to Alex. Still unsure as to the genuineness of their guests, she cautiously approached.

Attracted by the shield-like relic Alex held in his hand, she needed to obtain a better view.

Is this they key? she thought. *Unbelievable!*

The closer Christine walked, the weaker she became. The effects of her mental journey had not worn off as of yet, further exhausting her with each step. Attempting to focus on the Achilles Shield, she became light-headed and collapsed.

Marissa ran to her side and took out her medical bag. Placing a tape-like bio-strip on her head, she said, "Vitals stable. However, she's hypotensive and dehydrated. Plus, her NMDA receptors in the brain appear to have been overstimulated." She looked up at Alex. "I'd prefer to bring her back to our hideout in order to stabilize her. I fear she could start seizing."

"If there's nothing else down here for us at the moment," Alex responded, "we better take her and leave now." Pointing to the puck shaped device on the shield's surface, he then said, "This makeshift cloaking device I placed on the shield will only work so long, and I'd rather bring it back to our hideout and give it an upgrade before Julius finds us again."

William looked over at Murph. "The invitation goes to you, too, big guy."

"My home's here in Philadelphia." Murph responded. "I will live and die here. Plus, I bet no one in your hideout can make a good cheesesteak."

Cheesesteak, William craved.

Murph then knelt down next to Christine and placed his hand on her arm. "You take good care of her," he said, looking up at them. Realizing Christine was safer with them than remaining in the city, he felt no hesitation about her leaving.

"It's a promise," Marissa said, walking over to Murph.

William reiterated, "Last offer. You sure you want to stay?"

Before he could answer, Marissa placed a bio-strip on his head. Examining it for a moment, she noted, "He's medically stable. It doesn't look like the crystal had the same effect on him."

"I'll fend for myself," Murph responded. "Remember, my friend is now in your hands. Make sure she gets better."

Marissa gave a warm smile and nodded her head.

Christine slowly awoke. Her focus immediately moved to the shield Alex held under his arm. It was as if her momentary lapse of consciousness did little to hinder her train of thought. "Excuse me," she finally spoke up in a weak voice as she pointed to the shield, "What is that you're holding?"

Alex looked down at the shield. "You mean this?" he commented while turning it towards her.

Christine paused as Murph held her arm slightly tighter. It was as if he were subtly telling her that now was not the time to talk about it.

Realizing Murph's cue, she simply went on to say, "It's rather beautiful, isn't it?"

He must have seen the same vision as I did!

CHAPTER 24

"MR. WINDSOR," Drew stated while exiting the striker craft, "There is a lull in the Earth's electromagnetic instability." Examining the hologram above his wrist, he continued, "However, seismic activity across the globe is off the charts. It makes the great California earthquakes of 1909 and 2026 seem insignificant."

"Very well then," Jules stated. "Go tell our pilot to remove us at once from this God-forsaken barren island."

"Sir, as I attempted to explain before, this is not an island."

"Then what am I standing on out here in the middle of the Pacific?" Jules jested. "A figment of my imagination?"

"You would have to have one hell of an imagination then Mr. Windsor," Drew said. "This landmass is far too massive to be an island."

"As you can see," he continued to explain while expanding the size of the holograph above his wrist, "we are actually standing on a new continent twice the size of Australia."

A large smile lurched on Jules' face. Like a Cheshire cat or a giddy schoolgirl, he placed his arm around Drew and looked out into the barren landscape. "This is fantastic news! Think of the potential!"

Jules stood in silence and pondered the possibilities.

"This will be a new beginning," Jules stated boldly. "Out of the ashes of the old world, I will create a new one here on this continent. This whole place is one giant blank slate."

He began walking over the crusty surface thinking aloud, "We will first cordon off the entire continent and allow only authorized personnel on it. Then, I will construct a grand New Reality headquarters building complex that will serve as the centerpiece for not only this continent but also for my entire global initiative."

Jules grabbed the Achilles Shield emblem around his neck. "But first," he turned to Drew and said, "there is still one small nuisance that we must tend to."

"Small?" Drew noted, tilting his head.

"Men in general are quick to believe that which they wish to be true," Jules said, quoting Julius Caesar. "If you wish to think Alexander is a major problem, then in your mind, he will be one. If that is the reality you wish to create, let it be your downfall and not mine."

"Yes, sir," Drew said sheepishly. Feeling ashamed of himself, he wished he could be as confident, brave, and poised as Jules. As a child, he was taunted and belittled by his peers and made to feel insignificant. Occasionally, like now, those feelings of low self-esteem and self-doubt seemed to creep into his consciousness and negate his lifetime of success and achievement.

Jules again grabbed the emblem. After a brief moment, he unbuttoned his shirt and placed it against his bare chest with his hand. Pushing down on it, he gazed into the distance waiting for it to activate.

Nothing.

After a few more attempts, he let the emblem dangle from his neck.

"Sir?" Drew asked.

Jules placed his hand up to his ear. "Colonel, we are to board the striker craft immediately. Give the command to your men at once. I want them back on the ship ASAP."

"Yes, sir," responded the colonel.

Surprised that the auricular chip worked and not the key, Jules walked into the striker craft and up to the cockpit.

Drew followed without another word. He assumed the key was not functioning but dared not comment about the apparent problem.

Jules sat down on the copilot's chair. The pilot made a comment, which Jules summarily ignored. Taking the key with one hand, he then tersely placed it flat on the dashboard. He hoped that it would provide him with a more direct connection into The New Reality's computer system.

After a few minutes, Jules sat back in the chair with utter disgust. The key was not working; his means to track Alex had been lost. Looking down at his chest, he noted a large bruise behind the emblem. Recounting how he might have acquired such an injury, a solemn realization came to mind.

Alexander Pella.

Jules laughed to himself at the man's ingenuity. Somehow Alex's quantum entanglement image must have deactivated the key when it struck him in the chest.

If it's a chess match he wants, it's a chess match he shall receive!

"Drew," Jules said, "it seems as if the key has suffered some minor technical difficulties. Surely, there must be some other way we have to track Alexander."

Drew attempted to answer, but Jules held up a finger, curtailing his response. "First thing's first."

He then stood up and took off his dirty, ripped designer sports jacket. Placing it neatly over his arm, he pressed a button along the wall next to him. A door silently slid open. Jules then placed his sports jacket in it and removed a black leather designer jacket.

Drew realized that Alex must have certainly frustrated Jules. He had not seen him don this jacket since he personally squashed the English uprising just after he took office.

"And one more thing—" Jules said with a confident air to himself after placing on the jacket. He grabbed two glasses and a caramel-colored bottle from the drawer and poured them each a shot of whisky. "Drink up, my boy. It's Tennessee's finest."

Though Drew rarely consumed alcohol, he dared not refuse such an offer. Jules gulped the first shot and poured himself another while Drew sipped the whisky slowly.

"Now that I've cleared my mind," Jules said, "there is this matter of tracking our dear friend Alexander."

"Yes," Drew responded, attempting to finish the whisky. It burned as it slid down his throat, and he almost coughed while answering. "I picked up a peculiar quantum disruption exiting the island of Pohnpei. Let me show you on the ship's windshield."

A satellite image of the planet appeared. All three in the cockpit were stunned at the Earth's new landscape. While certain places such as Australia had grown, others such as Africa and South America were now half under water. Also new was an impressive land mass connecting North America and Asia through the former Bering Strait along with a massive Pacific continent, which they were currently standing on.

"As you can see from the small red dots heading out of the former Pohnpei Island," Drew explained after regaining his composure, "we can track the course of what I believe was some sort of vehicle of flight as it left the area. However, what is so peculiar about its quantum fluctuation trail is that the ship does not have the same signature under stealth as that of a stratoskimmer. It appears much smaller in nature."

"Alexander must have escaped on his aero-bike," Jules concluded, remembering how his foe used to race competitively.

"Well, that would definitely be compatible with the data," Drew acknowledged. He pointed towards the windshield. "However, I can only track the ship's quantum fluctuations about fifty miles at a time. In order to discover its destination, we will have to closely follow its path as if following a trail of breadcrumbs."

Drew looked towards the pilot. "And because of the Earth's unstable electromagnetic field, we will almost have to be right next to the quantum fluctuation even to see it." He shook his head. "That will almost be impossible with these flying conditions."

"I have a solution," the pilot chimed in. "This striker craft has the capability to reach orbital height. As the marquee ship of the fleet, it is designed for such extreme conditions."

He then looked at a few readouts along the windshield. "I think we can ride this zone of electromagnetic stability straight up into the exosphere. There, the Earth's electromagnetic instabilities should not affect us, and we will hopefully be close enough to these quantum fluctuations to detect them."

"Good show!" Jules applauded.

"Don't you think the people of the Earth deserve some explanation as to what is going on right now?" Drew asked, feeling less reserved after consuming a shot of whiskey.

"Right you are," Jules said. "I will prepare a speech as to how our former and misguided leader of The New Reality precipitated such a predicament. I will say that through her previous, catastrophic endeavors such as the Masjid Project, she destabilized the Earth's crust and upset nature's delicate balance in the process."

"Once you have made the video feed," Drew commented, "I'll send it high-priority to all the major and minor media outlets across the globe."

"And be sure to have all the usual political and scientific pundits *confirm* its validity to provide the story with some traction," Jules added with a wink on the word *confirm*.

"Understood."

"All aboard and accounted for," echoed the colonel's voice in Jules' auricular chip.

"Very good," Jules responded. Now turning to the pilot, he ordered, "Let's see what this ship can do."

CHAPTER 25

CHRISTINE SLOWLY AWOKE. Confused at first, she thought she heard Benjamin speaking in the other room. Her head pounded, and her mouth was dry.

Where am I?

The last few days seemed like a blur, and nothing made sense. For a moment, she was doubting her own sanity and questioned if any of it was real.

Christine heard the male voice again. She sprung up in the bed. Coming to her senses, she noted two IV drips attached under each of her shoulders. Her body was also under a thick blue comforter, and she was changed into clean, new clothes.

When she went to grab one of the IV lines, her hand was gently restrained.

"Who are you?" Christine asked, staring at the vaguely familiar face next to her.

"I'm sorry I did not properly introduce myself. My name is Marissa Ambrosia."

"Where am I?" Christine asked. "What happened to all my friends?"

"You are safe," Marissa said soothingly, "and among friends." Wanting to avoid overwhelming her guest, she slowly laid Christine's head on the pillow.

Details of the last few days quickly returned as she began to relax. As if reliving them again, Christine remembered the Art Museum, the earthquake, the cave, and the vision. She also distantly remembered flying over ice and snow before landing.

"Between what happened down in the cave and the biotag ablator I gave you," Marissa explained, "you may feel washed out for at least another day." She pointed to the two IV bags. "I'm rehydrating you now along with replenishing your electrolytes. You'll feel better soon."

On the contrary, Christine felt as if she were awakening from the worst nightmare she'd ever had.

"Rest," Marissa insisted, nudging the blankets closer to Christine's chin.

The softness of the mattress, warmth of the blankets, and coziness of the pillow were certainly attractive, especially after sleeping on a cold, hard floor for the past few nights.

Getting up from the side of the bed, Marissa said, "When you feel better, detach the IV stickers and come out for something to eat. We have a warm cooked meal waiting for you."

The door dematerialized in front of her as Marissa walked out into a large communal area. A rectangular table boasting an abundance of food stood in the corner of the room while other couches, chairs, and a few end tables filled the rest of the space. The crisp smell of coffee permeated the air.

"How's your patient?" a strong female voice asked.

Sitting on one of the couches and wrapped in a blanket, Samantha Mancini sipped from her large mug of coffee. Though the room was about sixty-eight degrees, she acted as if she were in the subarctic. With young olive skin, high cheekbones, flirty green eyes, a bright smile and petite build, she made many underestimate both her mental and physical ability.

"She'll be fine," Marissa responded. "Christine is just a little wiped out from the whole ordeal."

"Alex was just telling me of all the excitement that I missed," Samantha said. She looked over at him and sarcastically commented, "Next time, *you* guard our hideout while I go out and have a little fun."

"Fun?" Alex smirked with a raised eyebrow. He walked over and rubbed her shoulders. "Please, next time you can have all the fun you want. While you're out there, wish Julius and all his armed WOGs my best. I bet they'll want to know how I've been."

Samantha was not only Alex's first hire at his business, Neurono-Tek, but she was also a lifelong friend. Though a few years his senior—now in her late-forties—she grew up with him; the two were like siblings. Their families had been close friends, getting together regularly.

"I certainly will," Samantha jested.

"Not to rush you Alex," William said, taking a breath from an oversized plate of food, "but half of China is now submerged and seismic activity is tearing up this entire planet. Not to mention some Atlantis-like land mass suddenly appeared out of nowhere in the Pacific. You have any ideas before we are all swimming with the fish?"

Alex recognized that William's sarcasm was well founded. He then looked at the shield on the end table next to him, hoping it would bring him some inspiration. If the mysteries of this artifact were not soon discovered, there would be a mass extinction unlike anything seen since biblical times.

There must be something I missed, he contemplated as he stood and began to pace.

Finally, out of the WOG attire, Alex now donned black jeans with pockets down the side and a plain, equally dark aero-bike racing jacket.

Marissa wanted to tell Alex to relax and have a seat. However, she knew her fiancé sometimes worked better under stress and needed to pace in order to have his creativity blossom.

"Not a one," Alex went on to say, aggravated at himself for taking a moment to sit. Lives were at stake; if he did not do something soon, more innocents would die by the day if not by the minute.

"Orisihpa did not finish her story at Nan Madol," Terzin said, hoping to maybe shed some light on the situation. Sitting next to William on the couch, she had changed into a new set of clothes. No longer wearing a dress, she now donned a cream-colored sweater and black pants. Her long dark hair was also cropped into a ball on the back of her head.

Alex stopped pacing. "Go on," he said.

"Legends passed on to me by my family told of this great flood that cleansed the planet and almost erased humanity from existence," Terzin explained. She looked at everyone in the room before continuing, "This legend is not unique. In fact, it's prevalent throughout every continent on the planet. From the Hopi Indians, Aztecs, Jews, Mayans, Rapa Nui, Khmu, and Masai. In fact, there are hundreds of stories of a great deluge that almost wiped out all of mankind."

Christine listened on from the open door. The events of the past few days had become mentally too unsettling just to lie back and act as if nothing happened. Unable to rest any longer, she took off the IV bags and approached the door, which dematerialized upon her arrival.

As Terzin spoke, visions of the flood flashed through Christine's mind as if she were there. Her body shuddered at the memory.

"My grandmother used to say," Terzin explained, "that humanity is suffering from amnesia. They have forgotten their history and are disregarding all the clues left behind by past civilizations. The Aztecs along with multiple other cultures believed that mass extinctions like that caused by the last flood had occurred multiple times before and that we are now living in the fifth sun known as the Tonotuih Era."

William kept his mouth shut. Still highly skeptical of these flood myths, he chewed on his second slab of steak and stared at the storyteller.

"After this last great biblical flood," Terzin continued, "mass chaos ensued. New mountain ranges arose, lakes and seas were drained, rivers ceased to exist or flowed in different directions, large swaths of land crumbled into the sea, and great cities were lost. Plus, global volcanism caused day to become night. The Earth instantly chilled, killing off the large mammals, many plants, and choked the food supply. Surviving humans were left to fend for themselves on hilltops, or as the tribes of Bangladesh say, in caves, until the floodwaters subsided. The Aztecs wrote of being cold and hungry during these times."

As Terzin recanted the flood story, Christine recalled the image of Zorian on the Athenian mountaintop. The image seemed so real. It was like she had been there when the flood actually occurred.

Christine then turned her attention to the shield on the end table. It was undoubtedly what she saw in her vision. The chances that it was something else would just be astronomically coincidental. She wanted to go into the room and say something, but she couldn't bring herself to do it.

Though the proof stood right in front of her, she doubted her own sanity. *Were those visions in the cave just a bad dream? Or was I hallucinating?* Still not feeling completely well, Christine remained silent and continued to listen.

Plus, can I even trust these people? Christine contemplated. *Can I trust anyone ever again?*

"Let the stone age begin," Samantha chimed in. Always one with great insight, she anticipated the conclusion of the story.

"Exactly," Terzin agreed. "Mankind had to start again. Stone tools replaced lost technology. Humanity had to relearn to farm, breed, and cultivate the new Earth like babies have to learn to crawl, walk, and then run after being born. The rest of mankind's story you already learned in history class."

"They should make a movie out of that," William said with a mouth full of food. Wanting to act interested but not knowing what to say, the statement was all that he could think of at the moment.

"How about the shield?" Alex commented, attempting to keep his frustration at bay. "Was there anything mentioned about it or what caused this massive catastrophe?"

Terzin shook her head no. "Only bits and pieces. Over the millennium, major parts of the story were lost or forgotten. Legend has it that a shield—or rather *key*—which you apparently possess could have prevented it all from occurring. Other than that, Alex, I cannot help you."

"I—," Christine reached out her hand wanting to add something to the conversation but stopped as all eyes turned to her. "I, uh, feel better. Thank you, Marissa, for your hospitality."

"Help yourself to some lunch," Samantha chimed in, "before William over there eats us out of house and home."

Christine sheepishly walked over to the table. Almost ashamed with her actions, she bent her head and poured herself a glass of milk.

CHAPTER 26

DISCOURAGED, ALEX WALKED OUT of the room with the shield and into his lab at the end of the hallway. Not usually one to leave in silence, he felt the stress of the situation rising. If he could not figure out the mystery behind this ancient relic, another catastrophic event of biblical proportion would befall the entire planet. It was already occurring now, and he could do nothing to prevent it from continuing.

When he walked into the lab, the entire room acted as if it were alive. Every electronic device and invention stored in it was quantumly connected to a small subatomic analyzer chip Alex had implanted subcutaneously below his left ear. He could feel every piece of equipment in the room and knew simultaneously the status of each one of them. With almost a thousand different devices in the lab and electronic parts too numerous to count, the entire area vibrated with energy.

After placing the shield on a large circular metal plate levitating above a table, Alex analyzed all the digital readouts being transferred into his consciousness from the subatomic analyzer in the plate. He went over the numbers and calculations, attempting to make sense of what they could possibly mean. However, nothing new could be ascertained. Reconsidering the situation, he began to ponder if he were looking at the problem the wrong way.

Maybe the answer isn't from the inside out but from the outside in?

Alex stared at the constellations on the shield.

Do these constellations represent a clue? Why was the V-shaped Hyades star cluster of Taurus so prominent on the Mukulian Hall in Nan Madol? Do the esoteric scenes engraved on the shield represent something grander?

A kind hand touched his shoulder, breaking his concentration.

Alex turned. "Samantha."

"I saw your frustration back in the room," she responded like a concerned older sister. "While Marissa was caring for Christine, I thought it best to slip out. Is there anything I can do to help?"

"Unless you can tell me something about this shield here, we are in a stalemate," Alex said. He looked up at his oldest friend and let out a sigh. "Any update on the movement of the Earth's tectonic plates? I know you've been closely monitoring them since we left."

She placed her coffee mug down on a table. "Not good. It could be a matter of just a few days, hours, or even minutes before everything shifts again. The magma under the Earth's crust is churning and flowing like I've never seen before. It's like something's stirring up the mix and causing it to act erratically."

"Which is triggering the massive electromagnetic fluctuations across the globe," Alex concluded.

"If we don't do something soon," Samantha admitted. "What we've seen so far will be just the tip of the proverbial iceberg."

"Have you determined what's causing the problem?" Alex asked.

"No," she responded. "Not a clue."

Alex pointed to the shield. "The answer's here. It's a mystery a few millennia old."

Samantha smirked, subtly reminding Alex of his genetic heritage. "So are you."

Finally, a smile, she thought, watching a small grin form on Alex's face.

"Now, what can I do to help?" Samantha asked.

"Maybe it would help if I ran a few things by you." Alex held up his right palm, and a cross sectional image of the shield appeared above it. "As you see, the shield is composed of five different layers of composite material that I have no means yet of fully analyzing. However, its centermost layer is entirely made of mercury. And when I subject the shield to a certain frequency of electromagnetic energy, it excites this mercury, causing it to levitate."

"Sort of like the Roman god Mercury," Samantha chimed in. "He was also called Hermes by the Greeks."

"I never thought of that," Alex said, impressed with Samantha's analogy.

"Wasn't he the winged god of flight?" she continued. "And didn't he hold that thing-a- ma-jig in his hand? A winged pole with two serpents coiled around it."

"You mean a caduceus?" Alex responded. "The symbol prominently posted around our entire Neurono-Tek research center and hospital? I believe one was even embroidered by your grandmother and is hanging in your former office."

"That's it."

"Never heard of it," Alex jested.

Samantha gave him a slight nudge on the arm. "I'm glad to see that your recent near-death experience hasn't entirely ruined your sense of humor."

"But seriously," Alex commented, with a more austere look on his face, "could the caduceus represent the remnants of some lost knowledge from a pre-flood era? And maybe this lost scientific wisdom was passed on to the subsequent post-flood era through myth and legend."

"Or maybe," Samantha concluded, "both myth and legend were meant to hide this knowledge the entire time."

"Good point," Alex agreed. Looking at the caduceus now in hindsight, he said, "You can now understand where truth and myth merge."

"The wings represented flight," Samantha continued, "while the liquid metal mercury somehow made this flight possible."

"Let me show you something interesting." Alex held out his other hand and activated a holo-projector above them with his thoughts. Odd-looking vehicles in the shapes of a fish, submarines, beehives, and domes appeared in front of them. Some had propellers while others appeared to have fins.

"What are they supposed to represent?" Samantha asked

"The ancient Indian text known as the Samarangana Sutradhara sums it up best," Alex said. "By means of the power latent in mercury which sets the driving whirlwind in motion, a man sitting inside may travel a great distance in the sky in the most marvelous manner."

"Are you trying to say that these images represent ancient flying machines?" Samantha asked.

"They might," Alex concluded. "These drawings were created from detailed descriptions found in Samarangana Sutradhara and other ancient Indian Sanskrit texts such as the Ramayana and Mababharata. Again, what was once considered myth may have, in fact been, the truth all along."

"Just like the city of Ur or the Hittite Empire in the Old Testament," Marissa chimed in from the doorway. "Until archeologists dug up evidence of their existence, people used to think they were old, fabricated stories."

Christine and Terzin stood next to Marissa. Both listened intently to the conversation.

Marissa's voice warmed Alex's heart. He could not help but go over and give her a squeeze around the waist. "Spoken from a true Sunday school teacher."

"I see your patient is feeling better," Samantha noted, gesturing towards Christine, who had wrapped herself in a blue blanket.

"She said there's something that she needs to tell us," Marissa commented.

Christine pointed to the shield. With a weak and cracking voice, she said, "I've seen that before."

She paused a brief second before continuing, "In Philadelphia."

CHAPTER 27

JULES SAT IMPATIENTLY in the copilot's chair, watching a holographic image of the world grid on the ship's windshield. Rapidly changing numbers and symbols surrounded the representation.

"Let's go," Jules insisted.

Half asleep, the pilot could not keep his eyes open any longer. After such a stressful day and now cooped up in a dark cabin of a striker craft in geosynchronous orbit over Philadelphia for over an hour, he could no longer stay awake.

Jules, however, needed little sleep. His body seemed to thrive on excitement. Awake the entire time, he had been watching the fluctuations in the grid as ardently as one would their favorite sporting event.

"This is no time for sleep, my boy," Jules chimed in, full of life. "We must seize this opportunity before it's lost. The grid has remained stable over this point for God knows how long now. I think waiting any longer would be most counterproductive."

"Yes, sir," the pilot said. Wiping his eyes, he turned on the lights in the cabin and took control of the ship's steering wheel.

Its lights erupted upon his touch as he brought the striker craft out of orbit.

"What?" Drew asked. Awoken by the commotion, he looked out the dark windshield towards the Earth below them. What would have once been littered with millions of dots of light, now only boasted a mere pittance of its former luminosity. Much of the entire East Coast was dark, while the western portion of the country fared not much better.

Drew shook his head at the sight. He could only imagine what the people on the surface must have experienced between the seismic activity and the electromagnetic instability.

"You say this is where the subatomic fluctuations ended?" Jules asked.

"Yes, Mr. Windsor," Drew answered. "The signal terminated precisely at the coordinates I provided."

Jules surmised that Alex's smaller aero-bike must have rendezvoused there with the larger and stealthier stratoskimmer, making any further quantum fluctuation undetectable.

But was there something significant about this place?

Luckily, as the striker craft descended into the innermost layers of the atmosphere, the ride went extremely smoothly. With no perturbations in the grid, at least for the moment, it felt as if they were gliding on ice.

Drew examined the holographic image above his wrist. "Set the ship down right on that mound," he pointed. "That spot right there."

After landing, Jules stood up and checked the pockets in his leather sports jacket. Fully equipped, he felt prepared for whatever awaited them outside the ship.

"What's the recon say?" Jules asked the pilot.

"The entire area within a 500-yard perimeter is totally barren except for one human quantum signal about twenty yards directly ahead, sir."

"Very good. Let's shed some light on the situation," Jules said.

"Yes, sir," the pilot answered, pushing a button on the steering wheel.

Light began to emanate out from the striker craft in all directions, illuminating the area.

Jules walked back to the ship's hull. The WOGs all sat at attention. The red light blinking in the ceiling indicated imminent deployment.

"Colonel," Jules ordered. "Deploy and secure this mound."

"Yes, sir!" he bellowed as his voice echoed through the hull. Pointing at the door, he barked, "Omega formation, go!"

As the door descended to the ground, the WOGs barreled out of the ship in silence. In a hunched position with their weapons drawn, their departure was quick and efficient. Within less than a minute the colonel reported back to Jules in his auricular chip, "Secure!"

Jules walked down the steps and onto a distorted layer of debris. The entire site was in ruins except for the remnants of a few pillars and the broken frames of a couple doorways. As he looked out into the city, it was almost completely dark. Only a few flashlights and the smoldering remains of earlier fires shed any light onto the area.

Despite, the poor visibility, Jules noted the broken skyline along the horizon and could only imagine the destruction that must have recently engulfed the city.

A man with his hands behind his head and two guns pointed to his back approached.

"We found him here," one of the helmeted WOGs accompanying him blurted.

"Good man?" Jules asked the stranger as if speaking to a friend. "Please tell me who you are and what you are doing up here on this hilltop all alone."

"My name is Murphy O'Neil," he responded. Upon raising his head, he recognized Jules. "And you are Jules Windsor, the President of The New Reality."

Murph was certainly excited at the site. His only thought now was that help had finally arrived. Despite the violence caused by Jules' Open Society policies and the recent seismic turmoil, most citizens were misinformed by The New Reality's controlled media about the true nature of the situation. Few blamed Jules for their current troubles and instead believed the narrative set forth by The New Reality: The problems now faced by mankind were a direct result of Jules' predecessor and her previous disastrous policies.

An uninformed, ignorant populace was exactly what Jules and his Open Society needed for its existence. Just like one of the many tenants set forth by the Illuminati handbook, Jules knew that if he could control the information distributed to the populace, he could control their minds.

"Thank you, Mr. Windsor, for coming to help," Murph went on to say. "My friends and I were trapped in the museum here, and then this enormous earthquake destroyed the city. I'm the only one still left up here on the hill."

Such a simple mind, Jules thought. *So easily manipulated.*

"Please," Jules kindly asked, "lower your weapons. Our friend Murphy here is in need of a helping hand—not a manhandling."

The WOGs complied with the order. However, a message from the colonel echoed in Jules' ear, "We have a lock on him just in case."

"Very good," Jules responded to the colonel as if thanking the WOGs. "Now, Murphy, what pray tell, happened here?"

"Thank you, Mr. Windsor," Murphy said. "It was awful. A massive earthquake killed all my friends and destroyed the city." He paused for a few seconds to compose himself. "However, I discovered something that you might find interesting. At least the other people who left here earlier today did."

"Other people?" Jules asked nonchalantly.

"Yea," he said rather gruffly. "These other people showed up out of nowhere just like you. Fortunately, one of them was a doctor or something and helped my friend Christine after she passed out." He pointed to the edge of the rubble. "And they all seemed interested in the crystals I found in the cave over there, saying they would come back later to have a better look at them."

"Alex Pella, sir?" Drew concluded.

Murph pointed his finger at Drew. "Yea. That was one of the guy's names."

"Was it just the two of them?" Jules asked.

"No. There was also this husky guy wearing a red hat along with some girl with long hair and a battered white dress. If you ask me, they all looked like they were in some sort of earthquake themselves."

"Well then, Murphy." Jules asked. "Do you happen to know where they all went? Because of the poor reception, I lost contact with mostly everyone here in this grand city."

"No clue," Murph responded. "I wish they would have waited a little longer before taking off in their stratoskimmer. If they thought the crystals were interesting, they would have been really impressed with what happened next in the cave." He again pointed to the edge of the debris. "You gotta see it."

"Please," Jules kindly obliged, "lead the way Murphy. I must personally see what has gleaned your utmost attention."

Murph scuttled through the debris to the edge where it fell sharply down an incline. A dim light emitted from the cave, helping Jules, Drew, Murph, and a few WOGs to negotiate their way into it and down the stairs.

"You ain't seen nothing yet," Murphy noted as Jules and Drew admired the maps along the walls. "He then turned to each of them. "And watch what you're thinking down here. It's like this cave is magical; we can read each other's minds." He then pointed at the blaring flashlights on the ends of the WOGs guns. "I'd put those down. Nothing electrical works in this cave."

"You heard the man," Jules ordered.

The WOGs complied as the group entered the ancient hall of records.

Reminds me of Pumapunku, Jules thought, admiring the area.

"Look at this," Murphy eagerly gestured to the ceiling. "It didn't appear until everyone left."

"What is it?" Drew looked up and asked.

"It looks like some sort of ancient treasure map," Murph concluded.

CHAPTER 28

"SAW WHAT?" Alex asked.

Still looking at the shield, Christine answered, "The key. That's the key." Scared and still shaken by the vision, she added, "It could have saved everyone."

Alex was taken aback by the answer. Stunned that she recognized the shield's identity, he asked, "How and when did you see this key?"

"Please," Marissa said, noting Christine's face growing pale and sweat forming on her brow. "Let me take you back to the lounge area. Sit down."

Christine brushed off Marissa's advice and walked over to the shield as if hypnotized. Dropping her blanket, she reached out and touched the surface of this ancient object. "I saw it all. The argument. The betrayal. The flood. It's like I was there, and it just happened."

Alex and Marissa walked to her side. Without pressuring her, they listened to the entirety of the vision she saw in the cave. Once Christine started speaking, the story flowed effortlessly, as if she had told it a thousand times in the past.

Tears ran down Christine's face as she finished the story. "They could have stopped the flood." She looked at both Alex and Marissa. "If they had just turned off the cradle."

Terzin stood with her hand on her mouth. Almost in shock, she now understood her purpose and the purpose of all the Keepers around the world. It suddenly made sense. "The cradle's still active," she concluded. "They never turned it off."

"We must turn off the cradle before the planet is destroyed," Terzin said, with some persistence to her voice. "What you saw was just a prelude to something even more catastrophic. We must get the key to the cradle before it's too late."

"Christine," Alex asked with some urgency, "can you tell us more about Dilmun and where the cradle is located? Think of everything you saw."

Christine's eyes widened as a smile crept onto her hardened façade. "It was beautiful, utterly beautiful. The cradle was located in the center of a tropical paradise. There were stunning gardens, flowering plants, trees overflowing with fruit, spectacular fountains, and a magnificent white, shining dome at its center."

"The dome?" Terzin asked. "Can you tell us anything about the dome?" Remembering legends told by her relatives, she recalled vague inferences to a white beacon representing both hope and death. However, most of the story was lost over the generations, and it was spoken only with a whispered tongue, as if taboo.

Christine turned back to the shield and pointed at the V-shaped star cluster in the constellation Taurus. "Engraved on the dome's door was a depiction of a young woman with glowing hair who appeared to be expecting a child. In her womb was this same V-shaped design overlying a door."

"I bet that's where the key went to enter the dome," Alex concluded, pulling everything together. "Was the dome what they called the cradle?"

"Yes," Christine answered.

"Were they attempting to turn off something in the cradle?" Terzin asked.

"Yes," she nodded.

"Can you recall anything particular to the Dilmun's geography or anything you noted that stood out in the area?" Alex asked. Grasping for straws, he realized the question was most likely not going to yield any viable information— especially after the Earth had already undergone enormous geographic changes as a result of the previous crustal slippage and subsequent flooding.

"There were four rivers flowing into Dilmun," Christine recalled, "providing this magnificent land with an abundance of water."

"The Pishon, Gihon, Tigris, and Euphrates," Marissa quickly concluded. She looked at everyone with excitement. "I know the place Christine is describing."

Alex skeptically glanced over to his fiancée, knowing what she was about to say.

"Don't give me that look, Alex," Marissa noted with a smirk. "I know it sounds crazy. But the pregnant woman on the dome, the V-shaped star cluster, the four rivers, and the magnificence of Dilmun. It can only mean one thing."

"Say it," Alex responded, not wanting to steal her thunder.

"The cradle is located in Eden," Marissa concluded. "It all makes sense. In the Bible, the Garden of Eden was located at the head of four great rivers. And the picture on the dome most likely represented Eve while the V-shaped star cluster signified her pregnant womb."

"And whatever is in this dome may still be causing the tectonic shifts," Terzin added. "But the Garden of Eden has been lost for millennium."

"What'd I miss?" asked William with his mouth full and a bulbous sandwich in his hand.

"Come on in," Alex invited sarcastically. "Join the party."

"But seriously," Samantha said. "Isn't the Garden of Eden just some sort of myth or fable written about in the Bible? I always thought of it metaphorically and never really believed it existed."

"No," Terzin disagreed. "Other cultures tell stories of this place. In fact, Eden originates from the Mesopotamian word meaning fertile plains. There is definite validity to the biblical account."

"Let's think of this logically," Alex interrupted. "Do any of you recall who Heinrich Schliemann was?"

Blank faces confirmed his suspicion.

"He was the gentleman who discovered the lost city of Troy in 1870," Alex said, answering his own question. "Most people up to that time thought the ancient Greek poem, *The Iliad*, was pure fiction, and that he was a madman for attempting to undertake such a futile expedition."

"And do you know how he discovered the lost city?" Alex asked before again answering his own question. "He used *The Iliad* as his source. Now, I'm not saying I'm completely convinced with Marissa's conclusion, but I do believe it's something we need to think about."

William raised up his sandwich. "And it's the only lead we have."

Alex gave his good friend a smile. "True. Marissa, can you recall exactly what it says in the Bible about the rivers?"

Marissa shook her head. "Not verbatim, but I do know the exact passage is located in the book of Genesis."

Alex held up his hand. Marissa read the passage, which holographically appeared above:

A river rises in Eden to water the garden; beyond there it divides and becomes four branches. The name of the first is the Pishon; it is the one that winds through the whole land of Havilah, where there is gold. The gold of that land is excellent; bdellium and lapis lazuli are also there. The name of the second river is the Gihon; it is the one that winds through the land of Cush. The name of the third river is the Tigris; it is the one that flows east of Ashur. The fourth river is the Euphrates.

A holographic map of the Middle East appeared next to the words.

Alex walked over to it and pointed. "As you can all see, the rivers Tigris and Euphrates flow down Iraq and meet at this exact point here before unifying and flowing as one into the Persian Gulf."

The rivers turned red on the map as he mentioned them.

"Which leaves the biggest mystery unsolved," Marissa said. "Where are the Pishon and Gihon rivers?"

"And did they even exist?" Samantha noted.

"Let's step back and start with the River Pishon," Alex noted, thinking aloud. "Where is Havilah, and is it abundant in gold?"

"Further on in Genesis," Marissa commented, "in the Table of Nations there is a reference that people of Havilah as being Arabian in origin."

The map of Saudi Arabia grew brighter than the surrounding area.

"By the records I'm accessing," Alex agreed, "gold, bdellium, and lapis lazuli are all prevalent in this peninsula."

"But where's the river that flows through there now?" William inquired.

"Maybe not now," Alex said, "but possibly over 12,000 years ago there once was one."

A new holographic image appeared replacing the map. "This is a satellite view of the area as it appeared before the recent seismic shifts." Spectral analysis blinked one by one, each in different colors until a single brown image remained.

"Wow," Marissa commented, examining this particular spectral topographical display. "It looks like Saudi Arabia was once filled with rivers which have long dried up." She then ran her hand along one particularly long river, which ran eastward and ended just south of where the Tigris and Euphrates joined. "Did this old river ever exist in modern times?"

The words *Wadi Al-Rummah* appeared above it.

"It appears as if this river dried up over the last few centuries," Alex commented. "Now only trickles of water in sporadic places remain. You know what is more interesting," he then commented, accessing more information about the former river, "is that it is referred to by locals as the navel of the Earth."

"But the story in Genesis distinctly says the rivers divided into four branches," Samantha pointed out. "And it clearly does not explain what Christine saw—navel or not."

"Bear with me," Alex said. "I have an idea. But first let's explore the last river, the Gihon flowing through the land of Cush."

"Which now leaves an even bigger problem," Marissa noted. "The Kingdom of Cush is believed to be modern day Ethiopia."

The satellite image widened to incorporate this country. Few remnants of any ancient waterways could be identified on the spectral display. Those that once existed terminated far from the other three rivers or ended in the Nile.

"Could Cush represent possibly a different kingdom or land?" Alex asked aloud, "or could it have been mistranslated through the years to mean Ethiopia?"

"Maybe Cush represented the land conquered by the ancient Kassites," Terzin surmised. "They were in control of at least part of Babylonia when the nation of Israel was founded."

"Overlay this map with that of the land believed to have been owned by the Kassites," Marissa asked.

A yellow area highlighted on the satellite image. Encompassing northern Saudi Arabia and leading up to southern Iraq and southwestern Iran, a single river soon became evident as the spectral analysis changed colors in order to enhance it.

Above the riverbed, the words *Karun River* appeared. Its path went southwestward through the Kassite Empire and joined just below to where Wadi Al-Rummah intersected the Tigris and Euphrates.

"The Karun River," Alex pointed out, "has been dammed for many years, leaving its previous paths almost unrecognizable."

"Did the flow of these rivers in your vision look anything like this picture?" Marissa asked.

Christine shook her head no. "I remember what I saw. It was as clear as day, and that's not it."

"I think we need to go back to the drawing board," Samantha concluded. "This is a dead end."

"Don't give up yet," Alex said. "What I showed you all was a satellite picture of the area taken over a year ago. While we've been talking, I've been able to obtain a current satellite view of the area."

"How recent?" Samantha asked.

"It's a live feed," Alex said. "Neurono-Tek placed multiple mini-satellites into space for different scientific purposes." He pointed to his contacts. "It's what my vedere lens links to when I'm receiving images of a particular area."

A new picture of the Middle East appeared, replacing the old one. Though the hologram was vivid in nature, its geography appeared completely foreign.

Samantha gasped at the sight. Over two-thirds of Africa was now underwater. Plus, the former lands of Saudi Arabia, Iraq, and Iran were also mostly inundated.

"It seems as if more of this area is being lost to the sea each minute," Marissa noted, comparing this image to that recently seen on the Maternal Mark. "Where's the Persian Gulf?"

"Let me overlay this picture onto a faint image of the area before the tectonic shifts," Alex commented.

A new image appeared showing the entire Persian Gulf now devoid of any water, with the Saudi peninsula currently connected directly to Iraq.

A tear ran down Terzin's cheek. *What have I done?* she lamented, still blaming herself for the catastrophe.

"Humor me on this," Alex said. "You see the locations of the four rivers highlighted here in red. What if I run the same spectral analysis profile on this current satellite image as I did on the previous one. Take a look."

The image changed color and contour until a brown hue overtook the entirety of the holograph.

"I'm going to enhance this image and take into account every contour abnormality on the Earth's topography, searching for any discernable pattern," Alex said, while making a few calculations.

After about a minute, a new image appeared. Intricate waterways lost for millennium suddenly relinquished their secrets.

Christine walked up to the map and ran her hand in the direction of the four previous rivers. What was not obvious on the preceding image became apparent on this one. Lost waterways no longer present from these ancient rivers suddenly emerged. As she followed them one by one, Christine noted how they now all converged on one spot that was once inundated by the former Persian Gulf.

"That's how it looked!" Christine said enthusiastically. "This is exactly what I remember."

"The great flood along with the massive tectonic shifts must have made these ancient rivers either change directions or completely cease to flow," Alex noted. "No wonder it was never discovered before. The evidence had been hidden for millennium."

"Eden," Marissa said in awe.

CHAPTER 29

"WHEN THEY ALL LEFT, this whole ceiling was dark," Murph explained. "Then, about an hour later, it lit up like a flashlight."

They all gazed at the dome above them. Brilliant stars forming constellations were set on a backdrop of an ancient but familiar planet. Hundreds of thousands of small, tiny crystals created the amazing picture. The vividness of the image made it appear to be more of a crisp picture than any type of etched drawing.

Each constellation was directly superimposed on a different continent.

Drew took a pen-like device from his pocket and held it up towards the ceiling. He shook it a few times as if the sudden motion would somehow activate it.

"I told you nothing works down here," Murph said. *Moron.*

"Excuse me?" Drew exclaimed. "Did you just call me a moron?"

"Ah, sorry," Murph said, slightly embarrassed about the thought.

"He did mention that this cave fosters one's telepathic abilities," Jules said, looking over towards Drew. As a warning, he added, "One must therefore control what one thinks, especially if it is towards another individual currently present."

Yes, sir, Drew thought.

"Very good then," Jules replied.

"If this picture is supposed to be the Earth." Drew noted, while pointing at the dome, "it's nothing like I've seen before."

"I think it's the old Earth before the great flood," Murph said.

He then pointed over to one of the crystals and began to relay in great detail the story that unfolded in front of his eyes after he grabbed it. Jules and Drew listened intently, not stopping to question or interrupt him.

"And that point right there," Murph finished, "looks like where the cradle was located."

"Middle East?" Drew commented.

"Persian Gulf area," Jules agreed. Turning to their guest, Jules said, "So you say this presumptive key that looks like a shield is the only thing that can nullify the cradle's effect on the planet."

"You got it, Mr. Windsor," Murph responded. "That's about as much as I can remember from what I saw."

"Did anyone else happen to stumble upon this cave other than those you mentioned?" Jules asked.

"Nope."

"Did you happen to tell any other soul about what happened here?" Jules again inquired.

"You guys were the first people I spoke with since Christine left this place with that guy Alex and his friends," Murph answered.

"Well then," Jules concluded. "I guess our work is complete down here except for one little thing I must tend to." He then looked over to one of the crystals levitating above the pedestal. "Let me ask you Murphy, was it that crystal that provided you with such an amazing vision?"

He turned away from them and pointed at a different one in the opposite direction. "Like I said," Murph noted, "It was that—"

His words were abruptly curtailed as he coughed up blood and fell to his knees. Turning around, he noted Jules with a bloody dagger in hand and a matter-of-fact look on his face.

"We certainly cannot leave any loose ends lying around here Murphy," Jules said as he sliced the man's throat. "I do hope you understand."

Murph reached out his hand as if to beg for mercy, but the rapid blood loss made him quickly lose consciousness and fall face down.

Taking a white rag from his pocket, Jules cleaned the knife and threw the rag on the dying body.

"Well then," Jules finally said after inspecting his weapon for cleanliness and placing it back into one of the jacket's side pockets. "I think we both know where we should be headed."

Drew was appalled at such a senseless act of violence. However, showing Jules any sign of disagreement, especially now, would mean both the termination of his career and possibly even his life.

Doing his best to act as if nothing unusual had just occurred, Drew pointed at the dome. "But this is so vague. Where exactly do we need to go? With the electromagnetic instability only getting worse, it's not like we'll have the luxury of scouring the entire Persian Gulf area without significant interference."

"Don't worry," Jules assured. "My dear friend Alexander will lead the way. Now let us cover up this place and hide it from any pesky trespassers while I'm gone." He stared at the dome one last time. "Let's be off before the grid lines shift and strand us in this God-awful city."

CHAPTER 30

"STAY STILL," Marissa said, holding William's neck. "I can't place this anti-nausea chip if you're moving all around."

She held him by the shoulder and steadied a syringe-like device along the nape of his neck. After giving it a little press, she removed the compact medical gadget and placed in in the black bag she wore around the shoulder.

"It's not me," William said, "it's Tom's flying and these jet engines. They keep going on and off every few minutes. I'd feel safer in front of a firing squad than having to fly another minute on this stratoskimmer."

"You care to take the wheel?" Tom commented, attempting to level out the ship. "I'll kindly hand it over to you at any time."

Marissa grabbed William's seat to stabilize herself as the ship began to rock. The jet engines fired as the electromagnetic dipoles in the native engines failed to depolarize properly in the unstable world grid.

"Can you see anything out there?" Marissa asked, pointing out the windshield. "There's such limited visibility."

"It's not good," Alex admitted. "When half of Saudi Arabia sunk into the sea, it caused a chain reaction setting off massive volcanic activity along the eastern coasts of Sudan and Ethiopia. The closer we approach, the denser the soot and ash becomes."

"As a result, we have to fly this ship as low as possible," Tom said.

"Between the soot-filled clouds and electromagnetic fluctuations, we can't utilize our geo-guidance at any higher altitude," Alex added, pointing to a fuzzy holographic image of the Persian Gulf above the flickering instrument panel.

"It's like you are flying blindly," Marissa observed.

"That's why I insisted Christine sit with us here in the cockpit," Alex admitted. "I suspect we may just have to eyeball the best spot to land, and she would be the best one to do it."

"Guys," Willian said matter-of-factly. "Is this really what we want to be doing right now?" Feeling a little less airsick, he leaned forward getting closer to both Alex and Tom. "What are we really getting ourselves into? Just look at it out there. The Earth's crust is crumbling all around, and we are flying straight towards a massive rift of active volcanos."

William took a deep breath. "I'm all for saving the planet. Hell. We've already done it before. I just think it's too late now."

Marissa turned and walked back to the ship's cabin without another word. She had no rebuttal for William's comments; deep down she felt the same. Though she did not want to doubt Alex's plan, it was difficult not to at least mentally second-guess it.

This is the only option, Alex concluded. He knew there was no other choice. No place on the planet was safe. Even as they were leaving their hideout, he noted increased seismic activity in the area, indicating something more cataclysmic was on its way. Staying there any longer would have eventually proven suicidal.

"Why don't we wait until the crust slips and whatever finally happens to the planet happens?" William concluded. "Then we can land this bucket of bolts on whatever is still standing and hope for the best."

"There may be nowhere left," Christine insisted. "If what I saw on the image was just a prelude, we're all doomed if we can't stop this."

William said no more. Letting the repercussions of her warning sink in, he slowly slouched back into his seat as he contemplated all their fates.

The ship continued its descent. Land started to become visible through the soot and dust. The lower they flew, the more their visibility increased.

"By my instruments," Alex said while examining the hazy map above the dashboard, "we should be right over the dried-up lake bed of the Karun River and heading southwest directly towards the cradle."

"Eden," Christine corrected.

"Call it what you want," William stated, "but I don't see a thing down there that looks like any old river. Hell, the whole thing just looks like dune after dune of black-tinted sand." He paused a second. "I hate sand."

As the holograph above the dashboard faded, Alex turned and asked, "Christine was there anything else we could possibly use to identity Eden's location? Can you think of something more specific? The best I can do is land us somewhere within a five-mile vicinity of our intended destination. With these electromagnetic fluctuations, I won't be able to pinpoint it more exactly than that."

"I just don't know," she admitted.

"The seismic activity is getting worse," Tom pointed out.

New red dots representing active volcanic activity appeared above the dashboard. These dots were accompanied by a few others that began to spring up in northern Iraq and sporadically in Iran.

"I don't think you'll have the luxury of walking five miles," Tom concluded. "This whole region may be gone by then."

Alex looked out the windshield as the sandy landscape turned more rugged and crusty in nature. The remnants of broken-down ships and hallowed out oil tankers speckled the ground as they passed overhead.

"We're over the former Persian Gulf now," Alex concluded. "I can't make out much more than that down there. Plus, I'm no longer able to receive an accurate satellite reading of the area."

Alex's voice rose in volume as the roar of the jet engines became more constant and monotonous in nature.

How could people fly under such archaic conditions? William bemoaned.

"Are you sure you know where we're even headed at this point?" Tom asked with some concern. "I'm not making out much from that holographic map any longer."

Alex remained silent, not wanting to instill any further concern amongst his friends.

"Wait," Christine blurted. "There was one more thing that I can remember about the vision." She leaned forward so that Alex and Tom could hear her clearer. "There were these three long, white pillars, each heading out in different directions, away from the cradle like separate rays of sunlight."

Alex thought for a second, recounting the history of the ancient pyramids of Giza.

"You know," he postulated aloud, "those pillars may have been covered with the same, polished white tura limestone that used to coat the great pyramids in Egypt."

"You mean the pyramids didn't always look like blocks of piled sand?" William asked.

"No," Alex responded. "In fact, the pyramids used to be completely smooth along their edges and capped at the top in pure gold." He contemplated the situation again. "I bet that's what they used. What else could it have been?"

"But that's all I can remember," Christine added. "Everything else you already know."

"It may be just enough," Alex said.

Tom looked in the distance, hoping to see any white line or evidence of what Christine was describing; in the soot-filled atmosphere, everything appeared gray, dull, and monotonous.

"I don't think that's going to help," Tom concluded. "It all looks the same down there."

Tom lowered the ship until it was flying only about 100 feet above the surface.

"I still don't see anything," Tom again admitted. "Wherever those pillars are, they've got to be under thousands of years of crap that fell to the gulf floor."

The ship rocked hard to its right side, surprising all aboard with the sudden movement.

"Everyone alright back there?" Alex shouted back to the hull.

"Spiffy!" Samantha yelled back. "Just land this ship in one piece is all I ask."

That's the goal, Alex thought.

A faint white line began to holographically appear on the windshield off to their right side. Noting its sudden presence, Alex said to Tom, "Do me a favor and take over all the flight controls while I try to hone in on that signal there on the ground."

Tom looked over and saw the faint line flicker in and out of view. Without prompting, he changed the ship's course and flew directly over its path.

"That's it," Alex said. "I'm locking onto the unique quantum signal emitted by the quartz in the tura limestones. Because of the unreliability of our sensors, we need to be right on top of it to obtain an accurate reading."

William patted Alex on the back, proud of his longtime friend. He knew that if anyone could find the proverbial needle in the haystack, it would be him.

"There's the other two lines," Christine exclaimed as their images became crisper. "They all converge on that one point. You found it!"

"Tom, are you able to safely land us down there?" Alex asked.

Tom turned his head towards Alex. "With my eyes open or closed?" he grumbled. "Try doing this at night, under fire, and with the cockpit instrument dark."

"I'd opt for eyes open," William interrupted.

With the landing gear now engaged, Tom cut the jet engines and deployed the parachute just before hitting ground. The ship jerked upon impact and slowly came to a complete stop about 200 feet from where the three white lines on the windshield converged.

The roar of the engines gradually faded, providing William with a measure of relief.

"Good job," Alex complimented.

He then grabbed a large tan bag from a drawer along the side wall of the cockpit and placed it over his arm. "Let's get out of here," he said, "before time runs out."

The ship rocked back and forth for a few seconds just as Alex began to stand. He steadied himself on the seat so as to not fall.

"I thought we landed already?" Marissa said, walking into the cockpit.

"That wasn't the ship," Alex noted. "We better find what this cradle does and do it now." He started to walk back to the ship's hull. Before leaving the cockpit, he turned to his pilot. "Tom, you'll be our eyes and ears out here. Good luck."

"As always," Tom responded. "I'll have the ship fired up and ready to go at your beckon."

"Samantha," Alex stated. "There isn't much time left. Do me a favor and grab the shield while I see what's going on out here."

"Sure thing," she responded. Hearing the urgency in his voice, Samantha understood the gravity of the situation. "Do you want me to take this contraption off of it first?"

"No," Alex responded as the stratoskimmer's stairs descended. "Keep it on until the last moment. It's concealing the shield's quantum signal. The moment we take it off, if Julius is watching, the shield will guide him to us like a homing beacon."

Alex then took a rectangular object, reminiscent of a gray deck of cards, known as an etherometer and threw it like a Frisbee outside the ship. Within a second, it began sending a spectral and visual analysis of the entire area directly to his vedere lens.

Grabbing an electric pulse gun from a pocket, he looked back to his friends in the ship's hull. Everyone was standing silently, awaiting Alex's next words. Their fear was palpable, and each time the ship shook from the instability of the ground underneath of them, it continued to escalate.

"Everyone," Alex said, "take one. These are modified pulse guns designed to send whomever it shoots into instant cardiac arrest." Alex reached into the tan bag and handed them each an identical weapon. He then held up his own gun and said, "Before you fire, flick this switch forward to reveal the red dot. It will fully arm the weapon."

"Red means dead," Samantha said.

"Exactly," Alex agreed. "And the rest is self-explanatory." He pointed the gun. "Aim, shoot, and hope you don't miss." He paused while his friends fumbled with their weapons for a few seconds.

"End of class," he then said abruptly. "I'm afraid we don't have time for more."

Alex gestured out the door and over to the crusty mound about 200 feet from them. "What you see over there is the cradle. Or what's left of it. Let's get there as quickly as possible. Watch your step and be careful not to break an ankle. The sediment on the ground will make walking somewhat unsteady."

As Alex spoke, William could not help but notice numerous red plumes of smoke and lava rising up over the far horizon. The thought of walking straight into Dante's *Inferno* crossed his mind.

"Let's go," Alex said as he ran down the steps while watching the readouts on his vedere lens.

The others followed without another word. In single file, they all rapidly exited. Upon departing the ship, Christine felt a great sense of remorse fill her soul as she gazed at the barren landscape. Now a desolate wasteland, the area was a far cry from its previous glory. No longer the land of plenty, it appeared as if death itself had descended upon the area. The dim light trickling through the soot-filled atmosphere added to the site's gray and foreboding appearance.

A passage from Genesis echoed throughout Marissa's mind the further they walked through this barren wasteland. Recalling God's warning to Adam and Eve, she thought, "You shall not eat or even touch it, lest you die."

The mound appeared much larger upon their approach. What once seemed to blend into the mundane background now appeared more impressive standing next to it. The pillars extending from it also became much more discernable.

Triangulating where all of these pillars converged on the mound, Alex surmised where the door to enter must be located.

William scoured the area with his gun, pointing it in all directions. Though still with its safety lock engaged, his thumb rested nervously on it, waiting to flick it into action. The others, too, anxiously reconnoitered the area, almost expecting someone to jump out of the crusted soil and attack.

Taking a monocle-appearing device known as an eavesdropper out of his pocket, Alex placed it on the front of the mound. He then ran it along the cradle's side until a holographic picture emerged above it. Luckily, the electromagnetic interference was much lower on the Earth's surface and allowed for such a device to work without significant difficulties.

"I recognize this image," Christine said. "Go a little to the left." Alex complied; as he moved it accordingly, a V representing Eve's womb came into focus. Alex turned to Christine. "Good job. You found it!"

Alex's words provided Christine with some vindication. Though her friends were all lost back in Philadelphia, her time in the cave and seeing the vision might in the end save millions, if not billions.

The ground shook once more as a new red flume of lava cracked open in the distance. The roar of Mother Nature reminded them that time was swiftly dwindling.

Alex then took out four spikes from his bag and jammed them one by one into the crust, forming a large square around the V. Once the last spike was in place, the tips of each began to glow green. A crisp red laser in the shape of a square formed between the four spikes. Slowly, the laser bore down onto the crust and vaporized the millennium worth of debris as it progressed. Smoke and dust spewed from the site.

After about a minute's worth of activity, the red laser disappeared, revealing a V displayed prominently on Eve's womb. They were all humbled by the ancient site, staring at it with awe. Feeling rejuvinated by their discovery, Alex dropped the bag around his neck and took the shield out of Samantha's hands.

He then checked his vedere lens one more time. No one was in sight.

"All clear?" Alex asked Tom, giving one last double-check.

"Good to go," the pilot's voice echoed in his auricular chip.

"Disengage the safeties," Alex then ordered his friends.

They all complied without argument. One by one their pulse guns hummed with activity.

Alex then placed the shield directly on Eve's belly, hoping for it to open the door. An indentation with the exact shape and dimensions of the shield let him know that it must be the correct area to place it.

Nothing happened. Alex then attempted to turn and push it, hoping that something would occur. However, all attempts led to the same result.

"I don't like this," William grumbled. "I certainly don't like this."

Nor do I, Alex subconsciously agreed.

"The decoupler," Samantha pointed out. "Maybe that's interfering somehow."

Alex both feared and hoped Samantha was correct. Though he certainly did not want to remove the only thing hiding them from Jules, he realized he had no other option.

"Keep your weapons handy," Alex warned. He then deactivated the decoupler and yanked it off the shield.

I just hope Jules is far, far away.

Alex again approached Eve's belly with the shield. Before he had an opportunity to set it in place, the artifact slipped out of his hands and stuck to the mound as if drawn by some unknown electromagnetic force.

The earth suddenly shook more intensely. Unable to balance himself, William fell into the mound. Upon impact, he accidently pulled the trigger on his pulse gun. With a sizzle, it discharged straight up towards the sky.

An extensive area of earth only miles away from their position had collapsed, creating a massive crater in the ground.

"This is getting insane," William said. "Why don't we just let Mother Nature take its course and destroy this entire place? That will certainly turn this damn cradle off."

"There's more to it than that," Christine insisted. "Destroying it will not help. In my vision, it was revealed to me that the cradle must be properly deactivated in order to re-stabilize the Earth's crust. Simply destroying it will do nothing."

"We must continue," Terzin agreed.

Gazing out at the ever-growing crater in the distance, William could not help but think the end was not much further away.

CHAPTER 31

"I LOCATED THE SHIELD!" Drew exclaimed, examining the holographic image of the planet's surface below them. "Quantum signal's 100% match."

"Good show!" Jules stated. "I guess we owe our late friend Murphy a bit of gratitude."

"If we weren't close to the signal," Drew said, "we would have never discovered it, especially in this electromagnetic instability."

Drew relayed to the pilot the shield's exact coordinates. Still in a geosynchronous orbit around the planet, he adjusted the ship's course so it headed directly above the spot.

"Signal the other striker craft," Jules ordered the pilot. "We're landing immediately."

As reinforcement, Jules recruited the only other striker craft in the fleet that could safely reach such an altitude. Together, the two ships had remained in orbit, awaiting Jules' next command.

The pilot turned to Jules. "No can do," he responded sternly. "We're dead in the water the minute we hit the stratosphere. The ship will drop like a brick."

"Must I do it myself then?" Jules cursed. "I need not hear your excuses. This ship must be landed."

"I can surely get us down there," the pilot replied, "but I can assure you it will be with a bang. There is zero percent chance of survivability. The grid line fluctuations are off the chart." He then looked solemnly at Jules. "Mr. Windsor, I will do as you say, but exiting orbit over this area will be suicide."

"He's correct," Drew agreed. "I don't see a window of opportunity to land at the moment."

"Well, when will that window arise?" asked Jules impatiently.

"Could be minutes, hours, or even days," Drew replied. "It's impossible to predict. I'm sorry, but I can't give you anything more precise than that."

"Plus," the pilot added, "the entire area is crumbling into the sea as we speak. Even if we could land, I would advise against it under these circumstances."

Not one to be thwarted even by Mother Nature, Jules unbuckled his seat belt and stood in disgust. *There must be another way!*

"Don't' worry, Mr. Windsor," the pilot assured. "If I see an opportunity, I will land this ship immediately."

Jules kicked the chair in disgust. Patience was certainly not one of his strongest points. Pacing around the confined cockpit for a few irritable moments, he then stopped moving and looked at Drew.

"How about the gravity-wing?" Jules asked. "Those contraptions are built to fly in the most inauspicious of circumstances."

"It would be too risky," Drew said.

"The wings are designed to fly in the most extreme flying conditions," the pilot chimed in. As a former high-altitude Special Forces jumper, he was aware of its capabilities. "But under these circumstances, I certainly could not vouch for their safety. Even so, that doesn't mean it can't be done."

"That's all I needed to hear," Jules responded with some gusto. Holding his finger in the air, he said, "Give the order to suit up. We deploy immediately!"

Jules, along with WOGs from both orbiting striker crafts, quickly donned their gear and were ready for immediate departure. With guns strapped to their sides, all were prepared for the plunge.

"I've set a laser guidance beacon over the target," Drew announced in Jules' helmet. "Descend directly on that spot."

"On my signal, we jump," Jules announced to the WOGs in both ships. "Set destination for the beacon." He waited a few seconds and then shouted, "Go!"

Turning towards the blackness of space, Jules propelled himself out of the ship using his wing's gravity accelerator. Once at a safe distance, he locked onto the signal and faced directly towards it. Again activating the accelerator, he jettisoned himself directly towards Earth. One by one, the rest of the WOGs in both ships followed.

"Right on course," the pilot said into everyone's helmet. "Make sure you keep the gravity dampeners on full the entire time you land, and I'd recommend you depolarize them well ahead of time to ensure your safety."

Like meteors hitting the atmosphere, the air around Jules and the rest of the WOGs began to glow red from the friction in the atmosphere as they plummeted to Earth. Despite the intense heat, the suits protected them all from the harsh environmental conditions.

As Jules descended, he and his fellow soldiers entered a soot-filled layer of the atmosphere that obscured their vision. Dark smoke and dust clouded their visors. Other than the red glow radiating around their suits, all was dark. It felt like descending into the belly of an active volcano.

The thrill of the experience gave Jules a massive adrenalin rush. "Yes!" he muttered to himself.

The further they descended, the more visible the ground became. After passing through the thickest layer of volcanic debris, the rapidly approaching land seemed to advance quicker than anticipated.

"Start decoupling the wings," one of the WOGs ordered over the helmets.

With a jolt, Jules activated the gravity dampeners, deploying the wings to each of his sides. Though they were in place, his decent continued without hesitation. It was as if the wings proved more cosmetic than functional.

Jules flattened himself horizontally to the ground and kept his back arched and head held high in order to increase drag and decelerate his fall. With his albeit limited experience of two prior space jumps, he was aware of how to handle such a precarious situation. With the control to the wings embedded in the glove of his right hand, he continued to activate the gravity dampeners, hoping for them to depolarize in time.

"It's not depolarizing!" shouted one of the WOGs over the static-ridden communication line. "I can't slow my fall!"

Other screams and shouts of terror filled Jules' helmet as they all continued to plummet unabated towards the ground.

CHAPTER 32

THE ENTIRE SHIELD began to glow, making the engraved scene on its outermost layer seem to come to life. As its radiance increased, the ancient artifact began to rotate counterclockwise without making a single sound.

"It still works," Alex said in amazement. "After all these millennia."

"They sure don't make things like they used to," William commented.

"They sure don't," Alex agreed while watching huge, foot thick clumps of crust around the shield crumble to the ground.

The entire mound began to vibrate as cracks spread like lightning bolts across its façade. As it shook, the entire image of Eve emerged from underneath the crusty debris that had long entombed her. Her beauty and splendor were just as Christine remembered. For a second, she felt as if she found herself again in the bountiful land of Eden, surrounded by the best that nature had to offer.

The shield continued to pick up velocity as it spun. A huge crack on the dome formed as massive chunks of crust slid down along its side and fell to the ground, crumbling in the process.

"Get back," Alex cautioned as they all took a few steps in the opposite direction.

As more of the crust collapsed to the Earth, the beauty of white stone covering the cradle became evident.

"So, you say that's what the pyramids of Egypt used to look like?" William asked.

"Would have been an amazing site," Alex responded.

A sudden thud from behind them broke their concentration.

"Get down!" Alex yelled. "Take cover. Hide behind a chunk of the crust!"

Four more loud thuds surrounded their position.

Alex ran to the mound while the others hid behind one of the largest pieces of crust. Grabbing four thin sticks that looked like miniature versions of dynamite from his pants pocket, he twisted each of their tops until they turned red and threw them in a semicircular area about fifty feet in distance from their position.

It was not until a WOG wearing a fully-deployed gravity-wing struck the ground in front of him that Alex realized the source of the commotion. He surmised that the electromagnetic distortion around this area must have made the WOG's gravity dampeners fail to properly depolarize. In his vedere lens, Alex could discern a few more WOGs strewn out along the landscape in positions that the human body should never make.

The shield stopped spinning as its glow faded. A door along the side of the mound then opened, revealing a hallway behind it. Light emanated out of the opening. Without time to appreciate its beauty, Alex pulled the shield off the door and looked over to a large pile of crust next to him.

"Get out of here!" Alex yelled to his friends. "Take the stratoskimmer and fly as far away from here as possible. "Tom!" he yelled into his auricular chip. "Try to depolarize the engines and ignite the jets. Immediate take off. Do you read me? Immediate take off!"

The roar of the jet engine was all Alex needed to hear. He then pointed his friends to the stratoskimmer. "Get out of here, now!"

From behind the piece of crust, William burst out shooting wildly in the air. Whether he was shooting at birds, WOGs, or figments of his imagination, it was uncertain. As he ran, the shots burst out into the sky in a chaotic formation.

"You're not going at it alone buddy," the big man then yelled. "I'm not leaving you again. We're in this together."

"Save yourself," Alex implored. Before he continued to say another world, he noticed two WOGs safely land on top of his stratoskimmer. Before he could fire his pulse gun, the WOGs placed detonation charges alongside the ship.

A shot zipped out from Alex's gun, sending one of them head first to the ground. With his neck broken and heart stopped, the man was dead within seconds.

A few wild shots pulsed around the remaining WOG. A direct hit from Samantha's gun killed the man on impact.

"Get out of there!" Alex yelled, attempting to warn Tom.

The ignition charges on the side of the ship detonated before his good friend and pilot had a chance to react. The stratoskimmer burst into flames sending out black smoke bellowing up and into the atmosphere.

Reassessing the situation, Alex knew there was only one option left. "Everyone into the cradle!" he shouted. Now was not the time to mourn the loss of his friend.

WOGs began to descend around their position. A few more thuds let them know not all made it down alive. Unfortunately, more were successful than not. Now on one knee, Alex and William fired their pulse guns nonstop, picking off WOGs before they landed and a few as they attempting to grab their weapons.

Pellets from the rail guns fired by the WOGs ricocheted all around them. Fortunately, the quantum distorters Alex threw around their position disrupted the functioning of most electromagnetic equipment within a 200 foot perimeter of their location. As a result, the rail guns utilized by the WOGs were far less accurate and failed to fire on most occasions. Only such equipment as his pulse guns and stratoskimmer had been set to the correct frequency in order to negate the distorters' effects.

"Into the dome!" Alex yelled as Marissa, Terzin, Christine, and Samantha ran through the door.

Samantha proved an accurate shot. With years of practice skeet shooting with her father as a child, she was no novice with a firearm. As each WOG at the wrong end of her pistol discovered, Samantha could shoot just as accurately on the run as she could while standing still.

Alex thrust the shield into William's hands. "Get in there and find out what this does!" he yelled.

"You coming with us?" William asked, crouching his way through the door.

"I'll be right behind," he responded, pushing his friend forward. "I have a few presents to leave out here for Julius and the rest of the WOGs. Now, go!"

William scurried through the door and into the mound.

A metal pellet tore through Alex's jacket shredding the shoulder area. With all the adrenaline flowing, Alex didn't even flinch. Instead, he continued firing until his pulse gun became too hot to even handle and his trigger finger began to cramp from such intense overuse.

As he threw himself into the doorway, Alex could hear more pellets whiz by his head. Despite the quantum disruptors, he realized that with the amount of WOGs now surrounding the area and firing, it was only a matter of time before there would be too many for him to stop.

Once inside the dome, Alex grabbed a handful of red sphere-shaped detonation charges known as motion induced explosives (MAIs) from his pants and threw them out the door in order to booby-trap the dome's entrance.

He then took the remaining few MAIs and attempted to slap them against the wall. However, they failed to activate and fell to the ground without sticking. Alex slowly backed up further into the mound as he continued to hear shots from the rail guns ricochet off the dome's thick façade.

Alex then took another quantum disruptor stick from his pocket and twisted its top. Again, there was no response. Realizing that there must be an electromagnetic neutralizing effect within the dome, Alex understood why the MAIs had failed to activate or stick to the walls.

Undeterred, he took the quantum disruptor stick and two others and threw them out of the dome. Alex hoped that outside they would all successfully activate without further interference.

As he peered his head near the door's opening, an ominous face greeted him in the far distance next to his burning stratoskimmer.

Julius Windsor.

Instinctively, Alex raised his gun and fired. The shot never deployed. He attempted a few more times with the same response.

"Alexander!" Jules yelled out. "You can run but you certainly can't hide!"

The man is insane! Alex thought. The ground was crumbling and new volcanoes were springing up by the minute, ready to engulf their position at any moment. *He won't stop!*

With his friends behind him, Alex knew that there was only one thing he could do. He would have to remain and fight.

Bring it on! Alex thought, ready for battle.

CHAPTER 33

"THAT WAY," William insisted, pointing forward. "Get going."

As Christine, Terzin, and Samantha continued to run down the slight decline in the hallway, Marissa kept turning back, looking for Alex. Her pace had slowed almost to a stop in the process.

She watched William barrel towards her. With the shield in hand, he grabbed under her arm and nudged her forward. He understood what she was feeling. But he knew they couldn't afford the time to lament. As the hallway shook and bits of shimmering stone fell on them from the ceiling, William recognized that if they didn't determine what was causing the instability in the Earth's crust, the planet was doomed.

The sound of ricocheting pellets from the rail guns faded the further they moved down the hallway. Marissa could not but help think of Alex alone, standing against an entire battalion of WOGs led by a man bent on killing him.

With Marissa in tow, William saw both Terzin and Samantha come to a stop about ten feet ahead of him. He prompted, "Keep moving! They could be right behind us."

Once he finally reached them, he understood why they stopped their retreat. His legs began to falter at the majestic site before him.

"What is this?" William asked, standing side by side with his friends in awe. "Where are we?"

"I don't know." Christine uttered, equally amazed. "None of this was in the vision."

"Any ideas, Terzin?" Samantha inquired.

She was at a loss, too. "I just don't know. My ancestors never spoke of such a place. Whether the knowledge was lost over these long years or simply never provided to us, I cannot answer."

William took a deep breath; the run had winded him. Upon inhaling deeply, he noted the air was surprisingly crisp and clean, as if filtered by the most modern system. In fact, it seemed to clear his mind and rejuvenate his body at the same time.

With a little extra energy, he asked, "Where to now?"

Though they all wanted to continue moving, no one knew where to go. The immensity of the area in front of them was daunting. The dome visible above the Earth was just a small preview of this massive room under it.

They stood at the edge of a colossal three-story staircase overlooking a circular area twice the size of an American football field. Bookcases spanned the entirety of the walls along each of the three stories. Filled with countless scrolls, boxes, and figurines, it marveled the greatest libraries ever erected. The floor in the center of the room was composed of innumerable tiles creating equally magnificent yet different mosaics. Statues, glass tables, and ornately-carved shelves from the finest marble were strategically placed on it so as to not ruin the magnificent artwork it displayed. There were also crystals levitating above pedestals, each carved with ancient symbols or depictions of animals.

At a loss of what to do next, William asked in an exasperated tone, "Christine, any hints?"

The room shook slightly as a few scrolls fell from a bookcase next to them. Upon hitting the floor, one rolled up next to Terzin and struck her foot.

"Amazing," she uttered. "Over 10,000 years old and the paper, or whatever it's written on, is still intact." Removing the brown tie around it, the two-foot-long scroll opened to reveal a picture of an animal unknown to her. Looking like a combination between a fox and a leopard, she could not identify it nor could she read the beautifully printed cuneiform-like print below it.

"There must be something in the air that can preserve such antiquities," Terzin concluded.

"I bet this is a massive depository of ancient knowledge," Christine said. "Just imagine what we could learn from it. The cave in Philadelphia pales in comparison."

"Unless one of these scrolls tells us how to get out of here or stop all this madness," William uttered, "I'm not in the mood to do some casual reading."

"I agree," Samantha chimed in. "Now's not the time for sightseeing." Feeling as if they had paused long enough, she insisted, "Let's start searching this place for any clues."

Two staircases leading in opposite directions away from the main banister overlooking the room descended to the second level. Leading the way, Samantha grabbed the marble railing and scurried down the steps. In her haste, she failed to appreciate the ornately-carved stone she touched on her descent. With different scenes, it told of an ancient story long lost to the grains of time.

William quickly followed her. Staring at the shield for some clue or inspiration, he was unsure of where to head next. The enormity of the room overwhelmed him, and he realized that it could take a lifetime to fully appreciate it. However, time was not a luxury he possessed. The clock was rapidly running out, and he also knew he had mere minutes to discover an answer.

"Terzin and Christine," Samantha looked back and said, "you look around the third floor while William and I head down to the first."

Christine pointed Terzin in one direction while she took off in the other direction around the massive perimeter surrounding the room. Inspired by Samantha's words, they both ran, hoping to find any clue. More glass tables, bookshelves, and carved depictions of extinct animals greeted them along the way.

"Maybe you can find a clue that looks like a V-shaped star cluster or a depiction of Eve," William yelled up to them as he and Samantha sprinted to the ground floor. "It got us this far."

Christine looked at every sculpture, mosaic, tapestry, and crystal as she ran, hoping to find an answer. However, nothing particularly grabbed her attention. Though in awe of the ancient history, none of it seemed as if it would help.

After running almost half way around the room, Christine stopped at a glowing crystal levitating above a glass table. She had passed about twenty others along the way. Not that this one called out to her or seemed unique in any way, but she hoped that one of them might reveal some answers like the crystal under the Art Museum.

As she moved her hand toward it, the ancient artifact began to glow brighter and become transparent. Inside, Christine could see a vivid scene of a bustling city. The pillars on some of the stone buildings reminded her of something that would be found in ancient Greece. However, with fluted ceilings and multiple levels displaying elaborate, multicolored carvings, they were also reminiscent of Indian architecture.

The closer her hand approached, the more vivid the scene became and the more she became absorbed in it. She felt as if she were there, living amongst the people. As she touched the crystal, her mind drifted slowly away from her body. Unlike in Philadelphia, she was not totally immersed in the scene and could still feel her body and move her arm away from it at any time.

Christine could hear the people speak, and she felt what they were thinking. Some were off to work while others conducted more mundane tasks such as shopping or even sightseeing.

A large blast in the distance sent a chill down everyone's spine as the mountain along the horizon erupted without warning. Though smoldering for years, this sudden explosion rocked the city and stopped her populous in their tracks. A bulbous plume of smoke shot up into the atmosphere, sending debris falling all around them. People began to scream and duck for safety in the surrounding buildings.

Nowhere was safe. Christine watched as a dense cloud of ash and lava flowing down the volcano sped towards the city. Known as pyroclastic flow, it quickly enveloped the entire area, instantly killing all life while burying the city beneath the ash.

Christine jolted her hand back, overcome by the scene.

The crystal then rotated slightly to reveal a different scene. This one brought not much more solace. Ancient ships locked in battle rammed one another while its soldiers were engaged in hand-to-hand combat. Christine wanted to see no more. Already haunted with scenes of death and destruction, she felt overwhelmed and distraught.

Backing her hand slightly further, the scenes slowly changed one by one. As if flipping through a magazine, she could stop at any time and view more. Hoping one of the scenes could provide some help as to what she was looking for, she continued to watch them scroll by in succession. While some remained violent, others appeared more mundane and depicted scenes of long extinct animals or even people doing daily chores on the farm.

With one eye on the entrance to this massive room and the other on the crystal, Christine cautiously continued to scan the scenes, ready to run at any second.

"You go that way William!" Samantha bellowed, pointing towards ivory-colored shelves full of small gadgets and scrolls. "I'll examine these statues."

"Got it," William responded. His eyes darted and head whipped back and forth, attempting to process as much visual information as possible. All the while, he felt an eerie sense that the room would erupt at any second with a barrage of rail gun pellets ricocheting around him.

"You find anything?" Samantha shouted, looking up at the third floor.

"Nothing," Terzin responded. Pulling out random scrolls and touching every statue, portrait, or table she passed, she hoped something important may jump out at her.

As Terzin moved from one item to the next, she did her best to remember any story she was told as a child that may help now. Recalling old myths, legends, and even bedtime stories, she rattled her memory hoping to jar something loose.

Samantha bolted over to a large mosaic. The closer she approached, the more magnificent it appeared. A large intricately designed globe that must have been created from a million tiny pieces of tile formed an entire map of the ancient Earth. Atop different areas on this mosaic were unique marble representations of megalithic cities. The details in each were utterly amazing and their craftsmanship must have been completed by a master artisan.

Examining them quickly, she hoped it would give her a clue as to how this room worked or where to look next. Her eyes were immediately drawn to the pyramids in Egypt. However, unlike the three that currently stood, a total of five megalithic wonders filled the space. There were also other spectacular ancient, architectural megalithic sites spotting the entire globe and a few on a large land mass in the Pacific that no longer existed.

There must have been a pre-flood megalithic society that spanned the globe, she concluded. Though completely fascinated, Samantha needed to move on to the next exhibit; there were no further clues to be found on this map.

A sudden tug on the shield pulled William to the side. At first, he assumed it was the rumblings of an earthquake but quickly realized the shield must have moved on its own.

"OK," he said, talking to the shield as if it were real. "What are you trying to tell me?"

William stopped moving for a second and placed the shield in front of him. Slowly, he rotated his body, attempting to feel where it pulled him next. He then looked in the direction where he felt the greatest tug. With his arms held straight while holding the shield, he shuffled forward in that direction.

The ancient artifact began to pull him harder towards a glass table standing on a single large marble stand. A magnificent representation of the solar system levitating above the table rotated around the sun. He could almost feel the heat emanating from the yellow glowing ball in the center. Orbiting around it were nine realistic-appearing planets.

Taking a quick second to see if this was the shield's intended target, William stopped to inspect it a little further. With spectacular detail, the solar system accurately portrayed the orbit of all eight known planets. It also had tiny little crystals representing the asteroid belt located between Mars and Jupiter. A multitude of tiny ice-like spheres orbited past Neptune's orbit, which most likely represented Pluto-like planetoids.

The object that astonished William the most was a Jupiter-sized planet that orbited the sun at an extreme angle and brought it between Earth and Mars at its perihelion and far beyond Pluto at its aphelion. Though interested in examining the display further, he knew that he had no time to marvel at its lost mysteries.

William held the shield closer to the solar system, waiting for anything to happen. It began to tug him further, towards a table about ten feet beyond this one.

As William moved around the solar system, the pull on the shield became more noticeable.

"Everyone," William shouted while looking around the room, "I think I've got something!"

As he scurried closer to the marble table in front of him, a large obelisk-appearing glass object in its center began to glow a brilliant red while the silver ball at its top sizzled and sparked.

"This is definitely it!" William again reiterated.

Wondering what he should do next, he remained still while his other companions joined him around the table.

"What did you do?" Samantha asked.

"You're looking at it," William exclaimed as sweat-filled anxiety poured over his brow. "I just walked over here and held up the shield. Then boom. This is what happened."

"Well, what do we do now?" Samantha asked.

"Maybe, this is all I have to do," William said. "Maybe the shield is doing its job."

A circular area on the floor around the obelisk slowly began to rotate in a clockwise fashion, moving William and his companions with it. Like a corkscrew, the obelisk seemed to grow in length as they slowly descended to a lower level.

"Keep holding the shield in front of you," Samantha beckoned. "Whatever you're doing, it's working."

"Not like there's any other option," William responded as they slowly rotated further down to the room below.

Silently, they continued to descend until low enough to reveal what the floor above them concealed.

"And I thought I'd seen it all!" William declared in awe.

CHAPTER 34

JULES THREW HIS SPACE SUIT and gravity wings to the side. Still goading Alex, he yelled again, "You and all your petty friends are trapped!"

He then adjusted his leather sports jacket and grabbed a compact rail gun from one of its pockets. Jules understood that Alex was a formidable foe and to proceed without precaution would be a foolish endeavor.

The entrance to the cave began to blur as the quantum disruptors Alex threw out of the doorway activated.

"Hold your advance," Jules announced to all the remaining WOGs. "This area is booby-trapped." He touched the auricular chip in his ear. "I want the immediate vicinity thoroughly scoured by one of our scouts for any undesirables. Use the utmost of caution."

"As always," a voice responded in the chip. "Consider it done."

Two WOGs still donning their spacesuits grabbed a pole attached to each of their legs. In unison, they threw them towards the door. A thin dome-shaped haze engulfed the area upon sticking in the ground. Green dots began to appear, spotting the landscape in front of the entrance along with four more in a semicircular distance from its opening.

As the two WOGs assessed the situation, Jules reconnoitered the area. Smiling at the site of Alex's prized stratoskimmer in flames and the charred remains of her pilot in its front seat, he felt great joy to see his foe's means of escape neutralized. Jules could not help but recall how the ship was once a gift to Alexander by his late uncle Albert Rosenberg.

What would my dear old uncle think of his gift now? He laughed to himself.

However, as he gazed upon the dead WOGs all around the surrounding area, his favorable mood came to an abrupt halt. Their mangled and distorted bodies revealed that many died upon impact while the sizzling corpses of others depicted an equally painful demise.

Alexander will not get away this time, Jules promised himself.

"Colonel?" Jules asked. "How many WOGs have touched down and are still operational?"

"Twenty-five, sir," he responded, "including myself and the two scouts."

"Very well," Jules responded. "I want sixteen of your men to surround the mound in order to make sure there are no surreptitious means of escape. I then want you along with four other WOGs to guard the door. When it is safe to enter the dome, I will personally take the remaining four to root out the pests inside."

The earth rumbled and shook, forcing Jules to speak louder for his orders to be heard.

"If I may suggest," the colonel offered. "How about I lead these men into the mound while you safely board the striker craft? This whole place is not safe, and you are too important to be lost if this area collapses."

"My dear boy," Jules scoffed. "One thing I've learned in my life is that if something critical needs to be done with perfection, then I must do it myself. Alexander is my responsibility."

"Yes, sir," the colonel responded without further argument.

A loud explosion tore in half the WOG closest to the door. The other scout standing nearest to him fell backwards from the concussion.

"Report," Jules insisted.

The scout on the ground slowly got to his knees. Because of the precariousness of the situation, protocol had it that he needed to remain unattended and alone until a safe distance from any undesirable anti-personnel weapons.

"The ionizing dome must have missed one of the MAIs located on the ground," the scout responded, still shaken up by the blast. "I'm not sure if the quantum disruptors concealed the device or if the MAI itself was designed to evade our detection equipment."

"Alexander," Jules said to himself.

The scout then slowly crawled back towards a group of WOGs who helped him to his feet. The man then said, "Mr. Windsor, I will have to neutralize the area before a single person sets foot anywhere near its entrance."

"Can't you just blast those damn quantum disruptors and MAIs," Jules insisted.

"No, sir," the scout responded. "Blasting the quantum disruptors could potentially create a deadly subatomic distortion, killing every living thing within a quarter mile radius."

"Confirmed," the colonel agreed. "The distortion would alter the basic quantum structure of all living matter, ensuring a gruelingly painful death."

Jules shook his head and threw his pistol on the ground. *Imbeciles*, he thought. *I'm completely surrounded by imbeciles.* "And how long, pray tell, will this ordeal take? It's not like Mother Nature will simply roll over and let us take our own bloody time."

"The effect of the disruptors will most likely last another few minutes," the scout responded. "The ionizing dome's electromagnetic field will quickly short circuit their power source. In the meantime, I will pulse the area in front of the mound with an additional subatomic destabilizing field. It will help ensure all undesirables are neutralized."

"Then let's not waste any more of our precious time" Jules said. "Begin immediately."

Jules turned in disgust and looked out at the hellish environment. He could feel the earth move under his feet. Yet, his mounting frustration made the crust's rumblings pale in comparison with what was brewing inside of him. Jules watched the smoke bellow out of the volcanoes as plumes of lava blasted into the air. In the far distance, the earth gave way and collapsed into the imposing sea.

What a wonderful new world I will create out of the ruins of the old one, Jules fathomed, watching the impending destruction with great expectation.

"Sir," the colonel interrupted after a few minutes. "Quantum disruptors are powered down and all undesirables have been neutralized. You may enter the dome at your convenience."

Jules turned and picked up his compact rail gun off the crusty ground. With it held tightly in his hand, he reveled at the thought of finally ridding himself of Alexander. "Let's go," he shouted. "Assemble!"

After barking out Jules' orders to his men, the colonel, three WOGS, and the scout ran to the dome's entrance with their rail cannons poised at eye level, aiming towards the door.

Jules walked over to the entrance. Two WOGs immediately stood in front of him while another two positioned themselves behind. Each holding their rifle-like rail gun pointed towards the sky, they were ready for the assault.

Jules looked ahead while raising his pistol up to his chest. "On a count of three we move half pace. One, two, three."

The five marched into the dome's entrance, each now with their weapon pointed in different directions in order to maximize their killing radius.

"Eyes open, soldiers," Jules said as they approached the looming light at the end of the tunnel. "Shoot anything that moves."

As the tunnel began to widen, Jules ordered, "Full march!"

Their pace quickened as they exited the tunnel and entered the vast domed room. Halted by the massive staircase's banister, they stopped to assess the situation. Moving their guns in all directions, Jules and his men searched the area for any immediate threats.

"Twelve o'clock!" shouted one of the WOGs.

They all instinctively pointed their weapons forward and pulled the triggers. However, the electromagnetic field in the area nullified the effect of their guns, making them completely useless.

Jules pulled the trigger on his weapon a few more times before giving the stand down order. "Holster your weapons," he said. "They will be useless in here."

The WOG in the front pointed to a turning obelisk in the far distance. "Sir, movement dead ahead."

"Let us—" Jules began to say.

An ear-piercing smash curtained his statement as a large, sparkling crystal mounted on the wall above them crashed directly onto an unsuspecting WOG, electrocuting him in the process. He fell to the ground on impact as his uniform sizzled and his body burned. Death was instantaneous.

The crystal's shimmering shards momentarily blinded the rest of them in a blaze of searing light. The heat it produced felt as if it would boil them alive.

Alexander! Jules surmised as his eyes watered in pain.

CHAPTER 35

"WHAT ARE THOSE THINGS?" William asked as they continued to rotate down to the lower level.

No other words were spoken as they descended another twenty feet. Too captivated to speak, they all admired in awe the ancient technology standing before them.

Christine pointed to a large beehive ship located in the distance. "They're aircraft," she said wide-eyed. "I saw this exact one in my vision. It flew like a bright ball of light through the sky and landed here in Eden."

She marveled at the ship's beauty. "It is far larger and more impressive in person than I remember."

Christine reached out as if to touch it. Still feeling trapped between the vision and the real world, she needed to physically feel the ship in order to validate its authenticity.

"They're called Vimanas," Christine explained.

Samantha grew impatient and willed whatever was driving this ancient elevator to move faster. She looked at the ground and estimated the distance was still too high to jump. Plus, she did not want to risk a possible broken ankle when she figured the last ten feet of their decline would take at most another twenty seconds.

"This whole lower level is filled with them," Terzin noted with great pride for her ancestors. "And they're all completely different in shape and color."

With designs similar to that of fish, cigars, and even tops, each ship was an original. "I wonder if they can still fly?" Terzin then went on to say.

"Looks to me like some sort of ancient showroom," William commented. "If they can fly, maybe one of these old contraptions could get us out of here."

Not a bad thought, Marissa agreed. However, without an obvious exit, she wondered if these ships were originally brought into here piecemeal and reassembled.

As the ancient elevator touched down on the sterile metal ground, they were met by the sight of two emaciated female corpses lying on the floor. Appearing to have died only recently, each had their flowing long hair well combed and laid out on the ground as if an undertaker had placed them there.

"They're both Keepers!" Terzin announced, recognizing the women. She pointed a trembling finger towards them. "You can tell by their white dresses and the gold rings in the shape of a bull's head." She looked at her identical ring and rubbed it instinctively.

Marissa knelt down next to one of them and checked the Keeper's carotid pulse. Though she assumed they were long dead, she had nursed worse looking patients back to life. "Maybe they ran out of food down here after the land was inundated with water. From what I can tell by their skin and obvious lack of body fat, they both must have died of malnutrition."

"Over 10,000 years ago," Christine uttered.

"It's simply amazing how there's not a single trace of decay on either of them," Marissa assessed. "There must be something in this air that preserves everything."

"Well," William noted indignantly, "if they were already here, why couldn't they have just stopped the flood before it happened?"

"Because they didn't have what you're holding," Samantha quipped.

The hanger began to rumble violently, curtailing further conversation. Holding on to the table, each attempted not to fall. Marissa, however, got down on all fours next to the bodies and braced herself throughout the ordeal.

One of the many large pillars arranged in three long rows and holding up the floor above them collapsed. Fractured near its base, the massive monolithic rock slammed down on a saucer-shaped Vimana and crushed it as if it were constructed from aluminum foil.

"The quakes are getting stronger," Samantha noted. She looked towards William, "Is that shield giving you any more hints."

"Not yet," he answered. "I'll have to walk through here and see if it leads me anywhere."

The roof creaked and different pillars sounded as if they were cracking the closer they approached.

Another rumble sent a second shock wave through the area. "Don't move," Samantha whispered, acting as if the mere sound of her voice could somehow add to the area's instability.

In the quietness, they could all hear the massive marble pillars around them crack and pop. The sound reverberated throughout the room, making it unclear how many of these megalithic stones were effected. Unfortunately, the loudest of the noises emanated from the pillar just in front of them.

As if viewing the scene in slow motion, they helplessly watched a huge spider crack make its way up the stone column. Before they could react, the marble shattered, sending huge stone boulders plummeting to the ground and filling the area with dust. Other pillars in the immediate vicinity fell like dominos as one by one, they came crashing to the ground.

Instinctively, William bolted forward, knocking Terzin to the floor, away from the falling debris. As the two lay on the ground, both prayed the ceiling would not collapse on them in the process.

"You alright?" William asked. With his arms wrapped around her on the ground, he attempted to shield her from danger.

"Thank you," she coughed as dust filled her lungs. "I'm fine."

"I think I broke my ankle!" yelled Samantha in pain.

"Stay still!" Christine shouted in the distance. "You'll only make it worse by moving."

William looked back attempting to localize the sound. The dust and huge blocks of marble blocked his vision.

"Samantha, where are you?" William bellowed.

"Behind the pillars," she said. "Don't worry about me. Take the shield and keep moving."

The shield! William thought. "Where is the shield? I can't find it!"

"Samantha!" Marissa yelled. "I can't find a way to get to you."

"Keep going," Samantha insisted. "Christine's with me. Other than a little pain, I'm fine. Plus, you have more important things to work out right now."

The once perfectly-aligned Vimanas were now scattered randomly along the floor. Many were damaged or hidden under piles of rubble.

"The shield!" William yelled again while jumping to his feet. "Where's the shield?"

He frantically scoured the area looking for the ancient artifact. Seeing Marissa in the distance, he yelled over to her, "Do you know where the shield went?"

"I got it right here!" Samantha yelled.

William grabbed Terzin by the hand and brought her to her feet before running over to the large chunks of stone separating them. He then scurried back and forth looking for any way to get to the other side.

"There's no way to get to her," Marissa said. "I've been searching ever since I first heard her voice."

William attempted to scale the fallen pillar between them. A jagged edge from the rock sliced his hand. Blood smeared all over the stone, making gripping it almost impossible.

"There has to be a way to get over this," William said aloud. Searching the pillar and pile of debris that separated him from Samantha, he unfortunately discerned no obvious safe place to pass. The massive stone obstacle seemed impenetrable.

Before he could attempt climbing a broken pillar once again, Marissa grabbed his injured hand and wrapped it in white linen.

"It will have to do," she said. "None of my equipment's working down here so I can't cauterize it."

Another small rumble shook the area. With bated breath, each of them stood still, hoping there would be no further collapse.

Samantha yelled, "Heads up!" after she was certain the imminent danger had dissipated.

The Achilles Shield flew over the rocks and landed with a clank on the metal floor about ten feet away from William.

"Nice throw!" William applauded in disbelief.

"I said I broke my ankle," Samantha responded, "not both arms. Now get that shield and find out where it goes."

"Yes, ma'am!" William responded.

After grabbing the shield off the floor, he pointed to the opposite end of the room. "Maybe there's something back there? I doubt these ships here are going to give us any answer."

"Agreed," Marissa said. "Is the shield leading you in any specific direction?"

"Not yet," he responded as he, Terzin, and Marissa maneuvered their way through the maze of rubble, broken pillars, and debris.

Upon reaching the far end of the room, each knew without a doubt that they had arrived at their destination. The scourge that caused the great biblical flood and was the source of the massive chaos currently affecting the Earth was fifty feet in front of them. A massive coil stood prominently in the distance, dwarfing the enormous marble pillars surrounding it.

"The cradle," Terzin said in awe.

The coil's long base was made of some sort if silver metal while its oblong sphere-shaped top that almost touched the ceiling was bronze in color. Thousands of football-sized crystals rotated around it, each in different, yet separate orbits. Electricity sparked from the bronze cap while four metal poles equidistant from one another lurched out near the coil's base and spanned to the ceiling in an upside down pyramidal configuration. As the crystals rotated, none collided with the poles or with each other.

The shield began to glow brighter the closer William approached. As he drew nearer, he could feel the massive power radiating from the coil. It was as if every cell in his body were vibrating in unison.

Another earthquake sent them all flying to the ground. This time William tightly held onto the shield and protected it

250

more than his own body. He was certainly not going to lose it a second time and jeopardize their last and only chance to save humanity.

As he was on the ground, William looked up just in time to see two pillars collapse next to the coil. While one completely missed it, the other sent chunks of debris directly into the coil and its swarm of crystals.

Sparks and electricity jettisoned out of it, electrifying the air. Crystals crashed down to the ground in blinding flashes of light, and those that did not fall began to orbit more rapidly. Bits of rock and debris also got caught up in the electromagnetic field around the coil and began to orbit along with the crystals. Occasionally, there would be a collision, which would subsequently bring down a single crystal or several of them in a chain reaction.

Looking over at Terzin and Marissa, William was relieved to see each was unharmed in the recent quake. He also noticed their hair sticking straight out from their heads in reaction to the electrical charge in the air.

Got to turn this thing off, William thought.

Grabbing the shield tightly in both hands, he began to walk towards the coil. As the energy being emitted by this ancient monolith flowed through him, he felt as if every single joint and muscle in his body hurt. The pain of walking increased the closer he approached.

Marissa grabbed Terzin's hand in order to pull her to her feet.

Crack!

As the two touched, a massive spark erupted upon contact, sending a bolt of electricity through both their bodies. The high voltage shock stiffened all their muscles, and they both let out a guttural groan as their diaphragms contracted.

The pain was excruciating. Marissa stood motionless for a few seconds before collapsing on the ground. Her entire body felt as if it were on fire.

"You…" Marissa gasped as she willed her jaw to open, "okay?"

Terzin rose to her knees and tried to stand. Unable to speak, she simply nodded her head and frailly waved. *Must deactivate the cradle*, she thought. *Must get the key.*

The ground shook once again. Terzin's trembling arms could no longer bear weight, and she collapsed awkwardly on her side. Upon impact, her left shoulder dislocated with a loud snap. She shrieked in pain as if it felt someone placed a hot dagger in the joint.

While attempting to stand, Marissa slipped on some fine rubble and fell directly onto her buttocks. The impact sent a bolt of pain throughout her spine. Though she willed herself to stand, her ailing body denied her the opportunity.

Helplessly, Marissa watched as another pillar slammed down next to the coil. Further fragments of rock and debris went crashing into the enormous monolith. Crystals shattered in blinding flashes of light and those that remained, along with stray debris, spun around the coil with increased velocity.

Marissa again attempted to stand. However, the coil's power was too intense. Its surrounding electromagnetic force had grown to such a force that it repelled any motion she made towards it.

As the coil's power increased, the electromagnetic force surrounding it began to push both Marissa and Terzin in the opposite direction. Their bodies slid helplessly across the floor. Marissa laid on her hands and knees in a feeble attempt to crawl. Her effort was futile and only caused her aching body to throb even worse.

Terzin held her shoulder. As she slid back into a pile of stone, she turned to the opposite side in order to protect her wounded joint from any further injury.

Where's William? Marissa thought frantically. Realizing her friend was nowhere in sight, she yelled his name at the top of her lungs.

William attempted to answer. However, he was caught in the electromagnetic vortex spinning around the coil. Its immense energy made it feel as if he were about to rip apart at any second. Debris orbiting this massive monolith struck his body at all speeds and angles. Instead of calling out to his friend, the best he could do was moan in horror.

William held onto the shield with both hands. With his hat lost somewhere in the fray and clothing slowly turning to shreds, he helplessly orbited the coil. Peering through the cloud of debris, he searched for any clue as to how to turn off this massive device. As each new piece of rock or crystal struck his body, the searing pain made him momentarily lose his concentration.

"William!" Marissa yelled once again.

Her body slammed against a cigar-shaped Vimana overturned on its side. Fortunately, upon striking it, no burst of electricity was produced in the process. She looked to her left and saw Terzin on the ground not far from her. Still clutching her shoulder, she appeared otherwise uninjured.

"Must have dislocated my shoulder," Terzin said as the two made eye contact.

"Have you seen William?" Marissa asked.

She shook her head no. "Last I saw, he was heading for the coil."

"Watch out for rock," Marissa warned as bits of marble debris from the pillars slid across the floor towards their direction.

"I have to turn that thing off! shouted Terzin. "All will be lost if we don't."

An eerie feeling in Marissa's stomach made it seem as if all was lost already. She realized that neither Terzin nor she had any chance of making it to the coil. They were essentially pinned down without a way to generate any forward momentum.

A red hat tumbled towards Marissa and landed on her foot. At first, she assumed it was debris, but upon closer inspection she knew exactly what it was and to whom it belonged.

"William!" Terzin shouted, pointing towards the coil.

Marissa's eyes darted forward, following her colleague's finger. "William!" she also cried out.

Her friend appeared unconscious. His hands and legs were dangling while his head slumped to the side. Marissa reached out as if to help.

There was nothing she could do. There was nothing anybody could do.

She let her hand fall to the side.

All is lost.

CHAPTER 36

ALEX JUMPED DOWN from the ledge above the room's entrance. Though his eyes seared in pain, he could not lose the element of surprise. The four remaining men in front of him each looked like a dark blur. Not expecting such an explosive emission of light upon the crystal's impact, he was still somewhat disoriented by the blast.

Not sure who was who, Alex thrust his right leg to what he suspected was one of their heads. His foot directly struck the throat of the WOG. The impact threw the man backwards and down the adjacent flight of stairs. He choked for air and spit up blood as he fell. The impact of Alex's boot caused the man to bite down on his tongue, mangling it as a result. Landing awkwardly on the last step, his neck snapped as it slammed against the side railing. Now choking on his own blood, the WOG suffocated to death.

Alex leaned back, placing his hands on the staircase's horizontal bannister overlooking the massive library. As he tried to support himself, the entire room began to shake violently. Bookshelves tumbled to the ground. Statues smashed against the floor. Crystals fell in blinding flashes of light.

Alex's hand slipped on the bannister, and he fell backwards. As he began to plummet to the ground, Alex reached out and grabbed one of the flute pillars supporting the railing.

With his vision coming back into focus, Alex noticed that he was precariously dangling three stories above the library's ground floor. Swinging back and forth, he felt as if his sweaty grip on the pillar would slip at any second.

With his right hand, he reached up and grabbed the adjacent pillar and began to pull himself up to the floor. A searing pain tore through his left hand as he managed to swing both legs onto the ledge. He could feel and hear his bones crush. Blood dripped down from the hand as it instinctively jerked open. Alex looked up and saw Jules removing a knife from his throbbing appendage.

Before his nemesis had a second opportunity to strike, Alex jumped over the railing and towards one of the WOGs. Grabbing his trusted ivory-handled hunting knife from his pocket, Alex thrust it forward, hoping to take the soldier off guard.

However, the WOG deflected the attack to the side with his rail gun. Using his forward momentum, Alex leaned into a roundhouse kick, which landed squarely on the soldier's chest. The powerful blow threw the WOG backwards, knocking the wind out of him in the process.

The WOG standing next to his fellow soldier thrust the butt of his rail gun directly towards Alex's head. Barely ducking out of the way, the weapon struck the bookcase behind him, smashing a carving of a dog-like animal and sending scrolls to the ground.

Seeing an opportunity, Alex thrust his knife into the side of his attacker's exposed throat, severing the man's carotid artery. Before Alex had the opportunity to dislodge his weapon, the earth shook violently once again. As the soldier fell to the ground, Alex lost his grip on his weapon and grabbed the nearest bookshelf to keep from falling.

Chunks of the ceiling above them collapsed as different marble fragments along the wall crumbled to the ground.

Jules charged towards Alex. With his knife gripped tightly in hand, he brandished it above his head, poised to attack. But the undulating floor threw him off balance. Not one to miss an opportunity, Jules utilized his forward momentum and lunged forward with his leading elbow as he fell.

The impact struck Alex directly on the chest, slamming him flat against the bookcase. Alex attempted to knee Jules in the gut but could not steady himself for the counterattack.

Jules' knife loomed precariously near his throat. As his foe attempted to thrust it forward, Alex grabbed Jules' forearm and pushed it to the side. The two struggled to gain advantage.

An aftershock from the earthquake broke the stalemate. As the floor shook, Alex was successfully able to thrust Jules to the side and lunge away from the bookshelves.

"You will not get away that easily Alexander," Jules grunted. He then leaned back on his left foot and kicked the other one forward.

Alex caught Jules' boot as it struck him directly in the gut. Though the impact hurt, he held onto to it as he fell backwards. Alex's left hand throbbed and ached in the process. Blood oozed from it and bones crunched in the process, making it difficult to maintain a strong grasp.

Jules could not stop his forward momentum. As Alex held on to his foot, his other one slipped. Falling to the floor, he accidentally dropped his knife and was swept down the steps with his foe. The two grappled as they descended the staircase.

With the superior position, Jules gained the advantage. Utilizing his MMA training, he interlocked his hands behind Alex's head and squeezed the sides of his face between his forearms. As they slid down the last few steps, Jules exploited a technique known as a *double-collar tie* and pushed Alex's head down while thrusting up his knee.

The first blow connected with full force. Alex's upper lip tore open. On Jules' second attempt, Alex was able to flip him over just as the two rolled off the bottom step. With his uninjured hand, Alex thrust his palm upwards, striking the bottom of Jules' nose.

Crunch!

Jules' nose shattered as blood spewed down his face. His eyes watered from the impact, blurring his vision. With a keen fighter's sense, he threw a jab directed towards Alex's rib cage. Hoping to stun his diaphragm, Jules swung wildly forward. Without a clear line of sight, he missed his target as Alex easily dodged the blow.

From behind, Alex could hear footsteps rapidly heading down the staircase. He could only assume it was the remaining WOG who had entered the room with Jules.

Alex leapt off Jules and sprinted towards a silver statue of a bull's head positioned on top of a slender pedestal. With his uninjured hand, he firmly grabbed the football-sized statue. Fortunately, it was far lighter than he anticipated.

Feeling as if the presumed WOG were about to strike at any moment, Alex turned back just in time to see the butt of a rail cannon swinging directly towards him. Maneuvering to the side, he swung the statue headfirst and thrust it into the WOG's side. One of its sharps horns punctured the soldier's jumpsuit and impaled his lung.

Alex pushed the statue further into the man's side, forcing the bull's horn to penetrate deeper. The WOG gagged on blood as his chest cavity flailed with each laborious breath.

Alex continued to push the man forward until the soldier struck the railing behind him. Upon contact, the WOG flipped over it and fell to the ground floor, landing on a translucent sculpture. Shards of glass and crystal from the artwork shattered upon impact, impaling the soldier in the process. The WOG twitched a few times before letting out a final groan, signaling his end.

After regaining his vision, Jules jumped to his feet and leapt forward, attempting to land a powerful roundhouse kick while his foe's back was turned from away him. Alex spun along the railing before Jules could make contact.

Alex's dexterity was far greater than Jules had expected.

Wiping blood from his upper lip, Jules breathed with exhilaration, relishing the excitement. Though he wanted Alex dead, he certainly appreciated both his foe's intellectual and physical prowess.

Alex then backed up and onto the steps, attempting to gain the higher ground. Realizing Jules would be too quick, he knew there was no time to grab another statue or simply run up the stairs.

Expectation, Jules thought. Suspecting Alex would presume his next move would be a simple, direct frontal assault, Jules, instead, dove for his foe's legs. With Alex on the higher ground, he needed to neutralize the advantage.

Alex swung his fist forward, attempting to land a square punch on Jules' face, which missed when Jules unexpectedly dove for his legs. Alex knew if they again were in a grappling battle, Jules' MMA training would certainly be superior to his fighting skills. Though trained in the martial arts and with numerous wins in boxing while in college, Alex was better at a distance than locked in mortal combat.

Jules tightened his grip on both of Alex's legs. Before he was able to bring him to the ground, Alex broke one of his legs free.

Alex spun his body up the stairs while thrusting the heel of his right boot down on Jules' forehead. The blow caused his foe to lose his grip, giving Alex space to move further up. His left ankle twisted in the process; pain seared through the joint. Grasping onto the railing, Alex pulled himself up the stairs.

Luckily, Alex was holding onto the railing when another earthquake struck the library. This time, its concussion was far greater than the last. The beautiful marble staircase began to crack as shelves and crystal smashed to the floor around the room. Pieces of the beautiful mosaic decorating the ceiling fell like rain as chunks of stone from the walls also collapsed onto the ground.

Alex looked down the stairs and saw Jules running towards him despite the commotion. With great agility, the man ascended the steps without faltering.

As Alex painfully made his way to the top of the staircase, Jules was directly behind him. With an overhead punch, similar to a baseball pitch, Jules greeted the back of Alex's neck with his fist. With his injured ankle, Alex could not dodge the assault.

The impact sent a lightning shock through his body when his spinal cord absorbed the blow. Alex's legs went momentarily limp, and he was unable to successfully run any further.

Seeing Alex stunned, Jules jumped forward, hoping to tackle him with a double leg take down. He grabbed Alex around the knees without much difficulty.

Knowing he was caught, Alex threw his weight back and against the massive fallen bookshelf next to him. Not allowing himself to be tackled to the ground, he instead struck the marble rock with his back. Already sore, this did little to add to his already mounting pain.

Alex then punched the side of Jules' neck where it met his shoulder. With two strong blows, he hoped to injure the man's bundle of nerves there known as the *brachial plexus* in order to weaken his grip.

Lighting sharp pain ripped down Jules' left arm. Despite the agony, he would not budge, even though his arm was now partially paralyzed. With his head in his enemy's chest, he took his other fist and pummeled Alex's rib cage with one quick jab after the next. With delight, he could hear bones break with the last punch. The sound only proved to rejuvenate him and fueled his will to fight even harder.

Winded, Alex could hardly catch his breath. When he attempted to take a large inhalation, pain seared through his chest. He then landed a third blow on Jules' neck. Feeling his foe finally relinquish his grasp, Alex took Jules' head with both of his hands and thrust it against the bookshelf.

Invigorated by the adrenaline rush of the pain, Jules spun and landed a direct roundhouse kick on Alex's chest. Connecting with deadly accuracy, he threw his foe backwards and towards the tunnel leading out of the dome.

Another rumble knocked Jules slightly off balance. Behind him, he could hear parts of the dome collapse to the floor. It did not matter to him if the entire placed collapsed. He had retrieved what he came looking for.

Jules attempted to make two fists. However, with his left arm and hand still partially paralyzed, he had trouble coordinating its movements. Opening and closing it to hasten its recovery, he slowly walked towards Alex with a sense of impending victory.

Alex fell to his backside. He could see the room collapsing behind Jules. His thoughts were more for his friends than himself. He knew there was only one option left—his fate at this point was sealed.

Backing up quickly until he was at the tunnel's opening, Alex crawled on his buttocks until he was outside the dome. The soot-filled air and dark clouds above only added to the ambience of death and destruction surrounding him.

"Hold your fire," Jules announced as he walked out of the dome. As if showcasing a prize from a safari hunt, he walked over to Alex and pulled out a rail gun from his pocket, smiling with pride.

Both Alex and Jules were battered and covered in blood. If death had not overtaken them by now, it certainly appeared to be just around the corner.

Alex continued to inch backwards further from the door. To his surprise, two elite striker crafts were now positioned to each of his sides. There were also a few WOGS standing about ten feet around him, each with their rail guns poised and ready to fire.

"Any last words, Alexander?" asked Jules.

With a cocky grin and air of victory, Jules happily waited for an answer.

"Expectation," Alex succinctly responded. "Expectation."

CHAPTER 37

"WILLIAM!" Marissa shouted, hoping he was still alive, "Wake up!"

She watched as he continued to helplessly orbit the large metal coil. Stony debris and the remaining crystals obscured her view. However, she continued to yell, hoping her dear friend would respond. Still pinned against the Vimana, she could do nothing else at the moment.

"I'm stuck!" Terzin yelled. Futilely, she struggled to grab a large slab of marble next to her and pull away from the Vimana. Her grip slipped at every attempt.

"I have to turn that thing off!" she bellowed.

The more she attempted to pull herself forward with her one uninjured arm, the more exhausted she became. Despite the mounting fatigue, Terzin continued to fight the invisible forces holding her back but had no success.

Multiple sparks shot out of the coil, sending electricity simmering throughout the room. With each new barrage, Marissa could feel her skin crawl and body tingle.

"William!" she tried once more.

This time, her friend seemed to respond as he slowly raised his dangling head. "Get out of there!" she then insisted.

"No!" Terzin yelled. "Turn off the cradle! It's our only hope."

More crystals began to crash to the ground as the floor shook once again. Fragments of the ceiling came crashing down in different parts of the room, adding to the chaos. With each new rumble, the coil's once barely-audible hum grew more mechanical and louder by the second.

A sudden jolt of electricity struck William, causing his whole body to tighten and his teeth to clench. It was a searing pain more powerful than anything he had ever felt before. Breathing became laborious as he recruited accessory chest muscles just to inhale a pittance of air. The intensity was so brutal that it awoke him from his semi-conscious state.

William saw the shield at arm's length just in front of him, also orbiting the coil. The speed to which he spun around this massive pillar produced an intense sense of nausea and motion sickness. He had never known such misery.

Got to get the shield, he thought as Marissa's and Terzin's voices echoed in the background. Though he could not decipher what they were saying over the coil's commotion, the sound provided him with the moral support he needed at such a time.

William reached out for the shield. It felt as if shards of glass were ripping through each of his muscles. He yelled out in pure anguish as his hands took grip of the ancient artifact; adrenaline helped him override the pain and dizziness he was experiencing. He understood that this was his last and only opportunity to turn off the coil.

As he spun around the massive monolith, William noted Marissa and Terzin plastered up against a Vimana, frantically attempting to move. He could hear their pleas but could not decipher what they were saying.

I'm not going to let my friends down, he thought as he willed himself to remain conscious. *I won't fail them.*

William began to rotate more quickly around the coil. Vertigo gripped him. In order to see without double vision, he closed one eye. It helped his vision but did little to curb the growing nausea. After a few dozen rotations around the coil, he noted a glass control panel attached to the base.

That must be where the shield goes.

He had to reach the glass display. What he would do at that point, he did not know.

One step at a time, William said to himself. The thought of a multistep plan was too much for his already overwhelmed senses. It was enough just to stay conscious, let alone create a complex strategy.

William stretched out his body, hoping that somehow it could change his orbit around the coil. His muscles and joints ached in the process, but the more he moved them, the less stiff they became as the aftereffects of the electric shock diminished.

A crystal shard of broken marble pelted his back. The jagged stone further tore apart his shirt and ripped a large gash in his back. Despite the injury, William barely felt the impact. Already experiencing sensory overload, the trauma added little to his already mounting agony.

William's attempt was futile. As he continued to spin, he took note of the four long metal poles positioned around the coil in an upside down triangular shape.

William reached out with one hand, attempting to grab one of them. By the time he extended his arm, his body was far past its intended target. He was spinning too quickly. Despite repeated failure, he kept trying. Occasionally, he would touch the metal pole. His hand vibrated in pain at each instance.

I need to take a different approach, William thought.

His heart pounded vigorously, and his carotid arteries pumped so dynamically in his neck that it created the sensation of choking.

William lurched his body to the side and reached out a leg. With the shield tucked tightly against his chest, he again stretched his body, hoping to make contact with one of the poles.

The side of his calf smacked one of the poles, sending him spinning as a result. A crystal smashed against the nape of his neck with a thud. The jolt made his vision blacken for a moment as he fought not to pass out. Blood oozed from his leg.

He felt so disoriented. Between the spinning and pain, he could barely focus. Not wanting to give up, William again lurched his battered leg forward, hoping to make better contact with one of the metal poles.

He barely knew which way was up or down. Other than fleeting glimpses of the poles as they whipped by him, he could not focus on anything else. Everything was a blur.

William's leg again struck one of the poles. Hitting just behind the kneecap, he instinctively bent his leg in an attempt to stop. However, his momentum was too great, and he spun once around the pole before slipping off of it.

The ordeal fortunately slowed his orbit and changed his trajectory. Before he began picking up speed, William's back slammed against the adjacent pole. With dwindling awareness, he intuitively removed one hand from the shield and locked his elbow around the metal edifice. As his body spun around it, William interlocked both his legs around the pole and pulled himself closer to it.

To his surprise, he was facing downward towards the glass console. As some of the spinning in his head began to subside, he could slowly bring his mind back into focus and concentrate.

Bits and pieces of debris continued to pelt his body, tearing through his clothes and momentarily diverting his attention.

Sparks of electricity spewed out of the coil every few seconds. Occasionally, William could feel its energy course through his body. The searing pain would temporarily paralyze him. He could smell the acrid scent of flesh burning and macabrely knew that it was his own.

Seeking strength from the depth of his soul, William inched himself forward. Each movement was painfully laborious.

I'm not going to fail my friends!

***

Tears streamed down Marissa's face as she watched her dear friend swept up in the whirlwind around the coil. She could only imagine the agony he must be enduring.

"Turn off the cradle!" Terzin continued to yell with a hoarse voice. Completely exhausted by her futile attempts to climb towards the coil, she was left drenched in sweat and pinned against the Vimana.

Marissa watched as William slowly pulled himself closer to the coil's base. She could not see what was there but knew it must be significant. She could almost feel every time her friend's body was pelted by debris or struck by a bolt of electricity.

"William!" she yelled more for moral support, hoping her words might bring him comfort of any kind.

Tears continued to flow down her cheeks. She could not believe William was taking such punishment yet managing to remain conscious. His clothes were ripped to shreds and exposed skin appeared deep red and bloody.

With a roar, she heard William yell and slowly extend his arm holding the shield. The sound of his voice reverberated throughout the space and sent chills down her spine.

The closer the shield approached, the brighter it began to glow. Like a beacon of hope, its radiance lit up the coil and made all the remaining crystals rotating around it sparkle with dazzling radiance.

Marissa struggled to place her hand above her eyes. The electromagnetic force pinning her against the Vimana had become so overwhelming that it made any movement virtually impossible. Squinting to overcome the glare, she watched William reach further, extending his body. Debris and crystals continued to ricochet against him. Marissa marveled at such mental and physical endurance. It was far beyond what she thought any human body could ever tolerate.

With a brief flash of blinding white light, Marissa felt the massive weight on her chest lift. Though her eyes were closed, she could still see the light even though it was gone. Its image was etched on her retina and showed no signs of dissipating.

The crystals rotating around the coil slowly faded until no light radiated from them any longer. As their orbit slowed, they, along with the other debris, gradually descended to the ground. The mechanical hum of the coil also faded away in a slow rumble, replacing the thunderous noise once echoing throughout the entire room.

Marissa fell to her knees and gasped for air. Her chest and abdomen ached. It was a relief finally to take a deep breath and expand her lungs without such immense electromagnetic force pressed up against her.

"Terzin," Marissa gasped, "are you OK?" While awaiting the answer, she crawled in the direction of the coil. White spots filled her vision, making it impossible to focus.

"It is done," Terzin wept in happiness. "The curse has been lifted."

Marissa continued to crawl. Jagged shards of marble cut through her palms and dug into her knees. The pain did little to deter her.

"William!" Marissa yelled as she moved blindly in his direction. Feeling her side to see if her traveling first aid bag was still with her, she continued to scurry without concern for herself.

"William!"

When she still received no response, Marissa knew that if her friend were still alive, he needed immediate medical help. Her vision slowly began to return as the spots in her eyes increasingly shrank until they were barely noticeable.

Now able to see, Marissa got to her feet and stumbled over to a pile of debris filled with rocks and crystals around the coil. She could see William's hand protruding from the mess.

Marissa ran the last few feet and began to push or throw the rocks and crystals away from William the moment she could reach them. "William," she pleaded, "stay with me."

The more she uncovered William, the more she realized what a beating he had received. Bruised and bloodied, there was almost no spot untouched.

Turning William to his back, Marissa scrambled to pull out a circular pad from her bag. After ripping its plastic undercoating, she placed it on his exposed and bloodied chest. Hoping against all odds for any signs of life, the initial holographic readings only confirmed her greatest fears: The symbols indicating massive internal bleeding, cardiac arrest, pulmonary edema and cardiovascular collapse all began blinking in red around the holographic image of a body.

There was nothing she could do. Administering shocks through the pad or injecting him with epinephrine or adrenaboost would be futile. With no other recourse, she simply touched the image, making it vanish.

Marissa laid her head down and wept. Terzin approached from behind and understood the reason for her tears. With a comforting hand, she placed it on Marissa's shoulder. "We owe him everything," Terzin muttered. "He saved us all—every single last person, animal, and plant on this planet."

Taking out a small white sheet from her bag, Marissa placed it over William's face while saying a small prayer aloud wishing his soul a peaceful journey over to the other side.

CHAPTER 38

ALEX CRAWLED BACKWARDS, creating a little more distance between Jules and himself. Out of the corners of his eyes, he could see that a few WOGs had assembled in front of the striker crafts positioned at either side.

"You could not possibly fathom the true meaning of expectation, Alexander," Jules cajoled. "In the words of the great Karl Popper, 'Our knowledge can only be finite while our ignorance must necessarily be infinite.'"

As Jules contemplated his words, the striker crafts slowly began to power up their engines and turn towards one another. With Jules and Alex in the center between them and the WOGs directly in front, they were poised and ready for action.

Alex laughed. "Expectation: What you believe will become your reality," he said with a confident smirk on his face. It's also called bias and can unduly infect your thoughts and cloud your decision making."

Jules' upper lip stiffened.

"You must understand, Julius," Alex scoffed. "Your belief in a great new world order created by Karl Popper's dream of a grand utopia is a fraud and failure. Your own bias has blinded you to the fact that Popper was a swindler who accomplished nothing in life but create disciples like yourself who continue to believe in his antiquated rants."

No longer able to tolerate such sacrilege, Jules raised his rail run and uttered, "Goodbye, Alexander."

He pulled the trigger, expecting it to fire.

Nothing.

Jules futilely pulled the trigger a few more times with the same response. Without another word, he grabbed a second mini-rail gun from his jacket. With a stiff arm, he pointed it towards Alex and pulled the trigger.

Nothing.

The engines of the striker crafts began to hum a little louder as the air around them tingled with their depolarization.

Alex smiled, revealing his bloody teeth. Taking a silver medallion out of his pants pocket, he held it in front of him for Jules to view. Similar to the Achilles Shield, this replica looked the same but had a Greek helmet instead of the constellations displayed prominently in its center.

"Bias," he went on to say. "Beliefs alter facts. Take for instance, you believed that I deactivated The New Reality master key hanging around your neck when my quantum entanglement image punched you in the chest back at Nan Madol."

Jules reached down his shirt and grabbed the key. Thinking that Alex had somehow stolen his prized possession in the fray, he confidently held it tightly in his palm. Hoping that it would activate, he concentrated intently on the medallion, willing it to work.

However, like the rail guns, the key proved just as dysfunctional.

"You believed that only the handler of The New Reality key could activate it," Alex went on to say with a little more gusto in his voice. You believed that I engaged you in hand to hand combat in the dome just to protect my friends."

Alex's words hit hard as Jules quickly realized how easily he had been fooled and led astray. Before Alex continued speaking, everything made sense.

Looking blankly at the striker craft to each of his sides, Jules stood motionless. Defeated and humiliated, he could not believe he could have been duped so easily by Alex. Jules slowly lowered his arm, letting the rail gun drop to the ground.

Alex pulled himself up and got to his feet. With the medallion still in front of him, he continued, "The truth is, my dear old friend Julius, that at Nan Madol, all I did was simply distort The New Reality key's subatomic access frequency so you could not activate it. The truth is that when we were fighting I placed a quantum transmitter on your body that allowed me full access to the key and everything with New Reality technology built into it. All your guns, weapons, ships—the entirety of The New Reality—is now under my complete control."

Alex looked at the medallion in his hand. It began to radiate a faint white glow, casting a dim shadow around him.

The stark implications of Alex's words dug and sucked the life out of Jules' badly battered body. All that he had worked for was lost. His dream of a great utopian Open Society had been vanquished. His globalist agenda of world domination by a select, elite few had come to a crashing end.

He knew Alex represented the will of the people. It was this will that he despised and thus reviled Alex for his belief in it. The masses were not fit to make decisions for themselves, nor were they capable of self-governance.

"The final truth," Alex went on to say, "is that you lost."

With the last statement, Alex grabbed a small flare-like metal device from his pocket and threw it into the ground. The air around him blurred as the magnetic pulse cannons on the underbelly of both striker crafts charged.

Jules could see the pilots in the ships frantically moving their hands across the dashboard controls. In the cockpit of the ship to his right, he noted Drew standing idly behind one of the crew members. As if he knew his fate was sealed, he did nothing but look blankly into the distance.

"Goodbye, Julius," Alex said.

The tips of the cannons began to glow red before simultaneously discharging. Jules and the WOGs standing between them were incinerated while the striker crafts erupted into huge balls of fire as they were thrown violently backwards.

The remaining WOGs surrounding the dome's perimeter also met the same demise. With complete control over the entire New Reality system, Alex set each and every weapon on their body to hyperpolarize. As the weapons reached critical polarization, they all exploded with an enormous force, dismembering the WOGs in the process.

Alex remained unharmed. The electromagnetic shield around him had diverted the cannon's blasts, protecting him from their devastating power.

Bending over, Alex took the flare-like device out of the ground and placed it back into his pocket. With a sense of both relief and grief at the same time, he dropped to his knees. The rumbling of the ground had ceased, but the reverberating pain of his sorrow had just begun.

He could hear Marissa's sobs in his auricular chip, and knew they had successfully deactivated the cradle. He also understood their triumph came at the expense of his dear friend William Fowler. Though he wanted to console her, no words came to mind.

Alex let out a big sigh as he dropped the medallion on the ground.

It was finished.

EPILOGUE

12 Months Later
Neurono-Tek Headquarters, Pennsylvania

PACHELBEL'S "CANNON IN D" always soothed Alex's nerves and had an uncanny way of bringing him calm even in the most stressful of situations. As his heart pounded and sweat clamored across his forehead, he was glad Marissa chose this music.

Though the building was relatively cool, Alex wiped his damp, sweaty brow. His face was flushed, and he felt somewhat uneasy on his feet. However, he knew it was the right thing to do, and he would never forgive himself if he decided otherwise.

The organ music echoing melodically throughout the building ceased.

Alex gulped. *Here we go!*

"I would like to welcome everyone to the Little Sisters of the Poor Chapel here at Neurono-Tek in this great Commonwealth of Pennsylvania for the most joyous of occasions," rejoiced the priest.

Holding a Bible in front of him and wearing a long red and white robe, the man looked around the chapel offering all present a warm smile.

Alex looked across from him at Marissa. The sight of her made him feel faint. She was so beautiful: her long white gown studded with tiny pearls, a flowery tiara on top of her cropped hair. The longer he stared at her the more his heart softened. He knew there was nothing else he wanted more in life.

"Dearly beloved," the priest continued, "we are gathered here today in the site of God, and in the face of this company, to join together this man and this woman in holy matrimony."

As Alex gazed into Marissa's green eyes, he could not help but recall their past few years together. It was on this very neuroscience campus where they met during the terrorist bombing of the Science Building. They had been inseparable ever since. From *The Disease* which plagued the planet to the financial collapse of the world's sovereign countries to the rise of The New Reality's world order to the massive human catastrophe perpetuated by the nanosplicers, Jules Windsor's institution of the Open Society, and the near destruction of the Earth, they were in it together.

He knew that none of the success in confronting these global threats over the past few years would have been possible without her.

Alex finally smiled, taking a ring out of his front pocket.

"With this ring," Alex uttered, holding it in front of him.

Looking back out into the chapel, he could see his two head security guards, Phil and Gil, sitting in a pew. Each extremely dedicated to their jobs, they wore their New Reality jumpsuits to the wedding. Though extremely massive and gruff in appearance, they both whimpered in joy, unable to control their emotions. Alex grinned, pleased to see the human side behind their brusque façades.

Both Terzin and Christine sat in the front row, glowing with excitement. Since leaving Eden, Alex brought them both back with him to Neurono-Tek. As a sign of his gratitude, he started financing Christine's medical school degree and offered her a top full-time job at his company after her training was complete.

Alex also brought on Terzin at Neurono-Tek. She was thankful to join him and start again in Pennsylvania. Still heartbroken at the loss of her home, family, and friends in wake of the recent massive tectonic shakeup, she found great solace overseeing Neurono-Tek's human displacement program. In this position, she could help others find their family and friends and hopefully rebuild a new life in this post-New Reality world. She loved the position and felt she needed to do it for both herself and everyone else she helped. She was, after all, a Keeper, now and always.

Alex looked over at Samantha. Her eyes were gleaming in pride. Though she was the second in charge at Neurono-Tek, Alex had not seen much of Samantha over the past three months. Taking the lead in the global resettlement program, she was helping to bring business, technology, and people to the ancient continent of Mu that arose in the Pacific after millennium on the sea floor. Her organizational skills and biomedical expertise were proving extremely helpful in cultivating the barren land and breathing life back into it once again.

Alex was also pleased to see that other friends and family had joined their joyous occasion. Even Dr. Harding, a physician who once worked for Jules Windsor, was there at the ceremony. Though their first meeting was tumultuous at best, he had become a recent friend and had moved to Pennsylvania to help run the genetics department.

"I thee wed." Alex placed the ring on Marissa's finger. Her hand felt soft and comforting.

She looked up and smiled, feeling how his hand slightly trembled at the simple action. She also felt great love and joy. Though Alex always said it was a matter of pure luck that they met, she believed the two were meant to be together, not just for themselves, but for the sake of the planet.

All seemed right at the moment. Despite the immense tragedy caused by the tectonic plate shifts and geological instability, the world also was righting itself after years of The New Reality's oppressive abuse.

Alex recalled how he destroyed The New Reality and its financial stranglehold over the planet once he gained access to the master key around Jules' neck. During those brief movements, he dissolved the business' equity and returned it to the people and countries to which it belonged. Within a mere second, The New Reality ceased to exist, and those who brought it to power were left in financial ruin.

With new financial independence, each country that survived the massive tectonic upheaval took back its sovereignty and arrested the corrupt bankers and financial elites who had made possible the takeover by The New Reality. So, too, went the politicians who had sold out their nations. No more would a few elites rule the many.

"Those whom God hath joined together," the priest went on to say, "let no man put asunder."

Even in his moment of great joy, Alex could not help but think of William and wish that he was present. William had saved them all; Alex would spend the rest of his life trying to express his gratitude. He also thought back to others that he had lost to The New Reality: his good friend and pilot Tom Flynn, Father Jonathan Maloney, and Guri Bergmann.

"I pronounce you man and wife," the priest announced. "In the name of the Father, and of the Son, and of the Holy Spirit. Amen!"

The organ music started playing once again as Alex and Marissa kissed for the first time as husband and wife.

Everyone in the chapel stood and began to applaud. A few people sitting next to Phil and Gil helped them to their feet. Overwhelmed, they wiped their faces with a handkerchief and blew their noses almost like a horn trumpeting the union.

With one arm, Alex embraced Marissa and turned to the congregation. Now a proud husband, he looked out and thought how wonderful it felt to be alive.

A he walked down the aisle, Alex took out of his pocket a grimy old red hat with only the worn *G* and *R* letters remaining. Placing it prominently on his head, he felt that this was but a small tribute to his late friend. Upon seeing it, Marissa and Samantha began to cry. They could not help themselves. They, too, still hurt from his loss and appreciated this nod to their fallen friend. Proudly wearing the cap, Alex also found it difficult to hold back the tears.

After composing himself, Alex began to wave to the many friends joining him on this beautiful day. Despite the smiles and laugher that greeted him, he could not but help wonder how the world would respond to a second chance. Would they learn from the past, or would they once more move toward destruction in the name of progress?

Alex did not have the answer. What he did know was that he had a beautiful wife to love for the rest of his life. In this moment, it was enough.

FACT OR FICTION?

VIMANAS. Stories of these ancient flying machines were mentioned in multiple ancient Sanskrit texts from India including the *Sumaranga Sutrahara*, *Ramayana*, *Mababharatam*, and *Harivamsa* amongst others. In the Sanskrit writings of the *Vaimanika Shastra*, it describes not only how the Vimanas were constructed but also how they were flown. It was written that there were different types of Vimanas, including the beehive-shaped Rukmana Vimana, the stubby rocket-shaped Sundara Vimana, and the submarine-appearing Tripura Vimana. These ships were the ones described in *The Final Reality* hidden under the dome in Eden.

    Mercury Flight. In the *Sumaranga Sutrahara*, it was written, "By means of power latent in mercury which sets the driving whirlwind in motion, a man sitting inside may travel a great distance in the sky in a most marvelous manner." In this writing, it describes the Vimanas flying "like a pearl in the sky." The Greek word for mercury is *hydrargos*, from which the periodic symbol *Hg* is derived. The word translates into *liquid gyro*. The Greek god Mercury, also known as Hermes by the Romans, was hailed as the god of flight and had a winged staff known as the caduceus to signify this attribute. Does the liquid metal mercury possess some latent antigravitational zero-point energy effect that it can exert when properly excited? I don't know, but ancient myth does make one wonder.

    Caduceus. Mercury's winged staff with two serpents intertwined around it has become the traditional symbol of medicine, especially in the United States. Is this staff more than just a mythical symbol? Does it represent an ancient sign of electromagnetic flight? Some hypothesize the ancients used such symbols as the means to convey information from one generation to the next.

The Great Biblical Flood. Though much of modern science has dismissed the biblical story written in the Torah and the Christian Old Testament, hundreds of flood stories circulate across the globe. The Berber in North Africa believe that their ancestors were refugees from a land to the west that was destroyed by the sea. Some hypothesize this land was that of Atlantis and that their language may be the only vestiges left of this lost continent. In the Mayan *Popol Vuh*, it tells of a great flood. The Babylonian story of Gilgamesh is very similar to that of Noah. Flood stories also abound in China, the Samoan Islands, Sri Lanka, Mongolia, Philippines, Tibet, New Zealand, native American tribes in the USA, India, and Egypt. To dismiss the idea that a great flood once ravaged the planet would be to dismiss hundreds of different accounts told of this event across the globe.

Eden. In the Book of Genesis 2:10-14, Eden is located at the head of four rivers, the Pishon, the Gihon, the Tigris, and the Euphrates. Many have searched for where the biblical land was located. However, only the Tigris and the Euphrates are currently present while the other two rivers no longer exist. It has been up to much debate as to where the Pishon and the Gihon were once located, and many scholars have written erudite articles explaining their point of view. In *The Final Reality*, I deferred to Juris Zarins' writings on the Garden of Eden as the basis for finding this lost biblical location.

Troy. In Homer's *Iliad*, Troy was defeated by the ancient Greeks and left in ruin. Interestingly, Heinrich Schliemann discovered Troy a few thousand years later using clues found only in this Homeric tale. It does make one think how much truth is behind these ancient myths and writings that we thought were purely fictional in nature.

Crustal Slippage. It is true that the Earth's crust is but a thin, solid layer of rock floating on top of a vast sea of magma. Albert Einstein once hypothesized that the crust could theoretically move like that of the skin of an orange. Because the crust is of much lower density while the mantle below it is composed of higher density magma, crustal slippage as described in this novel, is a theoretical possibility. Modern science of today ascribes to a more uniformitarianism view of crustal movements. Science describes the movement of the Earth's crust as slow and taking millions of years to create any noticeable geographical changes. However, the belief that the crust can slip more dramatically is a theory known as catastrophism and is not propagated by modern science. In some books such as *Cataclysm!: Compelling Evidence of a Cosmic Catastrophe in 9500 B.C.*, J. B. Delair believes Noah's biblical flood was caused by rapid tectonic shifts. He tells how the previous geographic North Pole was located in the Hudson Bay and moved fifteen degrees as a result of this cataclysmic continental shift.

The Ancient Continent of Mu. The belief in this continent began in the 1860's when geologists found similarities between fossils located in India, Australia, South America, and Southern Africa. They believed that an ancient land bridge must have once been present to allow such similarities in the plant and animal fossil records. Tales of a great, lost continent in the Pacific known as Mu or Lemuria are told throughout the Pacific in ancient folklore and song. Some Polynesians call this place Hiva while Hawaiians refer to it as Ka-hoopo-kane. The Rapa Nui of Easter Island believe they came from a land that sank into the sea. Other natives along the Pacific share this idea and believe that their island is a remnant of this once great continent. Also, the Mayans and ancient epics from India describe such a lost continent. *The Lemurian Fellowship Chronicles* go on to further hypothesize about this ancient land. However, no objective evidence has yet to be found to confirm their claims.

Ancient Maps. The ancient maps described in *The Final Reality* under the Philadelphia Art Museum, in the dome located in Eden, and in different Keeper outposts were not a figment of my imagination. However, the cave under the Art Museum was. These maps, drawn up by sixteenth through eighteenth century geographers, cartographers, and priests such as Philippe Buache, Athanasius Kircher, amd Oronteus Finaeus, are believed to show Antarctica without ice, the Island of Atlantis in the Atlantic Ocean, and geographical features on the Earth that are no longer present. I used these maps as the basis for much of what was depicted in *The Final Reality*.

Nazi Germany's Expedition into Tibet. The expedition of the Nazi Germany's zoologist, Ernst Schäfer, and team occurred between the years of 1938-1939. This was Ernst's second trip into this forbidden land. Unlike the details described in *The Final Reality*, he had a large entourage including a film crew accompanying him on this expedition. They did meet with a Tibetan royal known as Rajah Tering as described in *The Final Reality*. Ernst Schäfer promoted this trip as a scientific expedition while the SS of Nazi Germany utilized it as a form of propaganda and a method to propagate their Aryan race beliefs. There is still much mystery about this journey and many unanswered questions remain as to the reason why it was sanctioned by the Nazis. Were the Germans looking for some secret technology, the lost ark, or an ancient library? Some have hypothesized more sinister motives. In *The Final Reality*, I draw on these possibilities and combine the expedition by Ernst Schäfer with that of a fellow non-Nazi German by the name of Theodore Illion. In Illion's works, *In Secret Tibet* and *Darkness over Tibet*, he describes how he infiltrated Tibet by himself, disguised as a wandering nomad. I must acknowledge Illion's works, because much of what was described in the prologue of *The Final Reality*, including his meticulous preparation, was written about in these two fascinating novels.

Zero Point Energy (ZPE). ZPE is essentially the fabric which creates the universe. It is the energy that remains when all physical energy is removed from a system. It can be calculated using Heisenberg's uncertainty principle where ZPE $= 1/2hf$ when h represents Plank's constant and f represents the oscillation frequency. It explains why liquid helium does not turn into a solid even at the most extreme cold temperature known as absolute zero. Some believe that gravity is directly related to ZPE fields. There are also books available such as *The SS Brotherhood of the Bell* by Joseph Farrell, which give evidence how the Nazi Germans attempted to create a super weapon, *wunderwaffe*, called Die Glocke, that exploited ZPE.

Pyramids of Giza. The pyramids of Giza were once not dull, step-like sandstone-colored megaliths as we see today. Just like Alex Pella explained, they were once covered in white tura limestone and were smooth and shimmering along their sides. Vestiges of this limestone can still be seen on the pyramids and have been described many times in the chronicles of history.

Bagdad Battery. The Bagdad battery does exist. However, no one knows how or for what purpose it was used. Experiments conducted today show that it could produce anywhere between 1.5 to 2 Volts of electricity.

World Grid. The world grid is a theoretical electromagnetic grid that surrounds the Earth similar to lines of longitude and latitude. It is believed to be created by the internal magnetic, radioactive, and kinetic energy within the Earth and is released around the planet in the form of flow lines which form a geographic pattern.

Bloch Wall. The Bloch wall is named after physicist Felix Bloch. They are neutral zones that represent the transition region at the boundary between magnetic domains. It is also characterized as non-spin energy. In a polarized universe, non-spin energy is rejected and theoretically, an antigravity effect is created. Viktor Schauberger utilized such a non-spin vortex physics to make non-buoyant logs float down a flume. It is theorized that where the lines along the world grid intersect, a Bloch wall is created and there is less gravity present as a result. It is also theorized that the ancients utilized this antigravitational effect and built megalithic monuments in those locations.

Megalithic Structures. All across the globe there are massive megalithic structures which defy modern explanation. The largest cranes of today could not lift 200 ton stones. Plus, the question remains about how they were not only transported sometimes over fifty miles but also raised to such high levels or brought up mountains. The pyramids of Giza and Stonehenge are the most recognizable edifices. However, great megaliths stand across the globe including Mount Nemrut in Turkey, Baalbek in Lebanon, Ggantija in Malta, the Yonaguni Monument in Japan, Sacsahuaman in Peru, and the Carnac stones in France among others. Despite many theories, it still remains a mystery how such "primitive people" could undertake these massive projects with the exact precision and manpower that was needed.

Pumapunku. In *The Final Reality*, I included two of my favorite megalithic structures. The first was Pumapunku in Peru. If you have not seen this structure, please search for pictures of it online. If this place does not lead you to the conclusion that an advanced science once used by the ancients was lost, nothing will. The precision of the work is astounding. Modern science has absolutely no explanation as to how such works of magnificence could have ever been created. Even the lasers of today would have difficulty in generating such precision.

Nan Madol. This lost megalithic structure off the eastern coast of Pohnpei is described without hyperbole in *The Final Reality*. Though there is believed to be a much more massive underground city as described in my novel, this hypothesis has yet to be proven. It is called the Venice of the Pacific and still baffles modern scientists about how such a small population of people could erect such a massive structure. Again, please search for pictures of this island on the Internet. You will not be disappointed.

Alaskan Muck. As described in this novel, Alaskan muck does exist in both Alaska and in Siberia. No one knows what caused such devastation, leading some to give credence to the biblical flood story.

Open Society. The Open Society concept was popularized by Karl Popper in his work, *The Open Society and its Enemies*, which was originally published in 1945. Though heard of by few, its concepts permeate modern society and are extolled by modern media. Billionaire George Soros popularized this philosophy and has spread the concept to colleges, universities, and schools around the world. However, recent elections have shown how American and British voters have rejected many of its tenants such as open borders, the evils of nationalism, and a purely secular, atheistic state.

Illuminati. It is interesting how the defunct Bavarian secret society, the Illuminati, has grown to such notoriety. Popularized by the all-seeing eye on the back of the dollar bill, vestiges of this group are still evident today. Founded in 1776 by Adam Weishaupt, it was disbanded by the Bavarian government in 1786. In my previous novel, *The Hidden Reality*, the story begins with a fictional account of Weishaupt's clandestine meeting with one of the Illuminati's former members, Xavier Zwack. The nonfictional part of this story is that Illuminati documents were seized from Zwack's home and that is how we

THE FINAL REALITY

discovered so much about the group. Though the Illuminati was disbanded, many of its principles permeated into other secret societies of the day, including the Freemasons. Theoretically, this is the reason for how the all-seeing eye made its way to the dollar bill. Some of the basic tenants of this group include: the belief in a central banking system, control over the media with only a select few knowing the truth behind each story, atheism, abolishment of the Catholic Church, abolition of the family unit, and neutering of the average person from influencing government. These Bavarian Illuminati members were powerful men with great influence over government, media, business, and banking at the time. It thus comes as no surprise why such a group was disbanded. It also comes as no surprise why globalists such as George Soros were so disappointed with Brexit and inauguration of President Trump.

Quantum Entanglement. The quantum entanglement cube I created is purely fictional but the science behind it is not. Albert Einstein once described quantum entanglement as "spooky action at a distance". It is a concept where particles or groups of particles are quantumly paired no matter what distance exists between them. If the quantum state changes in one particle, the other linked particle would change accordingly, no matter how far apart, ever millions of light years, they are. Theoretically, the science behind this concept would prove an efficient means of communication through the vastness of the cosmos.

Georgia Guidestones. The Georgia Guidestones actually exist and were erected as described in *The Final Reality*. Inscribed in eight different languages, the guidestones display the ten commandments of their New World Order creator: 1. Maintain humanity under 500,000,000 in perpetual balance with nature; 2. Guide reproduction wisely —improving fitness and diversity; 3. Unite humanity with a living new language; 4.

Rule passion —faith —tradition —and all things with tempered reason; 5. Protect people and nations with fair laws and just courts; 6. Let all nations rule internally, resolving external disputes in a world court; 7. Avoid petty laws and useless officials; 8. Balance personal rights with social duties; 9. Prize truth —beauty —love —seeking harmony with the infinite; and 10. Be not a cancer on the Earth —Leave room for nature. No one knows who financed these guidestones or what purpose they serve. Speculation to this day still abounds about this controversial megalith.

Phrees and Katholes. These two factions were written about by David Hatcher Childress in his novel *Vimana Aircraft of Ancient India & Atlantis*. In his book, he cites the writing of *The Lemurian Fellowship* in describing the conflict and battle between the Phrees and the Katholes. He also references such ancient Indian texts as the *Ramayana* to corroborate the story.

ACKNOWLEDGEMENTS

I WOULD FIRST LIKE TO THANK Theodore Illion and his works, *In Secret Tibet* and *Darkness Over Tibet* for his inspiration in creating the prologue to my novel. His journey into Tibet in 1934 along with the German explorer Ernst Shäfer's 1938 exploration into this country provided the perfect backdrop for this novel. I also express my gratitude for the following works and their authors, for all the information they provided when creating this novel: *Liberty: The God that Failed* by Christopher Ferrara; *Forbidden History* by Julian Kenyon; *Soros: The Life, Ideas, and Impact of the World's Most Influential Investor* by Robert Slater; *Vimana Ancient Aircraft of India and Atlantis; Lost Cities of Atlantis, Ancient Europe and the Mediterranean; Lost Cities of Ancient Lemuria and the Pacific*; and *Technology of the Gods: The Incredible Sciences of the Ancients* by David Hatcher Childress; *Maps of Ancient Sea Kings* by Charles Hapgood; *The Illuminati Fact and Fiction* by Mark Dice; *The New World Order* by A. Ralph Epperson; *Lost Knowledge of the Ancients* edited by Glenn Kreisberg, *Creation Myths of Primitive America* by Jeremiah Curtin, *Cataclysm!* by D.S. Allan and J.B. Delair, *Worlds Before Our Own* by Brad Steiger, and the writings of Juris Zarin about the Garden of Eden.

I would also like to especially thank fellow Light Messages Publishing author Dave Edlund for his writings on rail guns. Last but not least, I would like to thank Light Messages Publishing for allowing me to once again pursue my writing career with the publication of my latest novel, *The Final Reality*.

THE AUTHOR

Stephen Martino holds an M.D. from the University of Pennsylvania and is a neurologist in New Jersey. When he is not working, he can be found with his five children doing homework or cheering them on at a soccer field, basketball court, or dance recital. Martino is a member of the Knights of Columbus, a Cub Scout den leader, and is an active public speaker, helping to educate the local community and healthcare professionals on the signs, symptoms, and treatment of stroke. *The Final Reality* is his third and final novel in the *Alex Pella Series*. Visit Stephen online at martinoauthor.com.

ALEX PELLA NOVELS

BY STEPHEN MARTINO

The New Reality
Book 1

The Hidden Reality
Book 2

The Final Reality
Book 3

...you might also like

PETER SAVAGE NOVELS

BY DAVE EDLUND

Crossing Savage
Book 1

Relentless Savage
Book 2

Deadly Savage
Book 3

Hunting Savage
Book 4

Guarding Savage
Book 5, coming 2018